W9-DBC-352

DEATH
AT
Charity's Point

WILLIAM G. TAPPLY

Charles Scribner's Sons NEW YORK

Copyright © 1984 William G. Tapply

Library of Congress Cataloging in Publication Data

Tapply, William G.
  Death at Charity's Point.

  I. Title.
PS3570.A568D4   1984   813'.54   83-20200
ISBN 0-684-18056-1

1 3 5 7 9 11 13 15 17 19 F/C 20 18 16 14 12 10 8 6 4 2

Printed in the United States of America.

For Cyn

Author's Note

Dr. Albert Saubermann shared his expertise with me with infinite patience and plain language. Any technical errors here are mine, not his.

I leaned shamelessly on Rick Boyer and Betsy Rapoport throughout the project—for their instinct for my story, for their unerring eye for the cliché and the dull, and for their spiritual sustenance.

Thanks, guys.

DEATH
AT
Charity's Point

Prologue

ABOUT TWENTY miles northeast of Boston as the bluefish swims, between Marblehead and Cape Ann, Charity's Point juts into the ocean. It forms a natural jetty at the southern end of North Cove Beach. At the tip of Charity's Point lies a great rock with a sheer hundred-foot face that drops straight down to the ocean. At the foot of this little Gibraltar, the confluence of tides and currents has eaten away a deep bowl where the ocean swirls angrily, high tide or low. The bottom of the bowl is lined with jagged rocks.

In the summer of 1692 a fourteen-year-old girl hurled herself from the top of the giant boulder to her death. Charity Coughlin chose that manner of death over the gallows to which she and the other accused witches had been condemned. She made her point, and in the process gave her name and a legend to an otherwise insignificant little chunk of New England coastline.

Nearly three hundred years later a middle-aged schoolteacher named George Gresham took the same route. If Charity Coughlin had died as George Gresham did, if she had known that her body would be flattened, crushed, and broken, that it would be sucked across the rocky bottom of the bowl at the base of the great boulder and flipped up against the face of the cliff by the churning surf—she might have chosen the gallows as a pleasanter way to die.

The route to the tip of Charity's Point isn't usually difficult, but when I returned there in August for my last look, it took me nearly an hour. I parked at the municipal lot at the northern end of North Cove Beach and followed the wet, packed sand along the curving water line. Then I cut back away from the beach through the dunes. The sharp beach grass cut at my ankles, and the soft sand shifted under my feet. There was no path. I clambered over and around the boulders. My knee ached, and my breath came hard.

I sat on the flat top of the huge rock out at the tip, where I could look almost straight down into the crashing surf one hundred feet below. Mist sifted up through the roar and boom of the breakers, filming the jumble of rocks around me with a slick, oily sheen.

I lit a cigarette and felt no qualms about the poisons I was sucking into my lungs. A month earlier I had been a living corpse, my jaw wired shut, electrodes taped to my skull, half choked by my torn and swollen tongue. My shattered knee had been packed in ice.

I shifted my position to ease the throbbing in my knee. The orthopedist said I had been lucky. Simply a matter of ligaments. It could have been worse, he'd said matter-of-factly. A blow like that could shatter the patella and pop the cartilage, dislocate the whole intricate structure, as when the quarterback catches his spikes in the turf and gets hit from one side at the shoulders, and then two hundred and seventy pounds of defensive tackle smashes him low from the opposite side.

The young doctor had demonstrated with his hands on me, and I'd shuddered.

Soon I'd be able to wade a gentle trout stream like Nashoba Brook or the Squannicook. And I'd try a round of golf, although I knew that driving my legs through the ball properly would hurt.

The pain I could bear. Hell, the pain would feel good. It would remind me I was alive.

George Gresham should have been so lucky.

I pulled my knees painfully up to my chin and hugged

them against the evening chill. A breeze sprang up. I cursed myself for leaving my sweatshirt in the car.

The moon had risen above the cloud bank. Its beams shattered on the ocean, a million tiny crystals of light. A beautiful, peaceful sight from Charity's Point. I was only dimly aware of the continual crashing of the surf below.

I gazed off to my right to the lights of Peach Point. Beyond that, tucked into the great cove of Massachusetts Bay, lay Boston, where I lived and worked, barrister to wealthy Brahmins and any others willing to pay my fees. Forty-two years old, and happy just to be alive.

Three months earlier, Florence Gresham had called me to report that her son had died. It had seemed at the time like a routine matter for her family's attorney. I could settle estates with my eyes closed.

But it had gotten complicated.

CHAPTER 1.

IT WAS Florence Gresham who had set my career—such as it is—on its present course when she called me for the first time back in 1969.

"Is this Brady Coyne himself?" she demanded.

I assured her that it was.

"Because I don't want to speak to some flunky."

"No, it's me," I said. I didn't tell her that there were no flunkies at Brady L. Coyne, Inc. Just me.

"Okay. I have an unusual piece of business for you, Mr. Coyne," she continued in that whiskey-hoarse voice of hers. In those days I was taking whatever sort of business came my way—and there hadn't been much of it for a determinedly lone-wolf attorney in Boston, a city of staid, old firms which recruited almost exclusively from Harvard. I rather valued what I had learned at Yale Law School, but I found eyebrows raised when potential clients realized I hadn't worn the crimson.

Florence never told me how she got my name. I suspect she wanted someone exactly like the way I was in those days: energetic, independent, hungry.

"How can I help you?" I asked her, hoping desperately that I could.

"One year ago my husband and I received notification from the United States Army that our younger son was missing in action. A 'routine patrol northwest of Hué.' it said. We have heard nothing more. I want to know what has happened to my son."

"I'm an attorney, Mrs. Gresham," I said. "This is not, strictly speaking, a legal matter."

"I'll call someone else, then," she said. I soon learned that Florence Gresham was always direct.

I quickly assured her that of course I could conduct an investigation, that a discreet attorney was probably exactly what she needed.

"Do whatever you need to do," she said, adding that I needn't concern myself with the expenses. "Your fee will be adequate."

Implicit was the promise that, should I perform satisfactorily, there would be more business available to me from the Gresham family.

Lt. Winchester Gresham's old CO, I was able to learn, had been rotated stateside and was attached to the Pentagon. He received me graciously in his high-ceilinged office, an imposing figure in his starched and beribboned uniform.

"Lieutenant Gresham," he said. "Yes, I remember him well. Of course. A superior soldier."

Major Henderson stood by a floor-to-ceiling window and stared out over a broad lawn, watching a figure ride a lawn-mower across it. "He was on patrol. They walked right into an ambush. There were twelve of them altogether. It was a routine mission, really. We hadn't heard of any VC activity in the area. We didn't think there would be any problems."

Henderson turned to frown at me. "Four of the boys came back. The two who could walk carried the other two. One, as I recall, died shortly thereafter. Lieutenant Gresham was not among them. When we sent a patrol back, we found no bodies." He shrugged. "That's all we know, Mr. Coyne. Officially, they are missing in action. Prisoners of war, although the enemy has not given us the courtesy of an official pronouncement." Major Henderson ran his hand over his close-clipped, military haircut. "You understand, Mr. Coyne, they are probably all dead."

One of the survivors of that patrol, the Major informed

me, was still recuperating from his wounds in a V.A. hospital in South Carolina. I found Corporal Lucas Potter sitting in a wheelchair in a big day room watching television the afternoon I visited him, a freckle-faced, red-haired young man with jug ears and sharp blue eyes. A blanket was thrown over him so that he looked like a disembodied head set atop a large brown sack.

"I'm Brady Coyne," I said, extending my hand.

He didn't shake it. "Hi," he said, not taking his eyes from the quiz show.

"You knew Win Gresham," I said to him, pulling up a folding chair.

"Sure."

"You were with him when . . ."

"When we got it. Yup."

"Can you remember what happened to Gresham?"

Potter's eyes wavered from the television screen, and his head turned slowly to face me. "Listen Mr.—what was it?"

"Coyne. Brady Coyne."

"Okay. Mr. Coyne. There were machine guns and explosions all around us. I was flat on my belly, digging my face into the dirt the whole time, I don't mind telling you. Wondering if I was dead yet, you know? I had been hit and I was hurtin', and I didn't see much. But I could hear the Lieutenant. He was swearing and yelling at us, telling us to fight, goddam it, to fall back. He was in charge. Wasn't for him, none of us would've gotten out."

"But *he* didn't get out."

"He didn't?" Potter frowned at me.

"According to the Army."

"The Army," repeated Potter. He looked as if he had bitten into a bar of soap. His eyes slipped back to the television. "They say so, I guess it's true. I was hurt bad. What the hell do I know about it?"

"You think he got out?"

"Nope. Not me. The Army says he didn't get out, he didn't get out."

"You never saw him, then, after that patrol?"

"I told you, mister. I was injured. Still am, in case you couldn't tell. They shot me up with morphine and loaded me onto a chopper, and I don't know what happened to anybody."

"Do you think Lieutenant Gresham's dead?"

"Could be. I guess so." He turned his head slightly toward me. "That's what the Army says, ain't it?"

"Yes."

"Then that's what he is."

"Okay." I paused. "Tell me. What kind of a soldier was Gresham?"

Potter's head swiveled around to look at me. "He was a good fuckin' soldier. A killin' machine, the Lieutenant. That's what he was. A killin' machine. He talked funny. Like an intellectual, you know? A college boy. But he was one mean son of a bitch. We all obeyed him. Oh, yes. He'd of shot us if we didn't. We all knew that. He hated everybody. He hated us, he hated the gooks, he hated the officers who gave him orders. Helluva soldier, the Lieutenant. He say shit, you say where, sir."

I stood. Lucas Potter was again staring at the flickering television screen. I couldn't tell what might have been registering behind those unblinking blue eyes. His expression didn't waver. I bent down to his side and said, "Thanks, soldier." I squeezed his arm as I turned to leave.

Except there was no arm under the blanket. I wondered what else that had belonged to Corporal Lucas Potter was still missing in the jungles somewhere northwest of Hué.

After that I could learn no more. I wrote up a report and delivered it to Florence Gresham at her home in Beverly Farms. She read it with narrowed eyes.

"He called Win a killing machine. Were those his words?"

"Yes," I said. "But remember, this was an ignorant farm boy whose arms had been blown off. A bitter kid. I wouldn't put too much stock in what he says."

She shook her head. "No, the boy's right. That would be Win, all right. A killing machine. My son had a great capacity for hatred and cruelty. Just the opposite of George. George is a gentle boy. My Cain and my Abel."

Florence Gresham said this matter-of-factly, much as if she were discussing characters in a book. She peered at me. "He could still be alive."

"Oh, now, Mrs. Gresham . . ."

"No, he could," she said, nodding her head vigorously. "He's a survivor, Win. And," she added, her voice soft, "a killing machine."

I had not really done my job. The question of what had happened to Lt. Winchester Gresham in the jungles of Vietnam had not been definitively answered. But Florence Gresham seemed satisfied. She put me on retainer. Some of her wealthy friends began to do the same. I have, ever since, served the legal needs of rich folks.

A month or so after I delivered my report, two uniformed Army officers knocked at Florence Gresham's door. They presented her with a letter from the President of the United States, Richard M. Nixon, which purported to recount Lt. Gresham's courage in battle and to cite the manner in which he met his death. They handed her two small, velvet-covered boxes. One contained a bronze star. The other held a purple heart.

Lt. Winchester Gresham was now, officially, killed in action. Florence Gresham thanked the gentlemen and didn't mention her son, the "killing machine," at least in my presence, for another twelve years.

Throughout the Winchester Gresham affair, Florence never revealed to me the slightest hint of emotion. Win might just as well have been a stranger to her. Her interest appeared to be strictly intellectual. She had a question, she wanted an answer, and she was prepared to pay a persevering lawyer handsomely to try to produce that answer.

As I worked with her over the next several years, I learned to recognize her characteristic response to bad news: Her eyes would narrow, the corners of her mouth would pinch, and she would say, "Well, *that's* a bitch, ain't it?"

She didn't believe in God, or the stars, or bad luck. She simply felt that one did the best one could, and that regrets and second-guessing were a waste of time. That philosophy held equally true for her personal tragedies as for her business reverses. What happened one sultry July evening in 1974 showed me that.

Florence and her husband, Dudley, had been sipping gin-and-tonics in the living room of their summer place, which Florence insisted in calling a "cottage"—all twelve rooms of fieldstone, with its nine acres of manicured lawns and formal rose gardens high on a hill overlooking the sea in Bar Harbor, Maine. They were watching the United States House of Representatives conduct impeachment hearings and chatting idly after a day of sailing in their thirty-eight-foot sloop, which Florence called "the little boat." Dudley had painted its name and port of call in square black letters across its transom. It read: DAUGHTER, BAR HARBOR.

Dud Gresham was absently scratching the ears of his pair of field trial champion English setters, Boone and Crockett. Their surviving son, George, was upstairs reading Toynbee.

A Republican Congressman from Maine named Cohen was declaring his mournful duty to the nation. A Profile in Courage in the midst of the President's Last Crisis.

"Think he's Jewish?" Florence asked.

"Mmm," replied Dudley. "From Maine?"

"I think he's Jewish," said Florence. "That explains it."

Dud Gresham scratched Boone's ears.

Dud was happy to leave the management of the Gresham holdings to Florence. I worked for her, not them. In the five years since I had investigated Win's death, though, I had come to know Dud well. We never talked business. He preferred to tell rambling tales of grouse hunting in Scotland and Wales, quail shooting in Georgia, and bringing geese to the decoys over Chesapeake Bay. Florence and Dudley considered their division of labor equitable. They both did what they wanted to do. It was more than tolerance—they seemed to be genuinely in love with each other.

On that July evening, Dud Gresham smiled at the image of the young Congressman from Maine, set down his empty glass, whistled to Boone and Crockett, and went upstairs. Florence wagged her fingers at him without taking her eyes off the television set.

I have imagined what Dud did then. He unlocked the polished oak gun cabinet that stood in the corner of his study and removed his Purdy double. He sat on the ragged, overstuffed easy chair, rubbing his thumb along the oiled stock of the fine shotgun. Boone and Crockett rested their chins on his leg. Then Dud stood up. "Wait," I can hear him instructing the dogs. He slipped a shell into the right chamber and carefully closed the gun. It shut with the satisfying click of an expensive precision instrument. Boone and Crockett sat and watched, their tails twitching expectantly.

I can still see Dud in my mind's eye, striding down the hallway, gun slung under his arm, as if he were crossing a meadow on a frosty October morning. I imagine his purposeful stride, as if he were intent on keeping up with the dogs as they ranged wide, seeking the day's first covey.

He entered the bathroom, locked the door behind him, sat on the closed toilet seat, bit down on the business end of the gun barrels, and blew the back of his head all over Florence's monogrammed towels.

Florence refused to let the police break down the door of the bathroom. It took an hour for the carpenter to remove the entire frame. "Wouldn't do Dud any good to ruin the door," Florence said. "Dud's an excellent shot," she added.

Dud left a note. "Not because of him," is what it said. The summer people of Bar Harbor were divided on the interpretation of Dud's note. Some figured Dud was referring to Win; others figured he meant Nixon. A third school of thought held that Dud meant George, whose decision to pursue the ascetic life of a scholar—and who detested hunting—must have been a grave disappointment to his parents, and that the note was Dud's way of absolving him.

The carpenter replaced the door. Florence's housekeeper cleaned up the mess in the bathroom. I settled the matter of Dud's estate. For Florence, life went on. A week or so after they buried Dud, she was back in the bathroom soaking in the old-fashioned porcelain tub when she summoned the housekeeper.

Florence pointed into the corner behind the toilet. "That looks like a piece of skull. Clean it up, if you please. Really, my dear, you must do better."

Florence told me that story herself. The point, she said, was: "You just can't get good help any more."

It wasn't until several years later that Florence told me why Dud killed himself. "The prostate cancer had spread," she said. "It was into his bones. The doctor gave him two months to a year. He made it clear that Dud would be luckier if it were on the two months' side. There would be pain. Lots of pain. So Dud and I talked about it. It was his decision, of course. That's how we left it. He'd make the decision. And he did."

"I don't understand his note," I said to Florence. " 'Not because of him.' What did that mean, anyway?"

"Why, it was a joke, of course. A joke for all of us to enjoy. That's all. It wouldn't have been like Dud to *mean* anything very significant by a suicide note. He had already said what needed to be said." Florence paused then, I remember, and smiled wistfully. "Still," she said, "he really didn't have to make such a mess."

George Gresham remained an enigma to me. On the few occasions that I saw him, he seemed willing to defer to his mother in matters of the family fortune. Like his father, he did so without embarrassment. He made it clear that he simply wasn't interested in maneuvering large sums of money around. He was a small, balding man, a few years older than me. He taught history at a very swank little private school on the North Shore of Massachusetts, not far from the family estate in Beverly Farms. He drove second-hand cars, lived in faculty housing, and ate in the dining room with the students. He successfully side-stepped matrimony. For George, it always seemed more a matter of disinterest than active resistance to the lures that were trolled in front of the only heir to the vast Gresham fortune.

George Gresham did exactly what he wanted.

His mother, to her credit, supported George by accepting the life-style he had carved out for himself, satisfied that he spent his summers with her pecking out lucid articles for scholarly magazines from his study in the Bar Harbor "cottage." She asked no more of him. I suppose she knew his limits, respected them, and understood that he, in his way, was as tough-minded as she.

She wintered in Sarasota, continued to summer in Bar Harbor (still using the toilet where Dud squeezed off his last shot), and spent the spring and autumn months at the estate in Beverly Farms. She employed a cook, a maid, a chauffeur, a housekeeper (the same one who cleaned up Dud's "mess"), and two gardeners. Full time. Year round.

Florence Gresham is a leathery, shrewd old lady. I'm very fond of her.

When she called me on that rainy Monday morning last May, her tone was typically businesslike. "George is dead," she said.

"Ah, hell, Florence. What happened?"

"Drowned, apparently. Fell from some rocks by the ocean. They're investigating. I just wanted you to know. There'll be details, of course. I'll be needing you."

"Of course," I said. "Anything at all."

"They insist on doing an autopsy. Routine, they're telling me. And they've temporarily impounded his things. Damn inconvenient. Anyhow, until they're done there's really nothing. In due course, I suppose you and I will have documents to work on."

"The estate. Sure. Keep me posted," I said. "Are there arrangements?"

"For the funeral, you mean? I wish you wouldn't circumlocute, Brady. No, no arrangements, as you call them, yet. It's all up in the air. I'll let you know."

"Well, I'm terribly sorry."

"Yes. We all are."

Florence's stoic acceptance of George's death mirrored her response to Win's and Dudley's. It did not surprise me. I could picture her at the other end of the line, her tanned, craggy face grim, her strong mouth set. At seventy-two, she still wielded the Gresham fortune like a scythe.

The following Friday I found an uncharacteristically subdued Florence Gresham waiting in the anteroom of my office. She rarely visited me there. She summoned me to her if she needed me. We never met without an appointment.

My secretary, Julie O'Malley, arched her eyebrows at me and twitched her shoulders in a tiny shrug.

"Florence. Pleasant surprise," I said.

She took my hand and pulled me toward her. "I must talk to you," she said. There was an urgency to her tone that was not typical of Florence Gresham. "I took the chance that you'd have a minute for me. May we go into your office?"

"Of course," I said. "I'll get us some coffee."

I have the sort of office that befits an attorney whose practice caters to the very well-to-do. Julie calls my decor "neo-nouveau-riche." The panelling is solid mahogany, the furniture sleek chrome, glass, teak, and leather, the carpet imported from Afghanistan. I own two Wyeth pencil sketches, which hang unobtrusively over the sofa. My ex-wife Gloria, a professional photographer, contributed a sequence of shots of my two sons, Billy and Joey, one a year of each, up through the time of our divorce. Eleven shots of Billy, nine of Joey. They're both adolescents now. Their pictures are framed individually and hang in a mass on the wall opposite the Wyeths. I look at them often.

At one end of my office is my desk, my swivel chair behind it so that I sit with my back to the big window that looks out toward Cambridge. When I confer with adversaries in my office, I put my desk between us, on the theory that such an arrangement puts me in charge. I keep the top of my desk clear of papers. That, too, is a trick for negotiating. It gives the impression that I'm efficient and focused on the issue of the moment.

Actually, most of my adversaries know and practice the same tricks. We admire each other for being as shrewd as we are. None of us really thinks the tricks mean a damn thing.

Failure to employ them, however, would set one at a disadvantage immediately.

I do leave two mementoes on my desktop. One is a Titleist golf ball under a dome of glass, mounted on a white wooden tee. On the marble base a gold plate bears the inscription, "Stow Acres C. C., June 6, 1965." It's the ball I hit into the cup on the fifth hole of the North course from a fluffy lie at the edge of the fairway. A three iron for a double-eagle. Gloria made up the trophy for me. I keep it to remind me of the days when I could reach the par fives with a driver and an iron. It also helps me to remember the days when Gloria and I were too poor to afford membership in a private country club. When we were young, and happy, and in love.

The other item on my desktop is one of those clear, solid plastic cubes used for paperweights. Imbedded in it is a scarred, red-and-white Dardevle spoon. One prong of the treble hook is bent straight. I don't need an inscription to remember Manitoba in July of 1971 and the closest I ever came to catching a muskellunge.

I have a sitting area for my discussions with my clients—fawn leather sofa, glass-topped coffee table, and a couple of comfortable armchairs. That's where Florence and I sat.

She perched tensely on the edge of the sofa, her elbows on her knees, leaning forward. I pulled an armchair near her.

Normally she carried herself as if she were in the saddle—straight, tall, angular. Her face was always well tanned and craggy, her black hair streaked dramatically with white. The horsey-doggy look. A well-preserved woman on the far side of seventy. But now I noticed that her skin seemed blotched and pouchy, her usually sharp blue eyes watery and faded. Suddenly she looked like an old lady to me.

"Florence, you're looking well," I lied.

"I am like hell, Brady Coyne. I look terrible and I feel terrible and I'll tell you exactly why. They are now saying that George killed himself, that's why. Suicide! Can you imagine a less likely candidate for suicide than my George?"

The idea startled me for a moment. But as I thought about it, I felt that perhaps there were a great many less likely candidates. From what I knew of George Gresham's life, it allowed for few setbacks. He had, one might say, cushioned himself against them purposefully by withdrawing into the simplest possible mode of existence. No emotional ties, no financial commitments. A bachelor schoolteacher. Nothing to upset what might have been a delicate equilibrium. He could well have been perched on a knife-blade of sanity. The slightest disturbance could have pushed him off the edge. I did not share this perception with Florence.

"Who told you this?" I asked.

"Parker Barrett called me last night. Evidently the authorities—that's what Barrett called them—issued that verdict after some sort of inquest."

"Barrett," I repeated. "The insurance man?"

"Yes. He was all full of apologies, as though the damn money meant anything to me."

"What do you mean?"

Florence sighed. "A little over a year ago I took out a large policy on George. He was badly underinsured. Because he had a small policy with Jefferson Mutual—that's Barrett's company—which he had taken out when he was twenty, George could get favorable rates. It was convertible to an annuity at sixty-five. You know how George was about money. I figured he'd accept this sort of thing."

"How much?"

"The policy?" Florence shrugged. "Five hundred thousand."

I whistled.

"A lot of money." She nodded. "Enough to keep George very comfortable when he quit teaching. Without his feeling that he was living off his mother. And," she chuckled mirthlessly, "I, of course, was the beneficiary."

"And," I finished, "they won't pay off because it's suicide."

"Right. Not that it really matters. But, yes, there's a two-year suicide clause. Not only that, but there's also a double-indemnity clause for accidental death. You know how that works?"

"Sure. They pay double the face value of the policy in case of accidental death." I thought for a moment. "So if George's death was ruled accidental, Jefferson Mutual would have to pay you one million dollars. But since it's suicide, they pay nothing. I imagine your friend Parker Barrett was vastly relieved."

"Oh, he was as oily as ever." Florence waved the insurance man away with a flap of her hand. "But that's not really the point. This is the point: I do not believe that George jumped off any cliff into the ocean with the intent of killing himself. Not George. Dudley, yes. Dudley *could* kill himself. And did. That, as you know, I could understand. And even agree with. And Win, getting himself killed at war, that I can understand, too. It fits, if you know what I mean. But George? If George *did* kill himself, if he *did* jump into the ocean, that would mean that I didn't know my son, that I never did know him. I would find that hard to live with. His death itself—I accept death. But suicide?" She shook her head back and forth slowly several times.

"What can I do?" I asked.

"I want to appeal. I want you to take this thing to court and prove that George's death was not suicide."

"But, Florence . . ."

"Yes, I know. There must be a lot of evidence. But they've missed something, I'm sure of it. There has to be another explanation. I want you to find it."

"It's not really my line. Perhaps a private investigator . . ."

"No!" she said, with a vigorous shake of her head. "No sleazy private eyes. None of those trench coat-and-cigar types. I want you, Brady Coyne."

"Oh, come on, Florence. They're not all like that."

"The Greshams," she said, "do not hire private investigators. They retain attorneys." Her eyes narrowed. "Ten percent? Over and above your usual generous fee?"

"Now, Florence . . ."

"Yes, yes, I know," she said, waving her hand in front of her face as if flies were bothering her. "We're too sophis-

17

ticated to talk money." She leaned forward, hands on her thighs, her chin jutting at me. "The hell with that. Let's talk money. Ten percent of the policy, if we collect it. If you can prove that George's death was accidental, that'll be ten percent of five hundred thousand—doubled."

"One hundred thousand," I breathed, in spite of myself. She smiled. "Worth a shot?"

"Well, if you're dead set against a private investigator . . ."

"I am. It's settled."

At that moment Julie knocked quietly, then entered with a tray bearing coffee cups. "Milk and sugar, Mrs. Gresham?"

"Yes. Thank you."

Julie fixed me with her California smile. "Black, Brady?"

"Thanks."

Julie set the tray on the coffee table and stood before us, her hand on her perfect hip. "I was terribly sorry to hear about your son, Mrs. Gresham."

"I appreciate your concern, Julie."

Julie turned to me. "Anything you'd like?"

"Please. See if you can get Parker Barrett at Jefferson Mutual for me."

Julie touched her forehead with her forefinger. "Aye, aye, sir." She whirled and whisked out of the office, leaving in her wake the faint scent of mayflowers.

Julie O'Malley had unerring instincts for the law, charmed all my clients of both genders, and did all of my serious spelling for me. She was engaged to a radiologist at Beth Israel, a pleasant young man named Edward who assured me that he had no intention of interfering in Julie's career, and that, if I could consider a leave for her for perhaps three months should they eventually become parents, he and Julie did want her to continue her work. He, for one, had no objection to Julie and me continuing together well into the foreseeable future.

Julie and I established our relationship a few months after I hired her. We were working late, putting together the stuff for a nasty divorce case I had to argue the next day. We had

had tuna sandwiches out of waxed paper and Coke out of cans, and Julie was hunched over her typewriter, where she had spent most of the twelve hours of that workday. I stood behind her, waiting for her to finish the page. She paused in her typing to sigh and roll her shoulders to ease their stiffness. Tentatively I reached down and began to knead the muscles at the base of her neck. She leaned back against my hands, letting her arms fall to her sides.

"Oh, that feels good," she sighed.

Impulsively, I bent and touched the skin at the nape of her neck with my lips—not really a kiss, just my warm breath on her young skin. The wispy hairs tickled my nose. She didn't move, but I could feel the tension where I touched her.

Without turning, she said in a low, even voice, "I would consider becoming your lover. Or I will continue to be your secretary. I will not be both. Your choice."

I stood up and swiveled her chair around so that she faced me. I bent and kissed her forehead. "That's a difficult choice," I said. "But I'll take the secretary."

"I hoped you'd say that," Julie replied with a soft smile. Then she turned back to face her typewriter and resumed her work.

When I look at Julie, I find it easy to second-guess my choice. But it was the right one.

Florence and I sipped our coffee and shortly the telephone buzzed.

"Yes, Julie?"

"Mr. Barrett. Jefferson Mutual. I told him you were Mrs. Gresham's attorney. He's all a-twitter."

I chuckled. "Good." I pressed the button on the phone so that Florence could hear both ends of my conversation with Barrett.

"Mr. Barrett. How are you today?"

"I don't know what this is all about, Mr. Coyne. The clause in Mr. Gresham's policy is quite clear."

"Yes, yes. I know. Two years. How did you determine that his death was a suicide?"

"Oh, *we* didn't decide that. The verdict came from the Medical Examiner's Office. They are very thorough. There's no doubt their findings will stand up in court."

"No one said anything about court."

His sigh hissed over the amplified speaker. Florence smiled at me.

"Naturally, Jefferson Mutual will stand by its contracts," Barrett said, his voice assuming a new tone of confidence. "But I don't need to tell you, Mr. Coyne, that a contract is binding on both parties. We will, of course, return to Mrs. Gresham the equity that has been paid on this policy, with interest. Plus, I might add, some nice dividends."

"What can you tell me about the verdict?"

"Open and shut, evidently. Dr. Clapp—he's the M.E.— issued the verdict yesterday. I have been in contact with his office from the beginning."

"I can imagine," I said.

"I phoned Mrs. Gresham immediately. Sorry to bear bad news, you know, but that goes with the territory."

"A tough piece of work," I said. "What exactly did the doctor tell you?"

"Mr. Gresham jumped from a spot called Charity's Point. Place not far from the school where he taught. It's a hundred-foot drop into the ocean. He drowned. They found his body the next morning on an adjacent beach. Apparently he was quite battered by the surf and the rocks, but the cause of death was drowning."

"How did they determine he jumped? Were there witnesses?"

Barrett actually laughed. His voice burst harshly over the speaker into my office. "There didn't need to be witnesses, Mr. Coyne. Mr. Gresham was his own witness."

"Don't be oblique, Barrett. What the hell do you mean?"

"The note. There was a suicide note, Mr. Coyne. That's what I meant. Open and shut."

I lifted my eyebrows at Florence, who seemed to collapse into herself.

"I see," I said. "A note."

"Yes," said Barrett. "That simplifies things."

"I suppose it does, insurance-wise," I said. "Well, I do appreciate your time. Perhaps we'll be in touch."

"I can't see why. But, of course, if there's anything I can do . . ."

"Thank you, Mr. Barrett."

I returned the receiver to its cradle and looked at Florence. The corners of her mouth drooped.

"He never mentioned any note to me," she said.

"Still want to go ahead with it?"

"You bet I do," she said, her eyes glittering with new life. "More than ever. If George did jump off some cliff, I've got to know why. Can you understand that?"

"Yes," I nodded. "I guess I can."

CHAPTER 2.

I CHERISHED the faint hope
that I might make the Great Discovery that would persuade
the Medical Examiner to reverse his findings. The ten percent of George Gresham's double-indemnity policy, I had to
admit, was most attractive. Specializing in keeping wealthy
people safely legal has its drawbacks. The work tends to be
boring, for one thing. I spend a great deal of my time remaining *au courant* on tax and antitrust law, scouring contracts, and writing and revising wills. I spend very little of my
time arguing interesting points of law in courtrooms.

I work on retainer plus fees. Generous fees. Outrageous
fees, really. However, since my clients demand personal attention, I am forced to limit my practice. They expect me to
be available. They expect me to make house calls. They expect me to take afternoon tea with them, to tolerate their
poodles jumping up onto my lap, to listen to their old war
stories again. So I rather liked the idea of visiting the Medical
Examiner, for a change of pace.

When Dr. Milton Clapp extended his hand to me as I
entered his office, his confident professionalism dimmed my
hope of unearthing New Evidence, of making that Great Discovery. This self-assured gentleman, with his blue bow tie and
crisp white smock, seemed unlikely to make a mistake. He

peered at me over half-moon glasses, his sharp blue eyes crinkled at the corners, his mouth drawn back in an open grin over what appeared to be a good set of dentures.

"Mr. Coyne. Have a seat."

His office was small, a place of work. I had the feeling that the state's Chief Medical Examiner did not ordinarily receive visitors here. One dirty window looked out across an alley at a blank brick wall. His scarred desk was littered with papers and journals, many of them folded back as if they were half read. On one corner stood a large glass jar. Inside it, a dark, grayish mass swam in a yellowish solution. It looked like a big, dirty jellyfish.

Dr. Clapp followed my gaze. "A smoker's lung," he said. "I keep it as a reminder. Better than will power."

I nodded.

The walls of his office were noteworthy by the absence of framed diplomas, documents, certificates, or awards. Instead, I saw a large chart depicting, as near as I could tell, the human nervous system. There was also a calendar produced by the First National Bank of Boston featuring an old Currier and Ives print of Haymarket Square, and still turned to April. Almost directly behind Dr. Clapp's head hung a small wooden plaque inscribed in fancy Old English scroll. I could barely read it from where I sat. It was entitled "An Angler's Proverb."

"Allah does not deduct," it read, "from the allotted time of man those hours spent in fishing."

I pointed to it as I squirmed into a comfortable position on the wooden, straight-backed chair he offered me. "You're a fisherman, then?"

"Oh, yes. When I can." He waved his hand, as if it weren't significant.

"I have a plaque hanging in my bathroom at home," I said. "It's called 'The Angler's Prayer.' Know it?"

He shook his head.

"It goes like this," I said. " 'Lord give me grace to catch a fish so big that even I, when talking of it afterwards, may never need to lie.' "

Dr. Milton Clapp, I noticed, smiled easily. "When I was your age," he said, "I felt the same way."

"The difference between youthful excess and mature perspective?" I suggested.

"The difference between lawyers and doctors, perhaps," he said. "What can I do for you, Mr. Coyne?"

He leaned forward on his elbows, his hands clasped before him, his eyes alert. Everything about him and his office said, "This is a busy and important man. Don't waste his time."

"As I said on the phone, I represent the estate of George Gresham. Because there is a sizable insurance policy, and because his mother is quite distraught, as you can imagine, I am exploring the possibility of appealing the finding of your inquest."

"I understand perfectly. You're on a fishing expedition." The doctor smiled. "Don't blame you at all. It's always a sad duty for me to find suicide. But I assure you that there is little doubt in this case."

"Of course. Still . . ."

"I'll be blunt with you, Mr. Coyne. There is no other reasonable explanation. The presence of the note leaves no question in my mind."

"I'd like to see that note," I said.

"And you shall. But why don't you just let me explain the whole thing in my own way, first. Then we'll look at the note. And then if you still have questions I'll be happy to answer them."

He peered at me over his glasses, his eyebrows arched.

"That would be fine," I said.

"Good." He hitched himself forward in his chair and glanced up at the ceiling for a moment before he spoke. "I was called on the morning of Friday, May first, by Dr. Berman, the local Medical Examiner. I suppose you understand that in Massachusetts each county district has its own examiner, what the quaint law of the Commonwealth calls a 'discreet physician.' They're not forensic pathologists—not usually pathologists at all, in fact, but simply M.D.'s appointed by the Governor for five-year terms. The police call them in cases of unattended, violent, or suspicious deaths. Their job is to determine the cause and manner of death. I emphasize the word 'manner,' Mr. Coyne. It's not enough to know *how* a person dies. The circumstances of his death are at least of equal importance."

I nodded, feeling very much like a college sophomore sitting at the feet of a distinguished professor.

His eyes roamed the walls of the tiny office as he spoke in his precise, clipped manner. "By the time I was called in, the police and Dr. Berman had done their jobs. The note had been found, and they had pretty well reconstructed the manner of death. Because the death had been unattended— not to mention violent—a forensic autopsy was required. Dr. Berman is not authorized to perform such autopsies. That is my bailiwick."

I leaned forward in my seat and nodded.

Dr. Clapp stared at me briefly, then shifted his attention to the wall over my left shoulder. "Here's what happened: On the evening of April 30, George Gresham drove his automobile to a place called North Cove Beach, outside of Manchester. He parked and locked it at the municipal lot there. He was wearing a suit and tie. He walked from the parking lot up to the top of a high bluff that overlooks the ocean. The view is spectacular from there. It's a popular spot for lovers." Dr. Clapp permitted himself a wry smile. "Also with jumpers. Nine suicides have been attributed to jumps from Charity's Point in the last twelve years. Ten, counting Mr. Gresham. Anyway, he climbed out to the tip of Charity's Point, took off his jacket, folded it, and laid it on the ground. The suicide note was in the inside pocket of the jacket, sealed. Then he leaped to his death. His body was discovered on the beach the next morning by a young lady who was out for her morning jog. Frightful experience for her."

"I can imagine," I murmured.

"Indeed. Mr. Gresham's body sustained quite a beating. It did raise some doubt about the specific cause of his death. Until the note was found, in fact, there was considerable doubt about the entire matter."

I was finding the discussion—and Dr. Clapp's clinical tone—a trifle disconcerting. I wanted a cigarette. But the black lung on Dr. Clapp's desk seemed to be staring at me.

"When I arrived, unfortunately, the body had been removed to a local funeral home," he continued. "I performed the autopsy there. Not ideal conditions, but that's how our system works. Although by then the problem was really academic."

"Academic?"

"A body washed up on the beach, a suicide note. Most commonly, that spells suicide. Logical, eh?"

I shrugged.

"We have a saying, Mr. Coyne. We say, 'The commonest things most commonly happen.' It's a guide, understand. We're not enslaved by it. It's not like your mystery stories, where what *appears* to be is dramatically different from what really *is*, where you need a slick sleuth to uncoil a tangled web of clues."

I averted my eyes. This mild gentleman had me properly pegged.

"We're not, as I said, enslaved by that principle," the doctor said, his eyes crinkling as if he had read my mind. "But we do find that, by and large, what seems to be, usually is."

"But not always," I said, perhaps a bit defensively.

"Of course not. We'd both be out of business, if the commonest things *always* happened." He chuckled, and I smiled at his joke.

"I'm afraid I was hoping that something uncommon happened to George Gresham," I said.

He shook his head. "Our findings don't seem to bear you out."

"Can you tell me what you did find?"

"Oh, yes. I have a report, of course. You're welcome to read it. But you'll find it pretty technical, I expect. Here's what happens. My first task is to try to estimate the time of death, which, as I'm sure you know, is a *most* inexact science. If you should hear a pathologist claim that he can say with any certainty when someone died—even committing himself to an estimate within a couple of hours—on the basis of examining the body, don't trust that pathologist. It's mainly a lot of guesswork. You see, for pathological purposes we define death as the cessation of the heartbeat. Brain death occurs subsequently within minutes. The organs begin to 'die' shortly thereafter. As they do, the body ceases to produce heat. Hence, our single most important tool in estimating time of death is the amount of heat loss. So, of course, we take its temperature, both external and internal."

He paused for a moment, adjusting some of the papers on his desk. I waited.

"But there are so many variables. The body does not lose its heat at a regular, predictable rate. It tends to retain its heat for a while—longer or shorter depending on the temperature of the atmosphere. In the desert you might come upon a body with a 'normal' temperature that has been dead for hours. In the Arctic, it would lose its heat rapidly, depending on how heavily clothed it was, how much body fat it had, the position of the body, and so forth. Mr. Gresham's body posed special problems, since it presumably had been immersed in the Atlantic Ocean. Which is pretty cold in April. Suffice it to say that I recorded his temperature, but attributed no particular significance to it."

He peered at me. "What about rigor mortis?" I asked.

He smiled. "We place little faith in rigor these days, partly because it's difficult to measure, and partly because, as in the case of body temperature, there are so many variables that can intervene. Crudely speaking, complete rigor occurs within the first twelve hours after death, lasts approximately twelve hours, then gradually disappears over the next twelve to twenty-four hours. Rigor begins in the small muscles—mouth, eyelids—and progresses to the larger muscles. Again, crudely, it begins at the head and moves down the body to the legs. Nysten's Law." Dr. Clapp shrugged. "Of little practical value. Take Mr. Gresham's body. Rigor had only begun to occur. The chill of the ocean will inhibit rigor mortis. Conversely, of course, extreme heat will accelerate it."

"So you weren't able to estimate time of death?"

"I can put a frame on it. *You*, Mr. Coyne, could do the same." I frowned, and he allowed himself a chuckle. "On the basis of when he was last seen alive, and when he was found dead, you see. It doesn't take a forensic pathologist to draw conclusions from those data."

"When *was* he last seen? Alive, I mean."

"At the end of dinner. Around seven. No one we could find at the school could recall seeing him after dinnertime." Dr. Clapp peered at me over the tops of his half-moon lenses. "We have investigated this case very thoroughly. The local police have been most cooperative. Everyone of any consequence—and several of no consequence whatever—at the school has been interrogated. Mr. Gresham's room has been secured and thoroughly searched and examined. Everything that has been found—and there really wasn't much; Mr. Gresham appears to have lived a simple life—only seems to confirm our conclusion."

"Please tell me about your medical—your pathological—findings."

Dr. Clapp removed his glasses and rubbed them absentmindedly on the front of his white smock. Then he placed them back on the bridge of his nose, hooking them over each ear with the crook of his forefinger. He moved some papers on his desk, then held up a manila folder. He peered at the writing on the tab. "Here it is." He opened it in front of him and extracted a sheaf of black-and-white photographs. He handed them to me. "Police photos. The body as it was found on the beach." One showed Gresham's body curled fetally on the shimmering wet sand, necktie loosened around his throat, dress shirt with cuffs rolled halfway up his forearms, oxfords laced to his feet. A close-up focused on what had been George Gresham's face—a white, pulpy mass, oddly bloodless, jagged bits of bone around his nose and eye sockets, forehead laid open so that a big flap of pale flesh hung down over his brow. And his eyes—his eyes were gone. The photos showed dozens of tiny sandcrabs in the act of pecking and jabbing at the empty places where Gresham's eyes had been. There were pockmarks on his face and the backs of his hands. "What you see are mostly wounds made by seagulls. They had only begun on his face and the backs of his hands. If the body had washed up somewhere else, and had not been discovered by the girl jogging on the beach the morning after he died, there would have been little more than a skeleton and teeth left."

I shuddered.

I held up one of the close-ups, which showed Gresham's fist clenched tightly against his chest. "What's the significance of this?"

"Cadaveric spasm," he replied. "Interesting phenomenon. That photo suggests that Mr. Gresham was immersed in the ocean at the moment he died. Notice—you can see it pretty clearly—" the doctor jabbed at the photograph with his blunt forefinger "—the string of seaweed in his hand. What happens is that the fists clench spasmodically at the precise instant of death. Different from the gradual stiffening of the muscles in rigor mortis. This is one powerful, final electric impulse from brain to hand. The grip can be superhuman. So we know with certainty that this man was clutching at seaweed at the moment his heart beat for the last time. Presumably somewhere at the bottom of the sea. That particular variety of seaweed, our biologists tell me, is a sort of moss that grows only on rocks under the water, so we can pretty well eliminate the possibility that he was out of water at the instant of his death."

I stared at the picture of George Gresham's fist for a moment, trying to imagine the frantic desperation of a man being sucked along the ocean's floor, grasping at the slimy rocks as death struck him. I passed the photos back to the doctor.

"Now these," he continued, handing me a second sheaf of pictures, "are the pathological photographs. You'll see immediately why we decided to autopsy the body."

I saw. George Gresham's nude body lay flat on a narrow chrome table. It was a mass of scrapes, tears, welts, and bumps. It had undergone a terrible beating from ankle to skull. Hardly a square inch had been left unmarked.

"It looks like he was beaten up and kicked around," I said.

"Doesn't it!" Dr. Clapp's voice echoed the horror that I

felt. I liked him for that. "The work of the rocks and the surf, we surmise. He took inhuman punishment down there at the bottom of the ocean before he died. Inhuman!"

"But how do you know? Couldn't he have been beaten up and thrown over the edge? Couldn't those marks have been made by a knife or a club or something?"

"No. Look." He took off his glasses and pointed at the photograph with them. "They're random, shapeless. The gashes are jagged—tears, really, not incisions like you'd get with a knife or similar weapon. And the welts—each different. Some blunt, some sharper, none alike."

"Fists couldn't have done that? A man with a rock in his hand?"

"No."

"You sound so sure."

"I am sure, Mr. Coyne. I've examined hundreds of dead bodies, and hundreds more that were living. I've studied for a lifetime. I'm a specialist. This is my business."

"So you're saying that most of this—this damage to his body—occurred after he actually died. Is that it?"

"As a pathologist, I admit I can't tell you for sure. We can't determine with certainty whether lacerations, abrasions, or bruises occurred immediately before or after death. In either case, there's going to be some oozing of blood and fluids into the area. Post-mortem wounds look like ante-mortem wounds. It's still an area of study for us. We have some hope that microscopic examination of the enzymes that flood into the area can help us identify ante-mortem wounds—but even then, our best hope is to distinguish wounds at least an hour old at time of death. No, if any of Mr. Gresham's wounds occurred before he died, I couldn't tell you which ones."

I held out my hands, palms up. "Then . . . ?"

"Right, of course, Mr. Coyne. Some of those wounds might have been administered prior to his leap into the ocean. That is possible."

"So how can you eliminate . . . ?"

"Foul play?" He smiled. "Of course, we can't. Not with absolute certainty. But the evidence doesn't point to it. Naturally, if we could place another person at Charity's Point with George Gresham on the evening of April 30, we'd have a different story. We need opportunity—that's the person—and motive. Then we might be talking murder. We found nothing remotely resembling either opportunity or motive. That left us with accident. The note pretty much dispelled both theories. My autopsy found no natural cause to suspect. The police found the note. Ergo, suicide. I'm sorry."

"Yes," I said. "Me too. So he drowned."

Dr. Clapp leaned back in his chair and made a steeple of his fingers. He stared up at the ceiling for a moment.

"Drowned. Yes, I guess you'd say he drowned." He looked hard at me. "In the sense that he didn't die from the fractured ribs, the fracture at the base of his skull, the punctured lung, or the burst testicle—yes, he drowned. His lungs and stomach were full of sea water. There was bile in his lungs as well, indicating he had inspired regurgitated material. Official cause of death is listed as cardiac arrest from drowning. You see, when someone drowns, he takes huge quantities of sea water into his stomach and lungs. And when he can't breathe, he suffers from hypoxia—lack of blood oxygen. He thrashes around, he gasps for air, he regurgitates and inspires water, and he panics. Large doses of adrenalin are secreted into the system. Adrenalin plus hypoxia produces cardiac arrest. The heart fails. That is death."

Dr. Clapp rested his chin on the interlaced fingers of both hands, as if in prayer. I imagined poor George Gresham flailing in the turbulent water. I could not imagine anyone choosing that manner of death voluntarily.

"We've developed some pretty sophisticated tests, incidentally," he went on. "Blood chloride levels in the chambers of the heart, for example. The sodium chloride level in the blood is higher than normal in the blood coming from the lungs in a salt-water drowning. And then there are diatoms."

I lifted my eyebrows. "Diatoms?"

"Yes. Microscopic particles found in water. Little silicate skeletons. Tiny fossils. When drowning occurs, they are circulated through the blood into the organs. It's one of the sure ways of determining that a body died from downing, rather than, for example, falling into the water *after* cardiac arrest. A dead body will absorb sea water. The lungs may well be full, even the stomach. But because the heart isn't pumping, the diatoms will not be found in the organs. We detect them by examining liver sections. Diatoms even can help us pinpoint where a body drowned. They're different in fresh and salt water, and different bodies of water contain their own characteristic diatoms."

I frowned. Dr. Clapp looked at me as if he were surprised to see me sitting across from him.

"Sorry," he said. "I do tend to get carried away sometimes. Suffice it to say that we can pretty much rule out a natural cause of death, and we're certain that none of the blows to Mr. Gresham's body was fatal. He did drown, all right."

I thought for a moment. "What about drugs or alcohol?"

"A fair question. Naturally, we test routinely for them. Poisons, too, if we suspect them. There were traces of pyribenzimine in Mr. Gresham's blood."

"Traces of what?"

"Pyribenzimine. It's a routine prescription. He evidently suffered from hay fever. He had taken a pill a few hours before he died."

"Funny thing for a man to do if he was planning to kill himself," I said.

Dr. Clapp shrugged. "I suppose. One doesn't necessarily expect entirely rational behavior from someone in that state of mind. Anyhow, we found nothing to suggest a drug- or alcohol-related factor. Nothing. From what we've been able to determine, Mr. Gresham lived a very clean life."

"Yes. I would have thought so."

"We did a thorough job, Mr. Coyne. I can appreciate your concerns, naturally. But we do have very sophisticated technology. I took sections from each organ, samples of all the bodily fluids, samples from each orifice, hair from all parts of the body, scrapings from under the nails. All were tested in my laboratories either by me or under my supervision. There was nothing countersuggestive. Nothing at all."

"And there was the note."

"Yes. There was, of course, the note. That made it all fit together."

"Very neatly."

"You still sound dubious." He tilted his head back and stared at me over his glasses.

"On Mrs. Gresham's account, I have to be. I must admit you make a persuasive case."

He snatched his glasses from his nose with a quick, almost angry motion of his hand, and leaned toward me. "Understand me. I make *no* case. My job is not to make a case. The evidence makes the case. I use my scientific expertise to draw the conclusions that the evidence points to. I have no axe to grind. None whatsoever. I am neutral. I am a scientist. Sometimes I am called upon to examine the tissues from a living body, you know. Sometimes I discover carcinoma. That doesn't make me happy. I do not make a case for cancer. I report it. Do you think I want George Gresham's death to have been a suicide? Do you think I *care*? My job is *not* to care. My job is to discover, interpret, conclude, and report."

I averted my eyes. "I'm sorry. I didn't mean to accuse you of anything."

"No, I suppose you didn't." His tone was gentler. "Personally, I am always saddened to discover suicide. I am, first and foremost, a doctor. Committed to life. Yes, even pathologists—*especially* pathologists, especially *forensic* pathologists—are solemnly sworn to the great cause of human life. A life senselessly or needlessly destroyed is reason for great unhappiness among doctors. When I think of the confusion, the misery, the hopelessness of a man who is driven to destroy his own life, I do mourn, Mr. Coyne." He paused. "But I still must report it."

"I know," I mumbled, feeling inane. I had had my hand slapped, and I deserved it.

"Please excuse my vehemence." Dr. Clapp cleared his

throat, indicating that the subject was closed. "Now, about the note. You'll want a copy of it, of course."

I nodded.

"The original remains with me, but copies are available. I've had a photocopy made for you. Perhaps you'll deliver it to Mr. Gresham's mother, if she is interested."

He retrieved a piece of paper from the folder before him and held it up. "Let me assure you that all of the appropriate tests have been run to authenticate this note. It was typed on the typewriter in Mr. Gresham's room. It was signed by him. And," he added, staring meaningfully at me, "the envelope it was found in was sealed by George Gresham's tongue. We were especially meticulous with these tests. Each was performed twice by different technicians. We are virtually certain that George Gresham wrote that note, signed it, and sealed it in an envelope himself."

"Hold on a minute," I said. "I understand about the handwriting and the typewriter. But how in the world can you tell who sealed the envelope?"

"That really is something, isn't it?" Dr. Clapp nodded his head, arched his eyebrows, and grinned. He seemed genuinely amazed himself. "Actually, I overstated the case just a bit. We are only ninety percent certain that Mr. Gresham sealed that envelope."

"Even ninety percent . . ."

"Yes. You see, serology—the study of the blood—has made wonderful strides in recent years. We now know that virtually all the body's fluids—perspiration, semen, urine, bone marrow, saliva, and so on—can be typed. Like blood. And the groups are the same as blood. Someone with Type A blood will have Type A sweat, for example. Saliva is really the easiest to type, since it carries such a high concentration of agglutinins and agglutinogens. Our folks in the lab can take an old cigarette butt and tell the blood type of the person who smoked it. We've eliminated suspects on the basis of the saliva residue on a bite mark. A recently sealed envelope posed no particular problem."

"But . . ."

"Ninety percent. Okay. As you know, there are four blood

groups—O, A, B, and AB. Mr. Gresham happened to be Type B. The residue of saliva on the gum of the envelope seal was also Type B. Now, since only ten percent of the white American population is Type B . . ." He nodded once, and leaned back in his chair.

"I believe you," I grinned. I took the paper he handed me. The words were constructed on the paper like a freeform poem.

> *Now*
> *I have nothing.*
> *The rest is silence.*
> *Regrets fly up*
> *Like unanswered prayers.*

It was signed in a small, fussy script: "G. Gresham." And he scribbled the date under his name—May 1.

"I thought he jumped on the night of April 30," I said. "He's dated it the first of May."

Dr. Clapp shrugged. "I wondered about that, too. I guess he knew that's when it would be found."

"I suppose," I said. I reread the note. "I'm not sure I get it. Some of it's Shakespeare, isn't it?"

The doctor nodded. "You recognize Hamlet's dying words, of course. 'The rest is silence.' There's another place in the play where the king, I believe—Hamlet's uncle, whom he suspects of killing his father, seizing his throne, and sleeping with his mother—is trying to pray. But his guilt prevents him, and he says something about his words flying up but his thoughts remaining below."

"I remember," I said. "Hamlet's watching him, and thinks he might kill his uncle then, while he's praying. But he decides not to, because then the villain would go to heaven." I looked at Dr. Clapp. "What do you suppose it means?"

He shook his head. "I don't know. It's surely about death, and I guess that's all that really matters."

"Gresham's mother would think it matters," I said. "It's sort of a strange suicide note, isn't it?"

He shrugged. "Not really. I've seen plenty in my line of

work, of course. Too many. Most of them, actually, are addressed to somebody specific—a husband or wife, a parent perhaps. Suicides don't generally announce their intentions to the world. Some of them are pretty cruel. 'You made me do it. I hope you're happy now.' That was one we had. A teen-aged boy wrote that one to his father before he hanged himself. Try living with that."

"God!"

"Yes." Dr. Clapp inclined his head. "Others, you know, are actually quite touching. 'I'll meet you in Heaven,' or just 'I love you.' And some, to be sure, are long, rambling, incoherent discourses."

"This one," I said, tapping the paper I held, "it's . . ."

"Epigrammatic." Dr. Clapp finished my thought. "Yes. It's eloquent, too. Poetic, really."

"Very sad," I said. Then I had another thought. "You found this in his jacket pocket, you said?"

He nodded, his eyebrows arched.

"Maybe," I continued, "it had nothing to do with his fall. Maybe it was just a coincidence. A sad poem he had written. A life of regrets. Middle-aged ennui, that sort of thing."

He nodded slowly. "It's possible, of course. But you must admit, Mr. Coyne, most unlikely. In any case, that's my verdict, and if the evidence seems circumstantial to you, well, it's all the evidence we have, you see. Besides, there was the matter of Mr. Gresham's father."

"Dudley," I said.

"He took his own life several years ago, you know. And that—statistically, at least—is very significant."

I nodded. "It does all seem to fit."

"Yes, I'm afraid it does." Dr. Clapp began rustling the papers on his desk. I accepted the hint and rose, extending my hand.

"Thank you, Doctor, for your time. And for the most enlightening discussion."

His handshake was firm. "Sorry if I lectured at you."

I shook my head and smiled. "It was fascinating. Wish I could say I enjoyed it."

He moved from behind his desk and walked with me the few steps to the door. "You know," he said, "if you're really concerned about Mr. Gresham's frame of mind—if you want to try to understand this tragic thing—you should talk to the people who knew him, who he worked with, who were around him before he did this. There are so many things we scientists can't know."

I opened the door. "I suppose I'll do that. At least on behalf of my client, I have to remain skeptical about the suicide. Not," I added with a smile, "that I don't trust you."

His eyes wrinkled playfully. "Don't trust anybody, Mr. Coyne. That's one thing that both of our professions teach us. Don't trust anybody."

"I try not to," I said.

CHAPTER 3.

I GOT back to the office a little after two that afternoon. Julie was on the telephone. She lifted her eyebrows at me when I entered, then quickly put a finger to her lips. I nodded. She was holding a client off for me. She knew it wasn't urgent. Maybe not even important. My clients tend to call just to chat. They usually seem content to chat with Julie. I consider that valid client service.

I grinned at her. She blew me a kiss, and then spoke into the telephone, her tone soothing. Her free hand twirled absently in her glossy, dark hair.

I went into my office and sat down heavily behind my desk. I had had no lunch, and I discovered that my stomach had hardened into a tight knot. It felt like a barrel knot. At least a clove hitch. As if I'd swallowed a double shot of Liquid-plumr. I was not used to being close up to death. Contracts, separation agreements, wills, citations, I was used to. But glossy photographs of cadaveric spasms and empty eye sockets were out of my line. Suicide notes didn't seem to lend themselves to loophole-picking rational analysis.

Julie rapped softly at the half-open door to my office. "May I come in?"

I nodded, and she sat in the chair near my desk.

"Want some coffee?" I asked. "My turn to get it."

"No, thanks. I've had my quota already. You know," she said, frowning at me, "you drink too much of that stuff."

"Yes, yes, I know. Ulcers, high blood pressure. Rots the brain. Ruins the bowels. You know, you get these little creases between your eyes when you glare at me. You don't watch out, they'll become permanent."

"It causes cancer of the pancreas, too," she persisted. "Edward says you're trying to destroy yourself."

"I thought Edward was a radiologist."

"He is."

"Not a psychiatrist."

Julie tossed her head. "He knows all those things. I worry about you. Cigarettes, coffee, bourbon. You don't get any exercise. You're not a young man."

I snorted. "He's right. I am the living exemplification of the Death Instinct. On the other hand, there was nothing instinctive about George Gresham's death. It seems to have been painstakingly conceived, scrupulously executed. I wonder," I added, ostentatiously firing up a Winston, "if George regretted his clean living as he tumbled to his death. I bet his last thoughts were of bourbon Old Fashioneds and Lucky Strikes and shrimp scampi. Sad, huh?"

"You're being perfectly ghoulish, Counselor," she said. "Have a bad morning."

"I had an accelerated course in more than you ever wanted to know about the abuse that can be heaped upon the human body. It takes a lot to kill a man. I don't know very much about death. Or didn't."

"It was suicide, then?"

"Seems that way." I summarized quickly what Dr. Clapp had told me. She listened intently, as I knew she would, sucking on the knuckle of her forefinger as I attempted to reconstruct the pathologist's explanation of how the human body dies from drowning. When I had finished, she stared at me for a moment.

"So it all hinges on the note?"

"Well, yes, I suppose it does. Without the note, I guess it would be a lot of conjecture. But there was the note."

I removed it from my jacket pocket and handed it to her. "Tell me what you think."

She read it slowly. When she had finished, she handed it back to me. "Shakespeare, isn't it?"

I nodded. "Some of it."

"I recognize the Hamlet. His dying words. What's the other mean?"

I shrugged. "Who knows? It means whatever George meant it to mean. His father wrote a suicide note that was a *joke*, for God's sake. The point is, the man who wrote it ended up dead on the beach."

"If you want to know *why* he ended up there, that's not the point at all," said Julie. "This note doesn't say he's going to *kill* himself. For heaven's sake, it doesn't say he's going to *do* anything at all. It just—well, it says he's sad."

"Right. Very sad. Depressed. *Very* depressed, I'd say. Very depressed people commit suicide a lot."

"No. People who commit suicide may tend to be depressed. But that doesn't mean that depressed people tend to commit suicide. There's a difference."

I waved my hand. "Whatever. George's dead."

"Sounds like you've bought it all."

I shrugged. "Guess I have. It fits."

"Hell," said Julie, her eyes flashing. "This could mean *anything*. It's a poem. It's not even a note."

"Except, you see, George did kill himself. And he left this behind. That makes it a suicide note. *Q.E.D.*"

Julie grinned in triumph. "Correction, learned Counselor. George *died*. That's all you *know*. What ever happened to reasonable doubt?"

"Ah, there's always doubt, Julie. How reasonable is reasonable? Dr. Clapp said to me, 'The commonest things most commonly happen.' Set reasonable doubt up against the preponderance of evidence here, and the doubt seems pretty unreasonable. Remember. The law does not say 'beyond all doubt.' They stuck the word 'reasonable' in there. It's the rule of reason that still makes the law work."

"You damn lawyers. Always think you can outtalk us lay

people. But it doesn't make you right, you know. Come on, Counselor. We're just having a little discussion here. We're not in front of any judge or jury now, so you don't have to conquer any adversaries or win points. Not with me. What do you really think?"

I touched Julie's hand. "I really think that George jumped into the ocean, that's what I think. But you are right in one respect. The lawyer in me should doubt it."

"The human being in me doubts it," said Julie. "I can't get Mrs. Gresham's face out of my head. So what're you going to do?"

"Go up to The Ruggles School. See if I can talk to some people. Try to make some sense of it for Florence. It's the least I can do."

Julie smiled. "Good. That's good."

"In the meantime, tell me about all the morning's excitement in the bustling offices of Brady L. Coyne, Attorney-at-Law. What happened while I was gone?"

She waved her hand around. "Nothing interesting. More coffee?"

There's a little restaurant along Route 127 south of Gloucester known as Gert's Place. The sign outside announces, in typical understatement, simply "Good Food." The tourists always miss it, of course, as they race along the superhighways for the glamorous spots on the Massachusetts North Shore—Gloucester, with its fishing fleets and its Moonies and its statue of the slickered fisherman at the helm, or Rockport with its famous Motif #1 and its boutiques on Bearskin Neck, or history-rich Newburyport at the mouth of the Merrimack.

The sun-worshippers miss Gert's, too, preferring to crawl bumper-to-bumper along Route 128 on a steamy Saturday for the dubious pleasure of lying cheek to thigh with similarly minded strangers on the glimmering sands of Crane's or Wingaersheek or Good Harbor or Singing Beach, in a mindless race to see who can contract the first case of skin cancer.

The folks who live hard by the ocean go about their

business, tolerant in their taciturn Yankee way of the strange people who drive long distances to broil under the sun on their beaches. They're happy to sell them old pieces of furniture and ice cream cones and gasoline along the way, and if they think it's damn foolishness, they keep it to themselves.

Gert knows what to do with bluefish and wine, and she performs saintly miracles with fresh ground pepper and lemon slices and striped bass. The halibut and the sole and the scrod she buys directly off the boats, and she gets the fillets into her ovens under a layer of breadcrumb and butter and bits of shrimp and crab before the fish realizes it's dead. She serves Gloucester lobsters and Ipswich clams. For those who prefer, Gert keeps in her head a portfolio of recipes inherited from her mother, who must have been a Neapolitan wizard. Gert's veal scallopine with mushrooms and peppers and a carafe of her musty house red remains my second favorite way of accomplishing sensual ecstasy.

The crushed-stone parking area alongside the rambling, cedar-shingled building was nearly full when I arrived at Gert's. It was about noon on Tuesday. I got there at lunch time, needing directions to The Ruggles School and having had no breakfast. I hadn't exactly planned it that way, at least not consciously, but it worked out just the way I wanted.

The dining room was crowded—local people, mostly men, some in shirt and tie, their jackets thrown over the backs of their chairs, and others in work clothes. Bankers and insurance salesmen, electricians and plumbers, clerks and a few young secretaries.

I was led to a small table with a checked tablecloth against a side wall. The place was noisy. The patrons all seemed to know each other, and laughter bubbled up frequently as the diners conversed, the men and women twisting in their chairs to talk with friends at adjacent tables.

My waitress was a hefty girl in her twenties. She dumped a pile of silverware in front of me, then straightened, pencil poised over pad.

"Help ya?" she asked. Beads of perspiration stood out on her forehead. The armpits of her white uniform, which she was jammed into like a fat sausage, were stained.

"Busy, eh?" I offered.

"Special today is fish chowder," she said, digging into her beehive hairdo with the eraser end of the pencil.

"What kind of fish?"

"Fresh cod. Off the boat this morning."

"Fine. I'll have a bowl. And a bottle of Beck's."

Then she smiled, and her round face was momentarily beautiful before she waddled away.

The chowder was delicious. Chunks of flaky white fish, hunks of potato, and slivers of transparent onion swam in a peppery, thick broth which I knew was pure cream. Bits of crisp bacon were sprinkled on top. I devoured it, and sat back with a sigh to sip my beer.

My waitress—Alice, the black plate pinned above her left bosom said—returned and plucked up the empty bowl.

" 'Nother beer?"

"Please. And tell me, how do I get to The Ruggles School?"

" 'Bout a mile and a half north on one-twenty-seven, take a left at the second set of lights. You'll see it on your right." She seemed to study me for a moment. "You a cop?"

"Me?" I laughed. "No. I'm not a cop."

"Oh. There was lots of cops around last week. The guy, what's-his-name there at the school who killed himself. Big hoop-de-do. Glad that's all over with. Next thing you know, all the tourists will be comin' to take pictures of Charity's Point, havin' picnics up there." She snorted. "Who needs 'em?"

I smiled in what I hoped was a disarming manner. "I'm not a tourist, either," I said. "To tell the truth, I'm an attorney."

Alice looked disgusted. "Attorney, cop, same difference. I'll get your beer."

CHAPTER 4.

I ALMOST missed The Ruggles School, although Alice's directions were perfect. The driveway was bounded by two stone pillars. The modest sign on one of them announced "The Ruggles School, est. 1923." The driveway wound under a canopy of giant maples. Along either side, green lawns rolled gently among the ancient shade trees. Pathways intersected the grassy slopes, and perennial borders sparkled with late spring bulbs and splashes of pot-o'-gold and low pink phlox. I drove slowly, minding the sign that ordered "15 MPH." Here and there, young people strolled the pathways or lay sprawled in the sunny patches, some on their bellies, chins propped in hands, feet waving in the air, open books in front of them, and others stretched out flat on their backs squinting at the spring sky. The girls looked fresh and healthy. The boys looked young.

The driveway ended at a cluster of brick buildings, constructed, I judged, some sixty years ago when the school was founded. They were solid, square, functional. I parked directly in front of a sign that read "Authorized Personnel Only." I had an appointment. I supposed that made me authorized.

I entered into a cool, dark corridor. The interior walls were brick, the floor a worn, checked tile. From somewhere inside came the reedy voice of Buddy Holly. "It's so easy to fall in love," he sang. "So doggone easy."

It comforted me to hear Buddy Holly still singing in the corridors of The Ruggles School.

I found an open door and peeked in. A girl—a student, I assumed—smiled up at me from behind a sleek, incongruously modern desk.

"May I help you, sir?"

"I'm looking for Mr. Elliott. I have an appointment."

"This is Mr. Elliott's office." She consulted a book. "Are you Mr. Coyne?"

"Yes, that's right."

"Come right this way, please. He's expecting you."

She got up from behind the desk and led me to a closed door. The girl wore stockings and high heels, used old-fashioned words like "sir" and "please," and I concluded that there was something to be said for private education after all.

There were two people in Headmaster Elliott's office. I took in Elliott at a glance: tall, beaked nose, thinning gray hair combed straight back and curled at the nape of his neck. Deerfield '44, Princeton '48. Something like that. The old school tie. Stroke for the lightweight crew. Number three man on the subvarsity squash team. Gentlemanly C's. English major. Thesis on Alexander Pope.

Just like his Daddy.

And now he exemplified Dr. Peter's well-known principle as he drifted around the sedate, vine-covered campus of a distinguished New England prep school. He would comfort the trustees, cajole the alumni, amuse the faculty, and fool none of the students with his vague banalities.

He extended his hand to me. "Mr. Coyne. Bartley Elliott. A pleasure, sir. So regrettable, the sadness of this occasion." The Headmster cleared his throat habitually as he spoke, as if phlegm were bubbling up there. He inclined his head toward the other person in the room, a slim young Oriental man wearing a corduroy jacket and a plaid flannel shirt opened at the collar. "This is Mr. Alexander Binh. The Dean of the Faculty. Mr. Binh is also a member of the History Department. Your secretary indicated, Mr. Coyne, that you'd like to talk to some of our people. Mr. Binh can help arrange that, I believe."

I took the hand that Alexander Binh offered me. His grip was hard, practiced, impersonal. He slipped his hand from mine quickly and bowed his head in acknowledgement of Bartley Elliott's introduction. "Happy to help out in any way I can," he said in a soft, flat voice.

"Seated, seated," commanded Elliott, waving his arms around. I sat.

"I'm here on behalf of Mrs. Florence Gresham," I began, "as I believe my secretary indicated. She's George Gresham's beneficiary. His mother. You know, of course, that his death has been ruled a suicide. We are exploring an appeal of that verdict. Mrs. Gresham has retained me to investigate and to advise her whether or not to proceed with this appeal. Anything you and your staff can tell me to shed light on this question would be appreciated."

"Do you doubt it was suicide?" asked Binh.

"I'm a lawyer, Mr. Binh. I'm trying to reserve judgment."

Mr. Binh nodded. His little smile seemed to say, "That's bullshit."

"George Gresham," said Elliott. "A fine, fine man. Hard to believe. Suicide, that is. Scholar, George. Real scholar. Even-tempered, mild-mannered man. Loved the books, George. Personal friend, I might add. Real shock to us all, Mr. Coyne."

"I'm looking for clues, Mr. Elliott. I'd like to try to understand Mr. Gresham's state of mind at the time of his death. For example, did he seem depressed recently? Did he have any financial problems that you were aware of? Or maybe a personal relationship that wasn't going well for him? Did you notice any changes in his patterns of behavior, anything at all that might, looking back on it, make his suicide understandable?"

"I told the police. Nothing. Goes to show. Think you know a man, and . . ."

"What about his work?" I went on. "Was it going well for him?"

"George was the bulwark of the History Department.

46

Could have taught in college. Had offers. Should have, maybe. But he said he preferred it here. Loved his books, the students, the place. No pressure. That was important to him. No. A credit to his school. Credit to his profession. Published, too. Distinguished man."

I looked at Alexander Binh. "What about you, Mr. Binh?"

He shrugged in what I was tempted to interpret as an effort at inscrutability. "I agree with Mr. Elliott," he said.

"Did you know George Gresham well?"

"As well as anybody, I suppose. We were colleagues. We both taught history. I'd say I knew him professionally, but not personally. I don't believe I can tell you anything that will help you."

"Well, okay," I said. "Did his suicide surprise you?"

Binh gave me that "bullshit" little smile of his, and said, "His *death* surprised me. That's all."

I gave up with him. I turned to Elliott. "Perhaps if I could speak with some of your staff . . ."

Elliott stood up, as if he were grateful for the opportunity to usher me out. "Of course. Mr. Binh, if you will be so kind . . ."

Binh inclined his head slightly, rose, and moved toward the door. I shook hands with Bartley Elliott and followed the young Dean of the Faculty. He was, I noticed, much taller than he had seemed, and he moved with the smooth grace of an ice skater.

He led me outside the old building into the May sunlight. He walked along a pathway leading away from the quadrangle of grass onto which the cluster of buildings faced. I had to quicken my pace to keep up with him. He spoke without looking at me.

"Warren Baker. The baseball coach. Also teaches math," said Binh over his shoulder, his words popping out in rhythm with his steps. "Been here about as long as George. Knew him as well as anybody, I suppose."

The path led us around the back of a square brick building. Before us lay an enormous flat expanse of playing fields, with what looked like hundreds of figures flitting across them.

There were girls in shorts and tee shirts, others in little skirts and knee socks. There were young people of indistinguishable gender in sweat suits jogging in groups of three and four. Several stood in small clusters. Shot putters, and discus and javelin throwers, I judged from the motions they made.

From the far end of the field came the sound of aluminum bat meeting baseball—not a crack, but a ping. I have never accustomed my ear to the sound, no matter how many of Billy's games I've watched. Horsehide and ash, that's what I wanted to hear. But, hell, I don't like the designated hitter rule, and I'd rather see a stolen base than a home run, so I guess I'm an anachronism.

Binh led me to the baseball diamond. A compactly built black man wearing a nylon windbreaker with a cap yanked low over his forehead was whacking fungoes to his infield. "Get your goddam *tail* down, McAllister. Stick your face in there, for crissake, or I can find a spot for your ass beside mine on the bench."

His voice rasped, as if he smoked too many cigarettes and yelled too often. He smacked another grounder at McAllister, a skinny kid at third base. He smacked it *hard*. I was standing close enough to him now so that I could hear his *umph!* of effort when he swung the slender fungo bat. McAllister managed to keep his tail down, but his face shied away from the wicked ground ball. It glanced off the heel of his glove and caught the kid flush on the Adam's apple. He collapsed in a heap.

"Barnett!" called Baker. "Where the hell is Barnett?"

A towheaded youngster playing catch off to our left came jogging towards us. "Barnett," said Coach Baker, "you get your body out there at third base and see if you can keep it in front of a grounder, will you? McAllister," he shouted at the boy who was now sitting on the ground where he had fallen, holding his throat, "get in here. Damn it, get in here *now!*"

The boy got up from the ground and walked slowly in toward the plate where his coach waited, leaning with one arm on the fungo bat.

Alexander Binh said to me, "Wait a minute, and I'll introduce you."

Baker glowered at young McAllister. "You wearing a cup, boy?"

"No, sir."

"I suppose you ain't got a jock on, either?"

McAllister looked at the ground and shook his head.

"Well, no wonder you're afraid of the ball. Lucky you took it in the *Adam's* apple and not your other apples. Go get yourself dressed for baseball, son." Baker's voice had softened, and the boy looked up at him.

"Now!" said Baker, more loudly. "Sprint, boy. You get back here, and I'm going to whack you in the crotch with this bat and it better ding like a bell."

McAllister nodded, and took off toward a building at the far end of the playing fields.

Baker turned and seemed to notice us for the first time.

"Say, Brother," he said to Binh.

"Hi, Token," replied Binh. They touched palms up in front of their faces and grinned at each other. "This is Mr. Coyne. He's George Gresham's lawyer. Got a minute?"

Baker handed the fungo bat to Binh. "Do the infield for me. And don't baby them."

Alexander Binh allowed his eyes to smile quickly. He laid his corduroy jacket on the ground and rolled his shirt cuffs up his forearms, which I noticed, were corded and thickly veined.

Baker held out his hand to me, and we shook. "What can I do for you?"

I gave him what had become for me a set speech. "And so," I concluded, "I guess I'm just trying to get a sense of what George had been feeling and thinking during the last few days of his life. To try to understand his suicide."

Baker led me away from the baseball field toward a small tier of bleachers. We sat on the bottom bench. He reached inside his jacket and pulled out a pack of Camels. He offered me one, and I shook my head and lit a Winston of my own.

"George was a tough man," Baker began, exhaling a long plume of smoke. "Exacting teacher. Demanded a little bit more of each of his students than they were capable of, if you understand me. Always pushed them to increase their limits. Would've made a hell of a coach."

I squinted at him. "How does that relate to his death, Mr. Baker? I don't get it."

"Well, hell—he was the same way with himself, you know. That's all. Maybe he discovered his own limits. Like the ballplayer who spends lots of years in the minors and finally finds himself twenty-eight, thirty years old and a two-fifty hitter and not good for much of anything. That could have been George. Would've been just like him. George couldn't have lived with the idea of being a two-fifty minor-league hitter."

Baker tilted his cap back to look intently at me.

"Would that lead him to commit suicide, do you think?" I asked.

"Shit, I don't know. Who can answer a question like that? You wanted to know what he was like, that's what he was like. Two-fifty hitters don't necessarily kill themselves." He dragged on his Camel and looked out over the baseball diamond. "Some do, I expect."

I nodded. "Were you aware of anything particular in his life that might have been different lately? A love affair, a gambling debt, illness—something like that?"

"Nah. I don't think so." Baker yanked the beak of his cap back down over his eyes. "Look," he said. "I really gotta get back to my team. My Asian friend'll have them thinking that all grounders come on three easy little hops. I'm sorry I couldn't help you more."

"It's okay. I appreciate your time," I said. We stomped on our cigarette butts and walked back to the diamond.

"Okay, you guys," Baker yelled, taking the bat from Binh. "Mr. Binh has given you a nice little rest. See if you remember anything. Knees bent, up on the balls of your feet, heads up, gloves down . . ."

Binh picked up his jacket and tossed it over his shoulder. We began to walk back toward the school buildings. "Warren Baker," said Binh. "You never heard of him?"

"No," I said. "Should I?"

"Halfback, West Point, class of sixty-three. Everyone said he could've made it in the pros. Football *or* baseball. But he owed Uncle Sam five years, and he spent one of them in Vietnam. Left two toes from his left foot over there. End of athletic career." Binh looked at me. His eyes seemed warmer to me. "Baker's a hell of a guy. We kid each other a lot, him a Vietnam veteran and me half Vietnamese. And he's spent more time in the country of my origin than I have."

I nodded, encouraging him to continue.

"I was born in Paris and educated here." It took me a moment to realize that "here" meant The Ruggles School. "So I'm the token Oriental, and he's the token black. At least, that's what we tell each other, though the truth, I think, is that we're both assets to this place. Warren'll always be here. It's his home, now. I've got better things to do."

I murmured "Umm," to encourage him to keep talking. But he evidently felt he had told me enough.

We walked the rest of the way in silence. I followed him back to the grassy quadrangle where most of the school's buildings seemed to be grouped. We took the path past the administration building where my BMW was parked, past a couple of plain-fronted brick buildings, which I thought either contained classrooms or served as dormitories, to a more modern structure. This one, also, was constructed of brick, but there was varnished wood and glass, too, and its facade offered more facets and angles to the eye.

"Student Union," said Binh. "Auditorium's around the other side. Rina'll be there, I think."

We climbed half a dozen wide steps, pushed through a set of big double doors, and found ourselves in a dimly lit lobby. Binh motioned me to be quiet, and pushed open another door. I followed him into a theater. The aisle sloped down toward a brightly lit stage where several sweatshirted and blue-jeaned figures moved around. Binh made his way down the aisle and took a seat in the front row. I groped my way behind him and slid into a seat next to him.

Up on the stage a tall young woman, indistinguishable from the others except by the clear aura of command which she emanated, was gesticulating with one hand while she held in her other a sheaf of papers. "You're a *clown* pretending to be a *wall*, Scott. The audience has to get the *humor* in this. Broaden it. Ham it up. It's supposed to be *funny. Slap*stick. Loosen up. Have *fun* with it, for heaven's sake."

"That's Rina Prescott," whispered Alexander Binh. I nodded.

"Okay, then," the woman continued. "Let's do it again. C'mon, kids. Let's pretend we're enjoying ourselves up here. Okay? Quince? Thisby? You guys with us? Okay. In your places. Let's take it from, 'Gentles, perchance you wonder . . .' Prologue, go ahead, now. Remember. It's supposed to be *silly.*"

Binh leaned toward me, his shoulder touching mine. I inclined my ear to him. "*Midsummer Night's Dream.* She thinks these kids can put Shakespeare over."

"Just a minute! Okay. Everybody stop." Rina Prescott interrupted the speech of the boy on the stage. She came to the edge, by the footlights, leaned over, and peered toward us. "Who's in my theater? Who's there, anyway? Hey, Peter. Give me some house lights, will you?"

Suddenly Binh and I were exposed as the auditorium filled with light. The woman squinted for a moment, then abruptly stood up: "Mr. Binh, what can I do for you?" She clearly indicated by her tone that she did not particularly desire to do anything for Alexander Binh.

"Ah, Miss Prescott. I have a gentleman here who'd like to talk with you for a moment?" Binh made it a question.

The woman dropped her hands against her thighs and shook her head. "Damn it," she said, her voice low and intended only for us, "I'm working. I know you can see that. I've got a show to put on in nine days, Mr. Binh. Do you mind?"

Binh stood and moved to the edge of the stage. Rina Prescott stood, hands on hips now, and glared down at him. She was, I estimated, in her mid-twenties. Short, black hair, and a good face under the scowl it wore at the moment. She looked fine in her jeans. After a moment she moved toward Binh and squatted at the edge of the stage. He spoke to her in a low voice. As she listened, she glanced in my direction, seemed to study me for a minute, then returned her attention to what Binh was saying. I saw her shake her head. Binh touched her shoulder and whispered something else to her, and then she shrugged. Binh patted her arm and came back to sit beside me.

"Take ten, kids," said the woman. "Don't go away." The actors, who had been sitting on the stage while their director conversed with Alexander Binh, stood and began milling around. Rina Prescott hopped nimbly down from the stage and came toward me and Binh. I stood.

She held out her hand to me. Her grip was firm, masculine. "I'm sorry to interrupt you . . ." I began.

"Me too," she said. "People think this is fun and games. They don't seem to understand. This is my *job*. They *pay* me to do this. I don't suppose you allow people to walk into a courtroom when you're delivering your summation to the jury or something so they can discuss their personal problems with you, do you? Or do you say, 'Excuse me, please, ladies and gentlemen of the jury, but I've got to go and have a little chat with this person I've never met before, and I've got to do it right now, because this person is very busy and has made a special trip to our courtroom just to talk with me, so take a break and I'll be right back?' Do you?"

"I'm sorry, Miss Prescott. I didn't . . ."

"Yeah, yeah. I know." Her voice was only a shade friendlier, but I thought I detected a smile crinkling in the corners of her eyes. "It was Elliott, right? Sure. Beef-witted sod!"

I grinned. She frowned. "What's funny?"

"Beef . . . what?" I said.

She smiled, then, and it transformed her face. Her eyes,

especially, glittered and danced. They were the green of spring leaves when they first burst open, bracketed by tiny wrinkles at the corners, as if they had stared at the ocean and sky for many hours from the tiller of a sailboat. Her tall, slim body had fooled me, and I revised my estimate. Early thirties, at least.

"Beef-witted," she said. "That's the Bard, of course. Best oaths you can find are in Shakespeare. Look, Mr. Coyne. Mr. Binh told me what you're after, here. I really can't help you, anyway. George was a nice man. I don't know anything about his death. Okay?"

"If I could just ask you a couple of questions," I said.

She sighed heavily. "Look. I said I can't help you. I don't mean to be rude. I'm busy." She turned away from me.

"If we offend," I said, "it is with our good will."

Rina Prescott whirled to face me. "You know the play?"

I grinned at her. "I played Quince once. Many, many years ago."

She stared at me for a moment. Then she shrugged. "Good for you," she said. "Hope it went over. Right now I'm worried about his particular production. We'll leave the house lights on for you so you can find your way out."

She hopped up onto the stage and stood, her back to Binh and me, and clapped her hands. "Okay, people. Back into positions. Let's go back to Philostrate. Come on, now. Move it."

Binh touched my elbow and jerked his head toward the exit. I nodded and followed him out. As we opened the door at the rear of the theater, I heard Rina Prescott call out, "Okay, kill those house lights. Come on, up there, lighting crew, bring up the spot. It's *night*, remember."

Binh and I walked out of the building into the bright sunlight. We stood for a moment before the building. I shook a Winston from my pack and lit it.

"Wow!" I said.

Binh shifted his eyebrows and flashed a quick smile. "She's right, of course. Anyway, you really didn't think you'd learn anything here today, did you? I mean, you are going through some requisite motions, I assume."

I looked at him for a moment. He returned my stare with neither hostility nor humor. Neutrality, I read there. Patience. Boredom, maybe. His look said, "I don't give a shit," but I didn't read "Up yours" in it.

Finally I said, "I understand you probably have better things to do with your time than escort me around your campus, Mr. Binh, and I apologize for putting you in this position. However, a man has died. We think it's important to understand that death."

Binh's expression didn't change. "You're doing your job. I'm doing mine. I'm instructed to introduce you to some of our staff. Fine. If you'll follow me, please, I'll take you to Miss Wolcott." He turned on his heel and glided away from me. I dropped the cigarette butt, stepped on it, and hurried after him.

"Who's Miss Wolcott?" I asked when I caught up to Binh.

"Latin teacher. Also Greek."

"And she knew George Gresham?"

"We all did. More or less."

He led me diagonally across the grassy quadrangle. Dandelions bloomed in clumps here and there, making bright yellow washes of color against the pale green spring grass. Big old oaks and maples and a few surviving elms grew up from the manicured lawn, casting broad areas in shade. Here and there young boys and girls sat or lay, some engaged in quiet, intense conversations, some dozing, and some with their faces close together and fingers entwined.

Binh stopped by one girl sitting with her back against a thick tree trunk. She wore a long, full dress. Bare feet peeped from beneath its hem. A notebook lay opened on her lap. Her face was lifted to a beam of sunlight which streamed through a hole in the foliage above her. Her eyes were closed. Freckles dotted the bridge of her nose.

"This is Jenny Wolcott." The girl's eyes popped open. "Jenny, Mr. Coyne would like to talk with you about George

Gresham. And," he said, turning to me, "if you don't mind, I'll leave you. I've got some things to do back at the office, and I'm not sure who else it would be worth your while to talk to, anyway. You can find your way out?"

I nodded. "Thanks for your time."

He shrugged and walked quickly away.

Jenny Wolcott patted the ground beside her. "Pull up a seat, Mr. Coyne. What can I do for you? And why are you looking at me like that?"

I laughed. "You know, I imagined you were—well, older. Like Miss Partridge, my old Latin teacher. She had a bald spot on the back of her head and a mustache that she bleached. I do have this unfortunate tendency to make stereotypes."

Jenny Wolcott smiled prettily. "Apology accepted."

"It wasn't exactly an apology," I said. "Matter of fact, it was supposed to be kind of a compliment. You're very young and very pretty. I didn't expect that."

She lowered her eyes. "Thank you."

"How well did you know George Gresham?"

Her eyes flickered, then met mine. She nodded her head slowly. "I knew him—I knew him pretty well, Mr. Coyne. He was, well, like a father to me, sort of. This is only my first year here at Ruggles. It's a pretty closed little world, you know, and a public school girl from Des Moines can feel pretty out of place in a dour old New England prep school. You know?"

I nodded.

"And George, he was really the only one who made the effort. Oh, there were the men—well, never mind that. You know what I mean. But George, he wasn't like that. I mean, he seemed to really care if I was happy here. There was nothing sexual or anything. He was just nice to me."

"Sure," I said. "Do you remember anything about the way he was before he died? Anything unusual about the way he acted? Did anything happen to him that you know of?"

She widened her eyes a little. "I know what you mean. I've tried to think about that ever since I heard that he—that he, you know, killed himself." She shrugged her shoulders and gave me a wan smile. "He was a sad sort of man, anyway. You never knew what he was really thinking, because he always seemed to be focusing on you. He was so concerned about how I was doing that we never really talked about him. I feel very guilty about that. I was so selfish. He must've been very unhappy, very lonely, to do that. And I never even thought about *him* and *his* problems. Maybe I could have helped him. I could have at least encouraged him more. To talk about himself." She flapped her hands in her lap. "Anyway, he didn't."

I nodded and smiled at her. I took my cigarette pack from my pocket, hesitated, and offered it to her. She shook her head. "Do you mind?" I said.

"No. Go ahead."

I lit the cigarette. "Did his suicide surprise you?"

"Oh, well, sure it did. I mean, no offense, but isn't that kind of a dumb question?"

"Yes. I guess it is. What I meant was, when you heard that his death was caused by suicide . . ."

"Can you imagine," she interrupted, "*anyone* you know killing himself *not* surprising you?"

"You've got a point," I said. "Okay, then, what about George's other friends? I've met some of them. Mr. Baker, the baseball coach. Mr. Elliott, of course, and Mr. Binh. I met Miss Prescott briefly."

She looked at me expectantly. "What about them?"

I waved my hands. "I don't know. Anything that would help me understand this."

Jenny Wolcott stared at the hole in the leaves over her head toward the sunlight that streamed down on her. She didn't speak for what seemed like several minutes. Finally she said in a low voice, "I don't think those people knew him at all. He never talked about them. I thought *I* knew him. I thought I was the only one." She turned to look at me. "Now I'm not so sure of that. Maybe no one knew him. Anyhow, it doesn't much matter, now, does it?"

I stood up. "I guess you're right, Miss Wolcott. I'll let you get back to your work. I appreciate your time."

"Sorry I couldn't be more help."

"That's okay. I enjoyed talking with you." I lifted my hand to her, then headed back for my car. My digital watch read 4:37. I calculated that, if I took my time, I could pass by Gert's at a little after five. A bit early. Still, I could nurse an Old Fashioned or two, and then, fresh-baked striped bass . . .

I sauntered across the lawn, enjoying the clean air with its hint of salt water and May flowers. I hadn't learned much to help Florence Gresham. Life at The Ruggles School went on, closing in on whatever void George Gresham had left in it, and I supposed the most responsible thing I could do for Florence would be to help her fill in her own void. If I hadn't discovered any definitive reasons for this solitary man to end his own existence, I certainly didn't feel I had uncovered anything that could contradict the verdict of suicide, either.

As I approached my car, I saw that a knot of perhaps a dozen young people had gathered in the parking lot, blocking my way. There seemed to be a great deal of loud conversation and arm-waving. I started to walk around them when I felt a hand on my shoulder.

"Take some literature, mister." It was a command, not a request. I do not, as a rule, take kindly to commands. I turned and faced a young man dressed in what appeared to be Army surplus fatigues—high boots, with baggy pants tucked in, a camouflage shirt, and a cartridge belt around his waist. I noticed that there were no cartridges in the loops. He wore a wispy adolescent goatee and a snarling grin. His head had been shaved bald.

I shook my arm where he gripped me, and he dropped his hand. His other hand waved some sort of pamphlet in my face. I took it from him.

Its title read *Do You Know Where You Stand?* in bold red letters. Beneath the title, in neon red against the black background of the cover, a large red swastika glowed. I held the pamphlet away from me with two fingers and dropped it to the ground as if it were a dirty diaper.

"Not interested," I said. I rolled my shoulders to get

around him. He stepped into my path, still grinning, his dark eyes glittering like a cornered rodent's. The other young people began to crowd around us. They wanted a confrontation, I thought. I wanted no part of it.

"Afraid of the truth, mister?" said the bald kid softly.

"Move," I said.

He held his ground. "I know your type," he said. "Feed the niggers, vote for the commies, give your money to the Jews. Well, it's gonna happen, and it's gonna happen here, and you'd better be ready for it. So why don't you just pick up that literature you dropped, huh?"

I tried again to walk past him. His hand gripped me hard by my arm. His fingers dug unerringly into a spot just above my elbow, sending a shaft of pain to my brain. "Pick it up," he said more loudly.

I turned around slowly and put my face up close to his. I reached up and grabbed the strands of hair growing from his chin. "I said," I repeated softly, "I'm not interested. Take your filth somewhere else, sonny." I gave his little beard a hard tug and was gratified to see tears come to his eyes.

"You'll be sorry," he muttered.

"I doubt that," I said, turning away from him.

"Asshole!"

This was a different voice. It belonged to a girl who, at first, I took to be no more than twelve years old. She had the vanilla complexion and naive blue eyes of a pre-adolescent, with a little rosebud mouth and a tangle of blonde curls piled on her head like a fluffy helmet.

Except those eyes were glowering at me, and that sweet mouth was twisted into a hateful sneer, and beneath her sweatshirt rose a pair of decidedly post-adolescent breasts.

"You talk that way to your father, young lady?" I said.

"Fuck him," she replied.

"Forget it, Barb," said one of the other kids. "He's too old to understand."

The bald boy spoke again. "It's for your own good, man. Prepare yourself. Our civilization is collapsing. This—" and he again thrust one of his pamphlets at me "—explains it."

"Why don't you kids go do your history homework or something?" I said.

"History's a lie," said the kid with the shiny head. "It's the future that counts."

I wondered what George Gresham might have said to this young fanatic. Something more rational than what sprang to my mind, I imagined.

I shouldered my way through the kids and climbed into my white BMW. As I pulled out of my parking space, I saw that they were all watching me, identical frowns distorting their young faces. For an instant my mind flashed images of Berkeley and Chicago and Kent State in a rapid television kaleidoscope, and the phrase "the future of our nation is our youth" sprang to my lips. I repressed the urge to say it.

"If you're not with us, you're against us," one of them yelled as I backed out of my parking space.

"God bless free speech," I whispered as I drove away.

CHAPTER 5.

"FIRM WRISTS, Coyne," I told myself. "Don't worry about being long." I set the blade of the pitching wedge behind the ball, opened up my stance, moved my weight slightly forward, and glanced up at the hole.

The pin was tucked right behind the big bunker that gaped temptingly in front of me. A devilish little pitch shot.

"Keep your stupid head down," I muttered. I looked at the ball, up at the pin again, then down, trying to lock my visual measurement of the distance into my muscles. A little flick, up and over, drop it down beyond the big lip of the trap with enough backspin to stop it near the hole, where Charlie's ball already rested a birdie putt away. I focused my mind on the imagined flight of the ball. Head down, balance, firm left elbow . . .

"Don't leave it short," said Charlie pleasantly.

I stepped away from the ball and looked at him. He grinned at me. He leaned on his putter, his legs crossed jauntily.

"Goddam it, Charlie," I said.

"Big hole," he replied. "You need it for the match."

"Jesus, I know."

I stepped back, took a couple of practice swipes at the grass, then stepped back to the ball. I tried again to visualize the shot I needed to make. Instead, I saw Charlie McDevitt's cocky grin.

I gritted my teeth, took the wedge back, shifted my hips, and began my short, compact swing. I knew it was all wrong. I glanced up to see the results of my shot. I glanced up too soon. The club head dug into the turf behind the ball, which popped lazily into the air and splatted into the sand under the overhanging lip of the bunker.

"Hard lines, old man," said Charlie cheerfully.

"Up yours," I said.

Charlie McDevitt had always planned to become a Supreme Court Justice, which has turned out to be nearly as funny as my becoming a public defender. He and I rented a big old house on the water in New Haven our second year at Yale Law nearly twenty years ago. Charlie had a whole bevy of girls. We'd gather in my bedroom on a Saturday night, Gloria and I and Charlie and whatever girl he had with him, and we'd sit on my bed in our underwear drinking beer and eating steamers and listening to the surf.

There was a hole in the plaster right above the head of my bed. Charlie's bedroom was on the other side. He or I used to put our faces up to the hole in the plaster when the other one of us had a girl in our bedroom, to do a play-by-play of the action in the other room.

"You can cut this tension with a knife, fans," Charlie would say, his lips flapping in his Mel Allen imitation. "Big Bumppo Coyne is up there with that big bludgeon of his. He tugs at his cap. He takes a couple of practice swings. He scratches his crotch thoughtfully. And now he eases himself into the box . . ."

I did a pretty mean Curt Gowdy, myself. Coitus was more often than not interruptus that year in New Haven, and the girls who dissolved into tears—and there were fewer of them than you might expect—weren't invited back.

Gloria tended to dissolve into laughter, for which I loved her enormously. Sometimes she was able to ignore Charlie completely; other times she joined him, commenting on my stance, grip, and the size of my bat. "It's high and deep," she'd say. "Going going—gone! It's out of here! And big Coyne is getting the congratulations of his teammates back in the dugout, having completed his triumphant jaunt around the bases. He got all of that one, baseball fans!"

Charlie hasn't become a Supreme Court Justice yet. He might one day, which is more than I can say for the likelihood of my becoming a public defender. Charlie still wants one of those robes. For now, though, he's an assistant of some kind to the Attorney General of the United States. Charlie has been with the Justice Department's Boston office since the days of Ramsey Clark, which is an awfully long time without moving if you want to join the brethren in Washington. And Charlie, being neither black nor a woman, is going to have trouble getting appointments. But he's a patient man with excellent ears that he keeps close to the political ground. He also has superior anticipation. He knows the ball takes a lot of funny bounces, and Charlie somehow always manages to be there to snag it. He's still a young man, politically, and he's stashing lots of credits in the bank.

Charlie and I play golf together weekly, as our schedules permit. I've envied his stable marriage, his home where he tucks his kids in every night, and the way he can hit a high, controlled fade that always seems to end up on the fairway.

He professes to envy my independence, the sex life he imagines I live, my income, and my long, wild hooks that generally sail fifty or sixty yards beyond his.

Charlie is just about my best friend, and he has been for twenty years. Ever since our years in New Haven. He gives good advice when I ask for it. And he knows when not to give any advice at all. Best of all, he listens to me talk, and somehow talking with him makes things clearer for me even when he says nothing.

"It was strange," I said to him as we walked toward the eighteenth tee, the match now officially his. "They all seemed to be projecting their own self-images onto George Gresham, somehow. The Headmaster saw him as a great academic, the Dean as mysterious and inscrutable, the coach as tough, and the pretty little Latin teacher from Des Moines as a scared, lonely man far from home."

"Seems natural enough," said Charlie. "My honor, right?"

"Of course it is," I said. "And then there was the kid in the guerrilla suit, spouting some kind of fascist bullshit, and those sweet little girls yelling 'fuck' and their anger just oozing out of them."

"Yeah. Survivalists, sounds like," he said. "Now hush up, there. I gotta concentrate on this shot."

Charlie stepped up to the ball, wagged his club once, and whacked his standard high fade into the middle of the fairway.

"Good hit."

"Yup. Listen, Brady, me boy. Haven't you got anything better to do than run around talking to people about some dead guy? That your idea of practicing law?"

I teed up my ball. "It's a living."

My big hook managed to stay in the fairway. "You do that regularly," said Charlie, "and you wouldn't be buying the beers all the time."

I ignored his comment. "It seemed," I said, picking up my bag and following him toward our balls, "like a closed little world there. No one really said anything. They were all nice enough, and cooperative—all except the play director. But they didn't tell me a damn thing. I got the feeling that there was more there than met the eye, you know?"

"A conspiracy of silence?"

"Yeah, kinda."

"More likely you got what there was," he said.

"You're probably right. Still, I've got to satisfy Florence."

"Like I said, that's a funny piece of work for an attorney. Yale Law, no less."

"Yeah, well, it keeps me in Big Macs," I replied, perhaps a bit defensively.

I had been putting off calling Florence. It was several days after my discussion with Dr. Clapp and my visit to The Ruggles School before I asked Julie to ring the Gresham estate in Beverly Farms. Charlie's assessment of my work still lingered in my brain, and I had to contend with the realization that I couldn't disagree with him. This task that Florence Gresham had set for me did not seem worthy, somehow, of a man with a degree from Yale Law School.

Florence's familiar voice rasped, "Well? What'd you find out?"

I summarized quickly what Dr. Clapp had told me and what I had surmised from my visit to the school.

"You think it adds up, then," she said.

"Seems to," I said.

"Suicide. Hmm."

"I'm sorry, Florence."

"You've missed something."

"But . . ."

"Keep trying. You can start by meeting me at George's room at the school. I'm supposed to pick up his things, now that the police are through with them."

I sighed. "When, Florence?"

"How's today?"

"Okay. Sure."

"Five-ish?"

"Fine."

George Gresham's suite at The Ruggles School gave the impression that he had just stepped out for a moment. Perhaps to go to the bathroom, or to take a telephone call. If the police had searched through his things, they had done it with uncharacteristic tidiness. The clothes were neatly hung in the closet, the bed made, the towels folded in the bathroom. In George's study, the chair was pushed back from the desk, the top of which was littered with a couple of open books and several others stacked carelessly on the corner.

Against one wall of this little room stood a floor-to-ceiling bookcase crammed with more volumes, mostly histories. It was an eclectic collection. Thucydides, Herodotus, Beard, Schlesinger. He had a big, unabridged Webster's Second Edition, a Rand-McNally Atlas, a United States Zip Code Directory, and a Rodale Synonym Finder. There was a volume of Frost poems and a thick, blue book with faded gold lettering entitled *The Complete Works of Shakespeare*.

I returned my attention to the open books on the desk

and picked one up, careful not to lose George's place. Its title was *The Terrorists of the Sixties,* by someone named Ronald Glazer. The other book bore the pretentious title *Up from the Classroom: The Growth of Radical Consciousness of Students in America 1965–1975.* It was written by one Allison Cohen-Brown.

Florence was in George's bedroom, sitting forlornly on his bed. I brought the two books to her, each closed on my finger to mark George's place.

"I didn't know George was interested in contemporary American history," I said, showing them to her.

She waved her hand tiredly. "George was interested in everything."

I shrugged. I was supposed to be looking for clues. To something. I imagined the police had scoured George's rooms thoroughly. On the other hand, if, as Dr. Clapp had suggested, they conducted their investigation from the theory that the commonest things most commonly happen, and assumed that they were looking at the living quarters of a man who had killed himself—they would find evidence that would tend to confirm that assumption.

My job, I decided, was to try to find clues that might support the contrary hypothesis, which, at that point, I could only phrase as: "George Gresham did not commit suicide." Florence, I knew, wanted something more definitive. "George fell accidentally," perhaps, or, "George had a stroke before he fell." Or even, "George was murdered."

The two books had been borrowed from the Boston Public Library, as had several of the other volumes that were stacked on the desk. I glanced through them, as well, and wrote their titles into my notebook. *Most Wanted* was one, subtitled, *Modern Fugitives from Justice.* Also, there was *American Extremists and the Anti-War Movement,* and *Underground: The Mind of the Fugitive,* and a thin volume whose title proclaimed in large red capital letters *Students Outside the Law.*

I knew George had been a compulsive researcher, an inveterate note-taker and collector of clippings, a writer of dry, scholarly monographs. I assumed that somewhere in the three-drawer file cabinet beside his desk I would find the notes or outlines or drafts for this work he was doing.

But there was nothing. Two of the drawers contained ditto masters—old tests, bibliographies, charts and graphs, outlines, and a seemingly limitless supply of meticulously typed excerpts—speeches of Thomas Jefferson and John C. Calhoun, succinct commentaries on human nature from Machiavelli, the entire Funeral Oration of Pericles as reconstructed by Thucydides, a letter written by John Adams, an eyewitness description of the storming of the Bastille. The sort of stuff a dedicated teacher would make into lesson plans. I imagined George Gresham maneuvering his students into fascinating discussions of historical cause and effect, diffidently probing with quiet questions. "But *how* do you know?" "Where's your evidence?"

His files did not indicate an interest in the twentieth century, never mind the contemporary scene. The third drawer in the file contained a dozen or so manila folders. Each held a draft of an article he had written. There was one on the influence of Thomas Hobbes on the authors of *The Federalist Papers*. Another purported to refute a Marxist interpretation of the American Civil War. A third was entitled, "Religious Symbolism in Enlightenment Florentine Poetry."

George Gresham's study persuaded me of two things: the man had many interests, all of them academic; and, he was a thoroughly prepared teacher. One other thing impressed me: the complete absence of any suggestion that he had a family, or friends, or indeed, that anyone at all shared his life. No pictures, no letters, no mementoes.

Tucked under George's desk I found a cheap, gray metal strongbox. I pulled it out, and, finding it unlocked, opened it up. It contained the usual documents—insurance policies, income tax forms, an automobile title. Some of the files were upside down, others backwards. It looked as if the police had sorted through this stuff with their usual attention to order and tidiness, which suggested that they hadn't even glanced at the rest of his things. One thin file attracted my attention.

It held Blue Shield benefit forms, indicating payments that had been rendered for medical services to a Leonard Wertz, M.D. I called to Florence, who was still in the next room.

"Was George sick?"

"Not that I know of," she answered.

"Must've been something wrong. Looks like he had to see a doctor twice monthly for a while last fall and winter. There's ten or twelve visits listed here. Dr. Wertz ring a bell?"

"No," she said. "He never said anything to me. Do you think it's significant?"

"Might be. I'll check it out."

I wrote Dr. Wertz's name into my notebook, along with the address in Danvers that the Blue Shield computer had thoughtfully provided on the form for me.

Also in the back of the strongbox I found what turned out to be a photocopy of a six-page, hand-written paper—a student's paper, quite obviously. The name on the front was Harvey Willard, and it was dated January 23. The paper bore the title, "The Radical Anti-War Underground."

The paper had received a grade of C, and George had scrawled across the title page, "Your thesis is interesting, but the paper suffers from inadequate documentation and mechanical errors. I suggest rewriting." Clearly it was at best an average piece of work. And yet it was the only student paper I could find among George's things, even after I went carefully through the files all over again. It seemed odd to me. Why would anyone make and retain a photocopy of this obviously mediocre piece of student writing? How did it relate to the research George had been doing in all those books that were piled upon his desk?

I folded the paper and tucked it into the pocket of my jacket and wrote Harvey Willard's name into my notebook.

It all seemed silly, somehow. But I figured anything that might explain George's suicide—whether it had some connection with a student or a mysterious illness that had escaped Dr. Clapp's detection—would help to get Florence back into living her own life again. And that, it seemed to me, had become my task.

I sat at the desk and began to open the drawers. They

contained the usual pens, pencils, reams of paper, boxes of paper clips and thumbtacks. I slid them shut, one by one.

Florence's voice startled me. "What do you make of this?" she said.

She stood in the doorway, a little notebook held up for me to see.

"What is it?"

"Addresses and phone numbers," she said. "Not many, at that."

"Any names you recognize?"

She nodded. "A few. He corresponded with some of his former students, I know. Most of these addresses are at universities. Maybe they're students, maybe professional acquaintances. That's not what I found interesting. Look at this."

I moved to stand beside her. She held the little book open to the last page. On it I saw a list of numbers. That was all. No words, no names, no explanation. There were eleven numbers in all, lined up meticulously in a row:

```
12-12929
199-12981
22109-11204
4K-24740
81-70360
93R-59072
7718-05478
909-27970
69-12901
44S-04845
22-03592
```

Florence looked up at me. "What do you make of it?"

I shook my head. "I don't know. Safe deposit box numbers, maybe? Bank accounts? Lottery numbers?"

"Think it means anything?"

"Well, it means *something*. Or at least it meant something to George, I assume. Whether it's relevant to his death is another question."

Florence shut the little book and handed it to me. "Why

don't you keep it? Maybe you can make some sense out of it."

I took it from her and tucked it into the inside pocket of my jacket. I could check out the names in it, anyway. It seemed futile. But it was the least I could do.

"Excuse me," came a voice from behind us.

I turned. In the doorway stood a tall, slim woman with short, dark hair. She wore a straight, black skirt and a pale green blouse that reflected the color of her eyes, and a shy smile.

"Miss Prescott."

"Hello, Mr. Coyne. I'm sorry to intrude . . ."

"That's quite all right," I said. "Turnabout is fair play. This is Mrs. Gresham. George's mother. Florence, this is Miss Prescott, the drama teacher here at the school. I chatted with her briefly the other day when I was here."

Florence held out her hand. Rina Prescott entered the room to take it. Then she looked at me. "I saw the cars outside. I hoped it might be you. I wanted to apologize for my behavior the other day. I was rude. I'm sorry."

I shrugged. "It's okay. We intruded on you."

She turned to Florence. "Mrs. Gresham, I'm so sorry about your son. He was a special person to all of us here."

"Thank you, dear."

"Well, I didn't mean to barge in here," Rina Prescott continued. "As I said, I saw the cars. And I did want to say I was sorry for the way I treated you at the rehearsal. Anybody who played Quince deserves *some* attention from a drama teacher, I think."

I bowed to her. "Perhaps I'll take you up on that. I don't know what sort of schedule you have here at school, and obviously this isn't a good time, but I'd still like to talk to you about George." I took one of my business cards from my pocket and handed it to her. "I'd like to hear from you."

She accepted the card, ran her fingertips over the embossed lettering, and tucked it into the breast pocket of her blouse. She backed out the door, bid Florence and me a courteous good-bye, and disappeared.

"Lovely young lady," said Florence.

I nodded. I thought she might tell me something about the Harvey Willard who had written the C paper that George treasured enough to copy and keep in his files. Perhaps she could also identify for me the young man with the shaven head and the aggressive manner who had accosted me on my previous visit. I hoped she would call me.

I persuaded Florence to let me drive her back to Beverly Farms and leave John, her chauffeur, to clean out George's rooms and cart the stuff home. She agreed without a fuss. Which was uncharacteristic.

I brought the library books with me. Since they were a week or so overdue, I told Florence I'd return them and pay the fine. The Boston Public Library was a short walk from my office. I also kept Harvey Willard's paper and the Blue Shield statements, along with George's little address book with the mysterious list of numbers.

All of that seemed to please Florence. She seemed to think I was being more useful than I felt.

She rode beside me with her head back and her eyes closed. She looked old, now. Her skin seemed translucent, and her forehead was faintly spotted with liver marks. I had never noticed before how the flesh sagged in wattles under her chin. Her hands, resting quietly in her lap, seemed bony and fragile. George's death had transformed her.

As I drove, I reached to touch her hand. "Maybe you shouldn't have come," I said.

"Why not?" she said sharply.

I didn't answer. We drove in silence for several minutes.

"I still can't believe it," she whispered in a voice so soft that I could barely make out her words.

"Come on, now, Florence. You've got to . . ."

"I *know* he's dead. I'm not senile *yet*, you know. But this suicide idea. I just don't know."

"Probably we'll never *know*," I said.

She nodded. "Did we learn anything today?"

"I'm not a detective, Florence, in spite of your efforts to

make me into one. I'm not good at this sort of thing—questioning people, assembling clues, making great inductive leaps of imagination. I have no idea what I'm even supposed to be looking *for*. It seems to me that at some point we've just got to accept the word of the experts."

"They aren't experts on my son," she said.

"No. I guess not."

"Will you keep trying?"

I patted her leg. "Sure. I'll talk to this doctor George visited, and I'll see what I can find out about the boy who wrote the paper. Maybe when John gets all George's stuff home you can go through it again. See if there's anything that strikes you."

"I'll do that."

Several more minutes passed. As we neared the Beverly Farms exit, Florence said, "George *wouldn't* kill himself, you know."

I nodded.

CHAPTER *6.*

THE GENERAL practitioner of the law, like our counterpart in medicine, is rapidly going the way of the brontosaurus. Attorneys, like doctors and most other professionals, must be specialists. We barristers have our own equivalent of proctology, histology, podiatry, and psychiatry—criminal law, probate, tax, corporate, and so forth.

As I've mentioned, my field of specialty happens to be the law of the wealthy. My specific expertise is service. I provide counsel, and I broker my clients to other appropriate specialists readily when I recognize the need. Julie calls me a "social worker," and I guess the description is apt. I lend a shoulder for leaning or crying, I offer a willing and sympathetic ear, and I dispense sound advice. My clients value the personal relationship. They come to me because, as one might expect of very rich people, they expect immediate attention and they tend not to get it from the large firms.

Frank Paradise was one of my clients, a short, swarthy man of about sixty-five with one of the world's most magnificent pot bellies. Frank has trouble keeping his shirts tucked in. People tend to misjudge Frank. They imagine him to be a concrete contractor, or the owner of a fleet of trucks. In fact, however, Frank Paradise amassed his considerable fortune by inventing things. He started with components for jet engines back in the 'Forties. Next came inertial guidance systems, those gadgets that took satellites into orbits in space. Later, it was computers. Most recently, Frank's thinking has run along more bizarre routes. Surgically implanted radios, for example, was his latest brain child—little chips which could be inserted under the skin behind the ear. "Simple office procedure," declared Frank. "Great for joggers and school kids."

Frank retained me to perform patent searches for him— "discreet" patent searches, he always emphasized. He had become paranoid about what he called "the pirates out there" who, he was convinced, wanted to steal his ideas. He thought I was good at evading the pirates.

Working for Frank made a nice break from my usual paperwork, even if it required a couple trips a year to Washington. Besides, he paid me well for my simple services.

So after all the time I had devoted to Florence Gresham, I heeded Julie's advice and returned the half-dozen "urgent" calls Frank Paradise had made in my absence.

Julie reached him at his summer place in Brewster. "He's at the pool," she told me over the phone. "Someone's bringing the extension to him."

"He tell you what he wants?" I asked her.

"You kidding? Very mysterious, as usual."

The big voice of Frank Paradise boomed over the phone. "You alone?" he demanded.

I heard Julie disconnect. "Yes, Frank. What can I do for you? Sorry to hold you up. I've been out of the office a lot lately."

"I know, I know. Damn inconvenient. Never mind. You gotta go to Washington for me."

"What've you got, Frank?"

He dropped his voice. "You don't think I'm gonna tell you on the phone, do you? Listen. Discretion, Brady. Discretion. Remember?"

I sighed. "Sure, Frank. I remember. Okay. Mail the specs to me and I'll get right on it."

"Mail them? Hey, I'm not mailing them. Jeez, Brady. You know better. You've gotta pick them up. There are pirates out there. You know that."

"Aw, come on, Frank."

"This afternoon, Brady. No fooling. You've gotta get right on this one. It's hot, I'm telling you."

I thought about it. Frank would feed me steamers and lobsters and lots of Coors. It wouldn't be bad. I could use some time away from the office. I could use the chance to clear my head of the Gresham case.

"Okay, Frank," I said. "I'll be there by five. If you're any sort of a host, you'll have the water already boiling and the beer iced up when I get there."

When I got into my car at the parking garage, dreading the three-hour round trip to Brewster, I noticed George Gresham's library books on the back seat where I had left them. I stood there for a minute, then with a sigh I reached in and took them out. There were eight of them altogether. I stacked them up and clumsily closed the car door with my knee, holding the pile of books against my chest.

I walked that way the several blocks to the Boston Public Library, a staid old stone and concrete edifice that frowned out on a modernistic park of fountains and pools in the middle of Copley Square. Around back is the new addition to the old building, lighter and airier and more twentieth-century. That's where I took George's books.

I dumped them up on the high counter and stood waiting. Three or four young people behind the counter—college students, I surmised—paid no attention to me.

I stood on one foot and then the other for a while, cleared my throat loudly, and finally declared "Ahem!" very clearly. The public servants behind the counter gleefully ignored me.

I hate waiting. I am a prompt person. I keep my appointments. I would prefer to do without rather than wait in line to buy something I want. Gloria used to get furious when we had hired a babysitter so we could dine out, only to be greeted at the restaurant where we'd made a reservation with the news that we'd have a fifteen-minute wait, sir, which I knew translated to three-quarters of an hour to two hours, and won't you visit our lounge—and I'd turn on my heel and walk out.

"We'd have a drink *anyway*," Gloria would protest.

"It's the principle," I'd tell her. "Rather go to Howard Johnson's."

Which is what we usually did.

Which helps to account for the fact that Gloria and I are divorced now. She never minded lines, she tolerated rudeness, and she detested Howard Johnson's. We were quite incompatible.

I fixed my gaze on the nearest boy who was shuffling papers behind the the counter and whistling tunelessly through his teeth. He had watery blue eyes and a wispy blond mustache.

"Hey! You, there. Yes, you, sonny."

The boy peered blankly at me, and as he did, a face popped up directly before me from behind the counter. The face belonged to a towering black man with a goatee and a tangle of gold chains around his neck. He looked like a young Wilt Chamberlain.

"Help you?" he rumbled. I immediately regretted having used the word "sonny."

"Oh," I smiled in what was intended to be a disarming manner. "Didn't see you there."

"Puttin' some stuff away," said Wilt. "Whatcha got?"

"These are overdue. I'd like to return them and pay the fine. They were taken out by a friend."

If Wilt wasn't very, very tall, then there was a very high platform behind the counter for him to stand on. And if that was the case, then the college kids were very, very short. Wilt flipped open the books and studied the cards in the inside pockets.

"Four-forty," he said.

I paid him the money.

"How is George?" he asked.

"You know George?"

"Oh, sure. Always comes on Saturdays. Haven't seen him for a few weeks. These were his books."

"Oh. Well, he's dead."

Wilt glowered at me. "Don't jive me, man. I *like* George."

"He *is* dead."

Wilt scowled, then slowly began to chuckle deep in his throat. "I told him he'd get into trouble," he said.

"What do you mean?"

"Little joke between us. Listen—how'd George die, anyway? Heart or something?"

"He drowned. They called it suicide."

He whistled. "George?"

"So they say."

"Damn! Nice fella, George. Suicide! God damn."

"How did you remember these were his books? I mean, you must stamp out hundreds of books."

"Thousands. But, see, we don't just stamp out books. We librarians *know* books. We *help* people." He glanced at the college kids behind him. "Well, most of us do. George was doing research. I helped him find what he wanted."

I nodded. "What did you mean—about him getting in trouble?"

"Oh, just a joke. See, George wanted to copy an article from a magazine, and he didn't have any money with him. Typical of him, you know? Never brought back books late. Meticulous, that way. But always broke. Forgot his library card half the time. Drive all the way down here from his school there to take out books, and leave his card home. I'd stamp them out on my card for him. That's how much I trusted him. So anyway, he brought me this article. 'I've *got* to have a copy of this,' he said, and I said to him, 'The Xerox's over there,' and he said, 'Yeah, but I don't have any money with me.' So I loaned him seven dimes. That's all. He promised to pay me back, and, of course, I knew he would, though it really didn't matter. But I said to him, 'You don't pay me back you're in *big* trouble, honky,' like that, rolling my eyes around and lookin' fierce. That always made George laugh, when I did my tough-dude act for him."

The big man stared at me, as if he were trying to decide

whether to do his tough-dude act for me. Then he said, "I haven't seen George since then. Probably the same time he took out these books. Hell, he didn't have to send you. I can spare the seventy cents."

He bared his big teeth and laughed loudly. I smiled. "What was the article about, do you remember?"

"Yup. *Atlantic Monthly*. Fall of 1971. October, November, around there. Something about terrorists or radicals. College kids blowing up post offices. *White* college kids." He stared at me for a minute.

"Okay," I said. "That makes sense. He was doing some research on that. That article probably was just what he was looking for."

"That's what he said. 'Just what I'm looking for.' Those were his exact words," said Wilt.

"You don't have another copy of the magazine, do you?"

"Hell, no. You got any idea how many periodicals we get in this place?"

I shook my head.

"Two hundred and seventy-eight. That's just the magazines. Then there's the newspapers. From all over the world. The *Times* and *Globe* go on microfilm. We used to do a lot more of that. Had to cut back. You know, budgets."

"Sure," I said. "You think that was October '71?"

"October, November, in there. Maybe September, I couldn't say for sure. But the fall, and '71. I'm sure on that."

"Okay. Thanks." I nodded, and turned to go.

"You say hi to George for me, now, hear?"

I stopped and turned to face the tall man. "He's dead," I said. "Really."

He chuckled. "Sure. Right. I wouldn't show my face around here again, either, if I owed the librarian seven dimes. Hey, you tell George it's okay. You tell him ol' Percy isn't mad, and the dimes were a gift, okay? You tell him that."

I shrugged. "Okay. I'll tell him."

"You tell George Percy says he doesn't *need* to be dead."

I walked out into the sunshine. I agreed. George Gresham didn't need to be dead.

Frank Paradise fed me the anticipated lobsters, steamed clams, and Coors at a long table on the patio by his pool in Brewster. Our conversation was frequently punctuated by the BZZT! of insects flying into their electrified death at the pair of big, blue lights hung at the corners of the house.

After we had eaten, Frank led me into his booklined den. He picked up a large manila envelope and clutched it with both hands against his great stomach.

"This is it," he said.

"This is what?"

"What's gonna revolutionize America's morning rituals."

"More computer stuff?"

"Nope. Better." Frank put his mouth close to my ear. "Coffee bags," he whispered, then stepped back to grin at me.

"Oh. Coffee bags." I nodded vigorously.

"Sure. Like tea bags. Only with coffee in 'em. Better'n instant. Quicker'n perked. Listen, that can be our slogan, once we get production under way. Quicker'n instant, better'n perked. Nice ring to it, don't you think? These—" he tapped the envelope—"are the manufacturing specs. Guard them with your life, Brady, my friend. With your life."

I told Frank I surely would guard them with my life, that it was a helluva idea, and then I listened to him rave about the uses that America would make of coffee bags. Campers, sportsmen, housewives, harried executives late for the train— the market, according to Frank, was unlimited—as was his enthusiasm for the project.

It was the middle of the evening before I got away. I felt bloated and sleepy. Frank's warnings of pirates rang in my ears. Route 3 cut straight and narrow through the sandy terrain of the Massachusetts south shore, and I fought to keep my eyelids propped open in the face of the headlights of big trucks in the opposite lanes.

It was nearly midnight when I pushed open the door of my waterfront apartment. The phone was ringing.

"It's Florence," she said. "I've been trying to reach you."

"Hi," I said. "I've been working."

"Humph," she said, implying with that syllable that I had my nerve giving my attention to other clients. "I found something. You remember the books George had? All those things on radicals and hippies?"

I unbuttoned my shirt and was pushing my shoes off with my toes. "*Atlantic Monthly*, October '71," I said.

"Brady Coyne! How in the world . . ."

"Like I said. I've been working. So you found the copy of the article."

"Well, yes. You seemed interested in George's research, so I thought it might—you know—mean something. How did you know about it?"

"Percy told me."

"Percy?"

"It's not important, Florence."

"So what should I do with it? The article?"

"I'll come by for it. Okay?"

"It's all marked up. Written on. Underlined, and some little abbreviations in the margins."

"Okay. I'll be out for it."

"Do you think it means anything?"

"I don't know, Florence."

"I'm sorry. It's late." I heard her sigh. "I just don't believe he killed himself."

"No, Percy didn't, either."

"Who is this Percy?"

"Just a friend of George's. I met him today. Nice guy. Thought a lot of George." I yawned loudly. " 'Scuse me. Gotta go. Good night, Florence."

"Well, all right. Good night."

I showered quickly, the hot needles of water driving the tension from my muscles. Then I crawled into my solitary bed.

CHAPTER 7

I PARKED again under the "Authorized Personnel Only" sign. I thought of that as my parking spot. When I stepped out of my car I glanced around. The bald-headed kid with his flock of adolescent sheep was nowhere to be seen. I had rather looked forward to another debate with him.

The girl at the desk outside Bartley Elliott's office blinked myopically at me from behind thick, round glasses and said that Mr. Elliott was out of his office for the afternoon, could she help me? I told her I was trying to find one of the students, a Harvey Willard.

"Oh," she said. "*Harvey.*" Her cheeks flushed.

"Yes. Do you know where he might be?"

"The track. He's probably at practice. You're not the guy from Duke."

"No. I'm not from Duke."

"U.C.L.A.? Harvey told me the U.C.L.A. guy's supposed to be coming this week. You from there?"

"No," I said. "I'm from Yale."

"Oh, wow! That's awesome. The *Ivy* League."

The girl wore a scent that reminded me of Gloria's bridge parties. I wondered what she looked like without her glasses.

I wandered out behind the cluster of brick buildings to the complex of playing fields where I had talked with Coach

Warren Baker a couple of weeks earlier. The track team worked out at the opposite end from the baseball diamond, several Mike Schmidt home runs away.

Track practice seemed to be a pretty haphazard affair. I saw no one who looked like a coach. Three boys were jogging slowly around the outside of the quarter-mile cinder track. The way their hands were moving, I could tell they were intent on the stories they were telling each other. On the far side of the track two girls were working on the hurdles. There was a pole vaulting pit, a broad jump pit, and an area where half a dozen large boys and a couple of slim girls, all dressed in shorts and little sleeveless singlets, were taking turns putting the shot.

I approached a very skinny boy who was sitting on the grass at the edge of the track. He had one leg stretched straight in front of him, the other straight back, and he was bending forward and reaching for his toes with his fingers, bowing his head so that his chin touched his thigh. Marvelously limber. He was grunting, and the perspiration shone on his shoulders and the back of his neck.

"Excuse me," I said.

"Just a sec," the boy panted. He bobbed his head a couple of times, then reversed the direction of his legs and repeated the process. Then he stood, legs spread, hands on hips, and bent sideways, left, then right, then left again.

"Okay," he said. He picked up the sweatshirt that was lying beside him and toweled his face and arms with it. "You want me?"

"Not unless you're Harvey Willard."

The boy lifted his eyebrows. "That's not even close. Nobody ever called me The Beast."

"That what they call Willard?"

The boy smiled. He seemed very young, his smile very genuine. "That's what the newspapers are calling him. The girls, too. It fits. Anyway, he's over there."

The boy pointed across the track to where I could see a cluster of young people talking to a giant of a kid. Then the large boy began running. He held a javelin cocked behind his right ear. When he released it, the balanced spear sailed in a majestic arc, landing far from where the young man hopped in his follow-through.

"That's Willard," said the skinny boy. "Throwing the jav."

"He's got a good arm."

The kid looked at me as if I were crazy. "He's like six inches from the state record. *Pretty* good arm. Where you from, anyway?"

"Yale," I said.

"Want me to tell him you're here?"

"Thanks."

The boy loped away around the track, toward the group admiring Harvey Willard's arm. I watched him as he spoke to Harvey, pointing in my direction as he talked. Then Harvey shrugged, picked up a sweatshirt from the ground, tossed it around his shoulders, and began to walk toward me. He took his time.

When he stood before me I understood why the sports writers called him The Beast. He was three or four inches taller than my six feet, and I estimated he weighed about two twenty-five, most of it massed in his shoulders and chest. The big-time football folks would bulk him up quickly, with weights and diet. He'd play at two hundred forty and not look too much different.

He greeted me with a big, practiced grin and an out-thrust snowshoe of a hand. He had been trained in the look-'em-in-the-eye-and-shake-firmly school. I returned his stare and answered his grip with a hard squeeze of my own.

"I'm Willard," he said.

"I'm Coyne."

"Yale, huh?" He looked me up and down.

I noticed that he had a little Band-Aid over his right eyebrow, and the top lid of his eye bore the greenish-yellow tint of a week-old shiner.

"Yes. Yale."

His grin was really likeable. "I'm not Ivy League material, Mr. Coyne. Guy from Princeton told me that. I believe him. I don't want to waste your time. I might major in busi-

ness administration, something like that, but I'm not interested in killing myself, if you know what I mean. Hell, I'll
bet Yale doesn't even have a P.E. major." He smiled broadly
to let me know he was joking.

I returned his smile. "I doubt it. Couldn't tell you for
sure. I'm not a scout. I'm an attorney."

Willard cocked his head. "Yeah?"

"Yes. I represent the estate of your former teacher, George
Gresham. Trying to clear up some things about his death. I
hoped you might answer a couple of questions for me."

"Me? What do I know about it?"

"Well, he *was* your teacher. And I found a copy of a
paper you wrote for him among his things. It occurred to me
that he must have thought highly of your work to save it. You
see, we're very interested in understanding Mr. Gresham's
frame of mind at the time of his death. I thought you might
be able to help."

I pulled Harvey's paper from the inside pocket of my jacket
and handed it to him. He took it and glanced at it.

"Oh, yeah. That stupid paper. So what about it?"

"Why would your teacher make a copy of it and
keep it?"

"I didn't know that he did. I got a lousy C on it."

"This *is* your paper, isn't it?"

"Yup." He handed it back to me. "I was working on it."

"What do you mean?"

"Rewriting it. Like he said. Fixing up the spelling. Stuff
like that."

"What about the research? His comment here seems to
suggest that you need to document your thesis better."

Harvey reached for the paper and frowned at George
Gresham's comment on the front.

"Oh, yeah. Well, I really don't have time for that. But
I *was* working on it."

"I see," I said. "Mr. Gresham had a lot of books in his
room that seemed to deal with the same subject as your paper. I thought perhaps you were working with him on it."

Harvey wiped his forehead with his sweatshirt. He had enormous forearms. "Naw," he said. "I was just going over the words and punctuation and stuff. Nearly had it done when he killed himself. Now I don't know what to do with it, and I got that damn C, and I've got to get better than a C. Duke says if I don't get better than a C in history I might have to go to prep school for a year. That means I'd be twenty-three before I got drafted, and that would cost me when I signed." He peered earnestly at me. "Know what I mean?"

"Sure," I said. The boy had it all figured out.

"Anyhow," he said, "that's what that paper is all about. Can't tell you why he kept it. One thing's for sure. It wasn't because I was his favorite student."

"He didn't like you?"

"Mister," he said, "he hated me. Anyone can tell you that. I'm sorry he killed himself and all, but Mr. Gresham, he had it in for me. Ask anybody. He insulted me right in class."

"He did?"

"Yes. Called me The Beast of Little Brain. You think that was called for?"

I smiled at George's Winnie-the-Pooh allusion. "Doesn't sound called for to me," I said.

"Aw, he was all right, I guess. He just took history too seriously, that's all. See, and now I've got this paper, and some new guy's taking over Mr. Gresham's classes, and I don't know what to do with it. I mean, I really do need to get that grade up."

"Why don't you explain it to the new guy? Give him your revision."

"Yeah," Harvey said doubtfully. "The thing is, I really need some help on it. Muffy would help me, only she . . ."

"Muffy?"

"My girl. *Maybe* my girl." Harvey laughed and pointed to his eye. "Muffy's a popular kid. I had this fight the other day. Kid was bothering her, so I laid him out."

"He got in a good lick, looks like," I said.

Harvey glowered at me. "You should have seen him. Anyway, turns out Muffy wanted to be bothered. That make any sense to you?"

"Women hardly ever make sense to me," I said.

Harvey smiled. "Right. So anyway, right now Muffy isn't speaking to me, and I doubt if she'll help me with my paper."

"Why not talk to your English teacher about it?"

He shrugged. I persisted. "Worth a try, isn't it?"

"Yeah," he said with a frown. "I guess."

I looked at his paper again. "What do all these marks mean?" He stood close to me and looked over my shoulder. "Like this. 'Ag.' What's 'Ag' mean?"

"Agreement," he said. "That means agreement. See, my sentence goes, 'None of the women's bodies were positively identified.' The verb should be 'was' there. 'None was.' That's agreement." He looked at me. "Right?"

I shrugged. "Sounds good to me. What about this? 'Ro.' What's that?"

"Run-on. A run-on sentence. Needs a period in the middle." Harvey looked at me. "See, I do know this stuff. I just need a little help. Maybe I will talk to my English teacher. That's not a bad idea."

I flipped through his paper. Gresham's interest in it still baffled me. "So, then, 'Sp' here means spelling. And 'P'—what's that? Punctuation?"

"Right. Lots of those little buggers, huh?"

"Seem to be," I nodded. Something on the page caught my eye that I hadn't noticed before. There was an "SP" notation beside a name that George had drawn a circle around. "What about this?" I said. Harvey leaned over my shoulder to look.

"Right. That's spelling. When he writes it all in capitals and draws a circle around it, I guess that means he's really mad about it. Dumb to misspell someone's name, I suppose. See, that's Carla Steinholtz, one of the women who was bombing post offices and stuff back there in the sixties. Real dumb, to misspell a name. I must've copied it wrong. It's probably 'ie' or got no 't' in it or something."

Harvey backed a step or two away from me and began jogging in place and rolling his bulky shoulders like a prize fighter waiting for the bell to sound. I figured I'd worn out my welcome with him.

"Look, Harvey. I appreciate your time."

"Hey, no sweat, Mr. Coyne. Always a pleasure talking with someone from the Ivies. Sorry I couldn't help you out with Mr. Gresham, there. And real sorry about Yale. I'm pretty well set at Duke."

I smiled. "That's okay. I understand. And I did think your paper was interesting. You ought to work on it some more. Really."

He toweled his hair with his balled-up sweatshirt. "Yeah," he said. "Probably should. Probably won't, though, to tell the truth. I don't know. Maybe Muffy will come around. You know how women are."

"Sure. I know how they are."

"I'll see if I can't fix up those dumb mistakes, at least."

"Do that." I pointed to his eye. "And you watch out, now, when you go around defending the honor of maidens in distress."

He frowned and threw his sweatshirt over his shoulders. We began walking across the field. "That asshole Spender doesn't scare me with all his guns and stuff," he said.

"Who?"

Harvey was rolling his shoulders as he walked. "Cap Spender. Who's been messing with Muffy. Just a jerk who goes to school here. Shaves his head, wears old Army clothes. A weirdo. Talks about guns and killing black people and Jews and—like that. You know?"

"I think I met him," I said. "What'd you mean about his guns?"

Harvey tossed his head. "Aw, some of the kids say he keeps guns in his room. I dunno. One kid tried to tell me that Spender showed him some kind of little machine gun that he kept in his closet. I mean, Spender's crazy, but, Jesus—a machine gun? I think he tells stories is all. Though this same kid was telling me that he knows for a fact that Spender belongs to some kind of military club or something, and that he sneaks off campus a lot to go to meetings. Said he saw Spender getting into a car with Vermont plates one night after supper a couple weeks ago." Harvey shrugged his big shoulders. "Just a weirdo, if you ask me."

"Cap Spender," I said. "What kind of a name is that?"

"Means captain, I guess. Like, he's trying to organize these kids here at the school. He's their captain. Some kind of military outfit or something. He shows them his guns and makes them read this fascist stuff and call him 'sir.' Shit! I don't know what Muffy sees in that freak."

"Me neither," I said with a smile.

Suddenly from behind us came a sharp, piercing cry which stopped Harvey and me in our tracks. It was the shout a black belt makes before he slices through a cement block with the side of his hand. "Hi-*yah!*"

I quickly turned. About fifty yards from us, five or six young men were racing erratically across the grass. They were grouped together as they darted from side to side, paused, skipped backwards, then sprinted forward. The object of their quick movements, I saw, was a soccer ball. It was being controlled by a boy who was clad in a tee shirt and shorts like the others, but was distinguished by the bright red bandanna he had tied across his forehead.

Harvey and I stopped to watch. The boy with the headband was being chased by the other boys, who appeared intent on taking the ball from him. They were having no luck at all. He tapped the ball from foot to foot as he darted and dodged among them. Then he stopped and flipped the ball up over his head. He feinted with his head, and at the same time managed to cradle the ball with his heel behind him. Then he whirled around and sped off in the opposite direction, leaving the others several steps behind him. As they sprinted to catch up, the boy with the headband raced full speed, all the while dribbling the soccer ball without allowing it to touch the ground. With his toe he nudged it to his opposite instep, then up to his knee, opposite thigh, chest, head, tap-tap-tap on his forehead. Then he dropped it to his foot again without pausing or altering his headlong stride. He reminded me of Bob Cousy bringing the ball down-court on a Celtics fast break, zipping through the entire Knicks team. The ball stayed at his feet as if it were tethered there with a big elastic. It obeyed his will as if his mind, not his body, controlled it.

He stopped to let the others catch up, so he could tease them some more. They kicked at the darting ball. They dived at it with their feet. They tried to bump the boy with the red bandanna with their hips, but he pivoted and pirouetted away from them gracefully.

Then he gave the ball a tremendous kick, again screaming "Hi-*yah!*" with the effort. The soccer ball shot upward, higher than I would have thought possible. It paused at its peak, a dot against the sky, then plummeted. All of the boys circled under it. But the one with the red bandanna somehow caught it with his thigh. He faked with his shoulders, whirled, dropped the ball to the ground, and kicked it again, this time straight ahead of him. The ball took off on a high, majestic arc and landed far from the boys. Then they all fell to the ground and I could hear their laughter, although by now they were more than a football field away from me and Harvey.

"Wow!" I said to Harvey.

"He's pretty good, huh?"

"Some foot on that kid."

"That's Mr. Binh," said Harvey with a grin.

"Alexander Binh? The Dean?"

"Yep. He helps out with the soccer team in the fall."

"I thought it was one of the students."

"Nope. That's Mr. Binh. He keeps in good shape. Real good shape."

I nodded. "I'll say."

Harvey glanced over his shoulder, then turned and shoved his big mitt at me. "I really gotta get back to practice, Mr. Coyne. A pleasure to have conversed with you, sir."

I took his big paw. "My pleasure, Mr. Willard. I appreciate your time."

He turned and ambled back to the javelin-tossing area. He seemed a gentle enough Beast.

CHAPTER 8.

WASHINGTON WAS hot and humid, and I was happy to be able to get all my work done in one day there. I phoned the office Friday morning to tell Julie I'd be in after lunch, then spent the morning scribbling out my report for Frank.

He was going to be disappointed. A firm I had never heard of in Louisiana had been granted a patent on a process for manufacturing coffee bags. I learned that they had already begun to market them, so I wrote to the company for samples. I suggested in my report to Frank that the *idea* of the coffee bag was unprotected, of course, and that there was therefore nothing legal standing in the way of his developing his own manufacturing process. But I knew Frank Paradise well enough to predict that he would never pursue it. If it wasn't his invention, he wasn't interested.

I wrote longhand on yellow legal pads, sitting at the pine trestle table at the end of my dining-living room overlooking the harbor. Sometimes I glanced out over the bay. It was the same ocean that George Gresham had jumped into, I realized at one point. The idea, for some reason, startled me.

My mind kept turning to George.

I finished my draft of Frank's report about noontime, showered, and pulled on slacks and a short-sleeved knit shirt. Then I called Julie again.

"Brady L. Coyne, Attorney," she answered.

"Hi. Me."

"You coming in, or what?"

"Just to drop off the Paradise report. I don't want to see anybody. No appointments, please. Any calls?"

"Mrs. DeVincent was all. She wants to know about the dogs."

"Still?"

"Yes."

"What'd you tell her?"

"Me? You're the lawyer. I told her you'd call."

I sighed. "Okay. That it?"

She hesitated. "A Miss Prescott? From The Ruggles School?"

When Julie transformed a declarative sentence into an interrogative by her rising inflection at the end, she was asking for an explanation. I chose to ignore this hinted request, for reasons I couldn't identify.

"Okay," I said into the phone. "I'll try her from here. Then I'll be in to drop off the report, and you can go after it's typed. That okay?"

"Is it long?"

"The report? Naw. You'll beat the Friday traffic, no problem."

"Sure."

"Honest," I said.

I hung up, found an ancient can of Black Label in the back of the refrigerator, and took it back to my desk where the telephone sat. I got the number of The Ruggles School from the operator and dialed it.

The girl who answered told me that I was in the most unusual good luck, that Miss Prescott just happened to be conferring with Mr. Elliott that very moment and that she'd instructed her to please interrupt if she received a call.

Rina Prescott's voice, as it came over the phone, was softer and huskier than I had remembered it being in person.

"It's Brady Coyne, Miss Prescott," I said. "I'm returning your call."

I heard a soft chuckle. "Tell you the truth, Mr. Coyne, I'm going slightly bananas with this play. The curtain goes up in—less than seven and a half hours, my God!—and there's another performance, quote unquote, tomorrow night. And then, good my lord, I intend to render myself blissfully and totally inebriated. I'm kidding. The lighting board is busted and our esteemed leader—oops, I can't talk that way around here—Mr. Elliott, our distinguished Headmaster, is telling me that we aren't budgeted for repairs to the lighting board, and anyway he doesn't think we can find an electrician who knows how to work on it, and without the damn thing the play just doesn't work. It'll be another high-school Shakespeare. Yuck! And that would kill me." I could hear her take in a deep breath. I remained silent, feeling more than a little overwhelmed by her outburst.

"Look, Mr. Coyne," she continued, her voice somewhat calmer. "I found your card in my pocket this afternoon and I remembered that I'd promised to call you. Obviously I'm in no condition to discuss George with you now. Or much of anything, for that matter. How about after this play is over? Would that be okay?"

"How about dinner? Sunday." It came out of my mouth unbidden. I didn't know I was going to say that. But there it was, zipping along the telephone wires from my mouth to her ears.

She didn't answer for so long that I assumed I'd offended her, which wouldn't have surprised me. I'm good at that.

"Look, Miss Prescott, maybe . . ."

"No. No, that would be nice. Terrific, in fact. Perfect. Marvelous. I was just thinking . . ."

"I didn't mean to be forward. I'm sorry. We can talk again, when things are less hectic for you."

"I'd really like the dinner, Mr. Coyne," she said, her voice low and intimate, as if there were other people in the room who she didn't want to hear her. "Really."

"Oh," I said. "Well, good. I know a good spot not far from your school. You probably never heard of it. Run by an old Neapolitan dame named Gert. Not much on atmosphere, but it beats the hell out of all the Gloucester places for seafood. And Italian, if you're at all partial to Italian. Authentic Italian."

"I love Italian," she said. "It sounds perfect. That is, if you don't mind having a zombie for company. Tell me how to find it. I'll meet you there. About when? Sevenish?"

I told her seven was perfect, and gave her directions to Gert's. "And good luck with the play, Miss Prescott. Remember, 'To show our simple skill, that is the true beginning of our end.' "

"At which point my kids want to moon the audience," she laughed. "Good old Quince. I had forgotten you knew the play."

"Break a couple of legs," I said.

"Thank you, m'lord. God dig you den. See you at Gert's."

I hung up the phone, drained my Black Label, and smiled. Damn! She had a good voice.

When I got to the office it was nearly three o'clock, about the time on a Friday afternoon in May when most respectable Boston businessmen are evacuating the city to gather up their wives and kids and dogs in the station wagon to set sail for points Capeward or Maine-coastward. I had no family, no wagon, and no destinations in Maine or on the Cape. I didn't mind moving against the traffic.

Julie, however, did. When I dropped the Paradise report onto her desk, her shoulders slumped.

"You really need this today?"

I shrugged. "Monday'll be all right, I guess. Tell you what. Get this Dr. Wertz on the phone for me, and you can go. Okay?"

She flipped me a little smart-ass salute. "Fair enough," she said.

Leonard Wertz, M.D., whose name appeared on the Blue Shield forms in George Gresham's files, I figured was his allergist. Maybe George suffered from high blood pressure, or hemorrhoids, or postnasal drip. Whatever. I had promised

Florence that I'd do what I could. A chat with George's doctor seemed reasonable.

Julie buzzed me in a minute. "Dr. Wertz will not consult with you on the telephone. So says his snippy little secretary. So you gotta see him in his office. I made an appointment for you for Monday. Okay?"

I sighed. "Aw, shit, Julie. I don't want to drive all the way to Danvers to talk with some guy about ragweed and house dust."

"Huh?"

"George's allergist. Wertz."

"What gave you that idea?"

"What idea?"

"That the doctor is an allergist."

"I don't know. Something Dr. Clapp said. It doesn't matter. Don't get picky with me, Julie. Not on a Friday afternoon. So he's an oculist, or a podiatrist, or an oral surgeon. I just want to find out what ailed poor old George, that's all. Simple question. So he's not an allergist."

"No. He's not. He's a psychiatrist."

"Really? No shit?"

"No shit, Counselor. Dr. Wertz was Mr. Gresham's shrink."

"Monday, huh?"

"Right."

"I think maybe I'll keep that appointment."

Weekends.

Once upon a time weekends meant The Great American Suburban Dream to me. I bought it all, the whole big package. And I loved it.

That was years ago, in another life of mine, when the boys were small and Gloria and I lived in the Garrison colonial in Wellesley, when Saturdays were family days and Sundays I played golf at the country club while Gloria and the boys went to the pool, and afterward we ate tunafish sandwiches together. Gloria and I would have gin-and-tonics, the boys Cokes, and I'd limit myself to one drink. Then I'd wander into the locker room to join the poker game for a couple hours while we watched the Red Sox, and later, when it got cooler, Gloria and I would take on the Stetsons for a couple sets of mixed doubles.

That was one of my other lives. The next other life came in the early years of the divorce. I had the boys on Saturdays, then. I'd pick them up early for a frenetic day of entertainment—the Stoneham Zoo, the Aquarium, Fenway Park, the Boston Garden, the Peabody Museum. We drove to Plimoth Plantation one Saturday, and another time to Sturbridge Village. I wanted to be a Worthy Parent, and acquaint my sons with New England Culture.

We tried very hard, all three of us, to be at ease with each other. And we were all relieved when the day ended and I dropped them off with Mommy.

Gloria always served me a drink on those Saturdays when I brought the boys home. In nice weather she'd sit me down on a wrought-iron chair on the brick patio out back and wheel out the portable bar she had bought for me for Father's Day shortly after Joey was born. While she mixed my bourbon and branch she'd chatter about the boys' school, her photographic assignments, people at the club, just as if we were still married. And I'd contemplate the hours—hell, the months—of labor I had invested in her place of residence. The one thousand six hundred and fifty bricks I had laid one by one in a basket-weave design over the two truckloads of sand, all smoothed and leveled. The twelve azaleas, yellows and oranges and reds, and six rhododendrons I had planted, dug up, and replanted under Gloria's narrow-eyed supervision, in holes cushioned with a mixture of pine needles and peat moss. The gutters I had oiled, painted, cleaned, torn down, and replaced. The clapboards I had scraped, primed, and painted. The lawn I had mowed, despising every minute of it. And the woman I had laughed with, loved, and reluctantly left.

I felt myself a stranger there. The shrubs had grown. Weeds poked up between the bricks I had laid. The house was a new color. And somehow it all seemed smaller, darker, more claustrophobic than when I had lived there, as if jungle animals might crawl out from under the azaleas in the darkening Saturday evening while Gloria and I sipped our cocktails.

"Did you have a nice day?" she'd ask, in much the same way she used to after I had spent a day pampering clients in Boston, and I'd say, "Oh, sure, just fine," the way I always had.

And Gloria would say, "The boys are getting big, aren't they?" and I'd reply, "Oh, yes, they're getting to be young men," understanding that what we both meant was that Gloria was doing a splendid job of bringing them up without my help.

Gloria and I had a very polite divorce. "Civilized," she called it. Gloria was very big on doing things in a civilized manner.

It gradually slipped away. It didn't happen by design, and in spite of the inevitable tension between me and my sons when we're together, the emptiness I feel when we're apart has never subsided. But as they got older it seemed that Billy and Joey had things to do on Saturdays. There were ball games they had to play in, parties to attend, weekends out of town with friends. Gloria remained civilized about that, too, so that I could visit on a Sunday, or even take them to McDonald's on a Tuesday night. But sometimes it couldn't be arranged. Maybe I could have pushed harder. But I didn't want them to resent me, to think of me as an interloper who disrupted their lives. And if we missed seeing each other for a week or two, they didn't seem to mind.

I minded. I minded when I didn't see them, and I minded even more that they didn't seem to.

And now I don't see them that often. I watched Billy play third base for his high school team a few times, and I went to the banquet at which Joey was awarded second place for his fruit fly experiment. We still go to restaurants together occasionally, but it has become ceremonial, and I wonder that

I feel compelled to take them to expensive places now. We are polite, awkward, restrained. We know we like each other, but we can't seem to feel it.

So now I dread weekends. They remind me of what's missing in my life.

The Harborside apartment complex rises against the waterfront near the old Commercial Wharf, right off Atlantic Avenue. I live in apartment 6E. Two bedrooms, a living-dining combination, and a closet they call a kitchenette, all for $980 a month. At one end of the living-dining room are floor-to-ceiling sliding glass doors which open onto a balcony with a rusting wrought-iron railing. There's room for two vinyl-covered aluminum folding chairs and a hibachi. I sit on one of the chairs when I want to drink Jack Daniels and watch the sailboats drift on the harbor and think solitary thoughts, which I do almost every evening. I use the hibachi on those rare occasions when I have invited a guest to sample my cuisine. I'm damn good at charcoal cooking, though I find it hardly worth the effort when I'm alone. Usually I feed myself a frozen pizza or a can of Dinty Moore's beef stew.

I use one of the two bedrooms for sleeping. My double bed is one of the few pieces of furniture I own. I need an extra-firm, orthopedic mattress to keep my vertebrae flexing properly. The rest of the stuff I rent from a guy named Burke who, I think, gives kickbacks to the realtor.

The other bedroom contains most of my worldly possessions: cartons of books I probably will never get around to unpacking, a broken vacuum cleaner, a pair of large speakers—Gloria kept the stereo; I got the speakers—a tool box, a table saw, a ten-speed bike with flat tires, an ironing board. Artifacts, mostly, of my other life.

The things I really care about I store in the living room where I can keep in touch with them. That's where I have set up my fly-tying table and my cabinets of bucktail, wood duck breasts, neck hackles, tinsel, yarn, thread, and hooks. I keep my felt-soled waders there, too, and my rack of split-bamboo rods, and the shelf for my reels. And in the corner, where I can pull out the five iron or the putter, stands my bag of MacGregor M.T. Tourneys.

I spent most of Saturday morning in my bathrobe reading law and smoking Winstons at the table near the sliding glass doors. Around noon I dropped a couple of sport coats off at the dry cleaners and walked back the long way. Then I mixed myself a tall Carnation Instant Breakfast for lunch, putted into a glass on the rug for fifteen or twenty minutes, showered, and took a nap. When I woke up I opened a can of Schlitz and tied a few Quill Gordons on number sixteen hooks while the Red Sox lost a close one to Baltimore on the tube, which I rolled behind me so that I could listen to Ned Martin and the crowd noises without being distracted by the picture.

I thought briefly of piling my waders and gear into the car and driving to the Squannicook in time for the evening hatch. But inertia is the curse of my middle age. So I had another beer.

Later, I changed into a jacket and tie and treated myself to a steak at the Scotch and Sirloin and watched the young people play mating games. I got home early and fell asleep to an old movie which had been advertised as an "early Bogie," but in which Bogart had only a bit part.

A typical, exciting Saturday in the life of the bachelor attorney.

Sunday I devoted to Mrs. DeVincent's case. Believe it or not, there are precedents in Massachusetts judicial history on the custody of Labrador retrievers. The DeVincents had five—the dam and her four pups. Jenny DeVincent, my client, wanted me to argue that she should retain custody—that was *her* word, not mine—of all five dogs, on the grounds that the puppies shouldn't be separated from each other or from their mother. Jenny's husband, Jack, countered that the dogs were personal property, like automobiles or jewelry, and should be divided equitably.

I happened to know that all Jack wanted was the mother,

who would swim the Klondike to retrieve a wounded duck, and I figured we could settle the whole thing out of court after we danced around the issues for a bit.

The DeVincents did not disagree on issues such as alimony or their eleven-room house in Dover or the boat or the three Mercedes. I suspected that, had their children not been adults, the dogs still would have been the main point of contention between them.

I understood that sort of thing. Marriages fell apart over major issues. It was the little things like Labrador retrievers which came along to eliminate the chances for repair.

I understood it well. I had lived it myself. The solution, I decided years ago, was to avoid having major issues in the first place, and if that meant avoiding major relationships, as it seemed to, I figured it was well worth it.

Hell. I was single, middle-aged, and I had a date on Sunday night. What more could a man want?

CHAPTER *9.*

RINA PRESCOTT was waiting for me in the foyer at Gert's when I arrived. She wore a pale green blouse with a round collar buttoned to her throat, a full, patterned skirt, and little gold hoops in her ears. She had on no other jewelry. The only makeup I noticed was a touch of green on her eyelids. She shook my hand, grinned, and said, "This is the first time I've relaxed in a month. My Midsummer Nightmare is over. Time for a drink."

There was a different crowd at Gert's on Sunday night from the one I had seen at the noon meal a few weeks earlier—several families with small children, a few couples dressed for the theater, one old man sitting at a corner table with his napkin tucked into his collar, hunched over a heaping bowl of pasta. Conversation hummed at a lower decibel level than at noontime. The clink of silverware, little bursts of loud talk, now and then a public, controlled laugh, the clang of pots and pans when the kitchen door swung open, and, over invisible loudspeakers, the lilt of violins, Respighi—all melded into a comfortable, warm background that invited intimacy.

We were led to a table against the wall by a slim young man with one gold earring. He seemed to glide around on ball bearings. "I'm Charles, your waiter this evening," he said, in an incongruously deep voice. "Would you care for a cocktail?"

Rina had Cutty on the rocks, and I settled for Jack Daniels the same way. Charles oozed away.

"So. How did it go?" I asked her.

"Oh, good, actually. It *was* good. The kids came through. The usual slips. You know. The curtain got fouled up on one of the props and when we tried to open it at the fifth act it ripped. Elliott was ripped, too, when I told him. 'That's a thousand-dollar curtain,' he screamed. I told him the kids would sew it up, but he wasn't mollified. And, you know, we had the predictable missed cues. But none of the audiences noticed, I'm quite sure. They were great, the audiences. I'm still on adrenaline. In case you didn't notice."

I smiled. "I know you're not always this way."

"Yeah, well, I'm sorry about how I acted that day. But he should know better than to interrupt a rehearsal."

Charles brought our drinks. "Care to order now, sir?" he asked.

I lifted my eyebrows, and she nodded. "What'll you have, Miss Prescott?" I said.

"I think, for one thing, I'll have you call me Rina, if that's okay," she said. "What do you recommend, anyway?"

I shrugged. "Feel like fish or Italian?"

"Either, m'lord. Order for us, please."

"That's not very liberated of you."

"I'm so liberated that that doesn't bother me at all," she said. "You can hold a door open for me, hold my chair, taste the wine. That symbolic stuff is okay. When you're really liberated, you don't mind being treated like a woman, is how I figure it."

I nodded and turned to Charles. "The scallopine, then. We'll start with an antipasto. Big carafe of house red. Cheese and espresso afterwards. And," I added, pointing to our cocktail glasses, "please do this again for us." I looked at Rina. "Okay?"

"Marvelous."

Charles permitted himself a small smile of approval and rolled away.

"I appreciate your calling me," I said. "I hope you didn't mind."

She looked down into her drink. "I *am* liberated, if that's what you mean. I don't mind calling a man. And if you hadn't asked me out I probably would've asked you. I always get wigged out right before a performance, and all I can think is, if I don't get the hell out of here I'm going to start throwing things. The idea of having a date—boy, that sounds old-fashioned, 'date'—anyway, the idea of getting away from there and doing something reasonably civilized with somebody totally disconnected from dear old Ruggles kept me sane through the whole thing. You can't believe how refreshing it is to talk with somebody other than another teacher or an adolescent. Sometimes it's hard to tell the difference." She shrugged and grinned. "But to talk to somebody from the real world. All caps. THE REAL WORLD. Besides, I owed you an apology. And I did say I'd call." She lifted her glass and downed the remainder of her Scotch. The ice cubes clinked against her teeth. She pursed her lips and sucked one into her mouth. "So I called," she mumbled around the ice cube. "Okay?"

She crunched the ice loudly.

I smiled at her. "Yes. Okay."

"What was it you wanted to know about poor George?"

"I don't know, exactly," I said. "Why would he take his own life? Or did he really take his own life? How well did you know him?"

"He was a friend. All of us there are friends." Rina paused as Charles set our second round on the table and deftly filched our empty glasses. "Most of us, anyway, are friends. It's a small school, we're thrust together a lot. We live together. It's like a family. There are the feuds, the jealousies, but also the dependencies. We're like siblings. I mean, I know George liked oatmeal for breakfast with big chunks of brown sugar on it. But I don't know a thing about his sex life. I know he detested television but secretly watched football on Monday nights. But I don't know whether he squeezed his toothpaste from the end or the middle. I'd guess the end, though."

"Did his suicide surprise you?"

She hesitated. "It surprised me, of course. If he'd had a heart attack or gotten hit by a car, that would have surprised me, too. Naturally. But—well, you think back on it, you try to figure it, and you say, 'Yeah, he could have.' You know? He was a melancholy person. No real joy in his life, at least none that any of us could see. We've all talked a lot about it. Jenny Wolcott, she's taken it hard. I think she had a little thing for George. Father figure, maybe. He could be that way with women. Not a sexual bone in his body." She squinted at me. "Is that mixing a metaphor?"

"Sexual bone? Hmm. Maybe. Maybe not."

"Anyhow, I guess, yeah, he could have. Of the people I know, I'd say George was one who might kill himself."

"And the others feel that way?"

She shrugged. "More or less."

"Binh too?"

"Mr. Binh doesn't tell us peasants what's going on in his head. He's too busy being inscrutable."

"Inscrutable?"

"Aha! You caught me. Prejudice, right? Or at least, guilty of a cliché." Rina frowned at me. "Don't get me off on the subject of Alexander Binh. He walked all over George to get that Dean's job. George should have had it. He deserved it. By seniority, if nothing else. But Binh played it cozy with the buffoon—Elliott, that is. Persuaded Elliott that if he, Alexander Binh, didn't become the Dean, Ruggles would be guilty of racial discrimination. So Elliott gave the job to Binh. Which, it seems to me, itself is a clear case of racial discrimination. Don't you agree?"

I shrugged. "You're not asking me for a legal opinion, I know. How did George feel about not getting the job?"

"You had to know George to understand. He never uttered a word. No complaint. Sincere, hearty handshake and congratulations for Binh. But his feelings were hurt. Deeply hurt, I know. At the same time, I think George understood that Binh had simply outsmarted Elliott—not a particularly difficult feat, of course—and he didn't blame our Headmaster for his folly. He was saddened by it, that's all. But hurt, too. All of us learned by George's example. Two lessons. One, don't trust Elliott. He's too dumb to trust. And, two, don't trust Binh. He's too smart."

Charles wheeled himself up to the table and slid our antipasto in front of us. Then he set the wine by my elbow. I poured a dash from the carafe into my glass and cermoniously sniffed it, then sipped.

"Ah, a brave little vintage," I murmured. "Pert, but not gaudy. A touch of the grape for m'lady." I poured Rina's glass full.

She inclined her head. "My thanks, good my lord. And God bless this our repast."

We touched glasses. Rina's sharp, green eyes glittered as she drank.

We attacked the antipasto. I dug around the anchovies and hunks of prosciutto and salami and concentrated on the tomatoes and cucumbers and bits of tuna. Rina aggressively monopolized the ripe olives. She crammed big leaves of lettuce into her mouth, so that the olive oil made a film around her mouth and on her chin. I caught her watching me, and after a calculating moment she gathered up the anchovies into a pile on her plate and attacked them methodically. When they were gone, she raised her wineglass and drained it. She set it down and arched her eyebrows at me.

"Those little fish are salty," she explained.

I reached across the table and refilled her glass. She smiled broadly and took another deep draught. "Bring on the veal," she said, dabbing her napkin at her mouth.

As if he had been listening, Charles materialized. He slid a heaping plate before each of us. Big slabs of veal swam in a pungent sauce. Little buttons of mushrooms and chunky pieces of green pepper were piled on top. Rina leaned over and sniffed deeply.

"Ahh," she sighed. She broke a hunk of bread from the warm loaf and held it in her left hand. She took her fork in her right and laid siege on the scallopine two-fistedly. She ate with the enthusiasm of the Dallas Cowboys at their training table. Her concentration was absolute. Little beads of perspiration broke out on her forehead. And when her plate was empty, she grabbed another hunk of bread and sopped up the rich juices. She finished her wine and poured herself another glass, paused, and refilled my glass as well. Then she looked up. Her expression seemed to say, "Oh. I forgot you were there."

I was smiling abstractedly at her, and when her glance caught mine she seemed to open her eyes a little wider.

"Like it?"

She nodded, grinned, and burped into her napkin.

"Excuse me," she said, rolling her eyes in mock horror. Then she laughed. "Hey, that was fantastic. More wine?"

"You just filled it," I said.

"Well, drink up, so I can fill it again." She gulped from her own glass, then set it down and said, "Poor old George."

"Here's to poor old George," I said, lifting my glass. She lifted hers, and we touched glasses and drank to poor old George. "Query," I announced.

She frowned solemnly. "Of course," she said.

"Enlighten me, if you can, on two gentlemen not from Verona. To wit, one Master Harvey Willard, and another, the Captain Spender, both scholars at the Ruggles institution of learning."

She lifted the empty carafe, wiggled it in front of her face, and said, "If't please my lord?"

I swiveled around in my chair and caught Charles's attention. He slid towards us. "More spirits, my man," I said. "And forget the espresso and cheese." He didn't smile, but he did remove the empty carafe. Rina sat smiling and drumming her fingernails on her empty wineglass until Charles returned. I refilled both of our glasses.

"Willard, Harvey," said Rina. "First, a toast. To The Beast."

"The Beast," I said. We both drank to The Beast. Rina topped off our glasses.

"Pulling guard. Projected as a linebacker. A Nautilus major, minor in wind sprints. A gentle beast, is Harvey, except on the playing fields. An indifferent scholar, though 'tis said his WAIS hovers around 140, which, I understand, is several standard deviations to the right of average." She stopped and frowned at me. "What's Harvey Willard got to do with anything?"

"Nothing, most likely. I don't know. I found a paper of his in Gresham's files. Something on radicals, antiwar groups. As a function of Vietnam, near as I could tell. It wasn't a great paper. Gresham gave it a C. Yet, for some reason, he kept a copy of it. Evidently he was doing some studying on the subject himself. Had a big pile of books about that period on his desk."

"Which explains it."

"What—that George was studying that era?"

"Sure. Don't you think?"

"Why keep a C paper, anyway?"

She gave me a great, exaggerated shrug and took a sip of wine. "Well, anyway, that's what I know about Mr. Willard. I've got him in a class. He gets a C there, too."

"Do you teach anything besides drama?"

She nodded. "English. What we euphemistically call 'College Prep English.' Our curriculum is imaginatively sequenced this way: English Nine, English Ten, English Eleven, English Twelve. Subtitled, in each instance, College Preparatory."

"What about this Spender kid?"

"A beast of a different color. This wine's good, huh? And not a gentle beast at all. Harvey may be smart, but Cap Spender is a bona fide genius. Used to drive George bananas. Liked to set George up in class. Ask him leading questions. The kid was clever as hell. He'd do a Socratic number on George, lead him down the logical primrose path until he had George at the point of agreeing that Jews and blacks should be shipped out of the country, that mentally deficient people should be abandoned on ice floes, that they should require people to pass a Mensa test before they can be allowed to vote. The boy's good at it, too. He's done his homework. He's read his Plato and Nietzsche and Spengler and Hegel. Elitism, nationalism, racism, all that stuff. And he's got this magnetic way about him. The girls seem to love that shaven skull of his and that wimpy little goatee, and there's a loyal cadre of boys who do his bidding. I suppose he makes them feel that they're a part of some kind of elite themselves. Kids who doubt themselves—and most kids do, you know—latch onto someone with the kind of power that Spender has. He's our own Reverend Moon, see?"

"But not Harvey, I gather."

"Oh, certainly not Harvey Willard. Harvey's got plenty of common sense. He told Spender one day—it was right in George's class, right in the middle of one of Spender's sly dialogues—Harvey said, 'Hey, asshole. Cut the bullshit. Let's get back to history.' George loved that, of course, though he felt compelled to bawl Harvey out for the language. But he told us all about it afterwards. It was funny to hear George use those words. 'Asshole' and 'bullshit.' He didn't talk that way himself, of course. You could practically see the quotation marks when he said them."

"Why do you tolerate a person like that? Doesn't he disrupt the educational process?"

"That's from the Supreme Court, isn't it? 'Disrupt the educational process'? You sound like a lawyer."

I covered my mouth in mock dismay. "Fie on me. My gracious. I sounded like a lawyer. Yes. *Tinker v. Des Moines,* 1969, if you want to know. But doesn't he?"

"Sure. He's disruptive as hell. Elliott has this philosophy about freedom, and kids needing to go through phases, as he calls them, and not forcing kids into more antisocial postures, and crap like that. George complained to Elliott all the time. He'd say, 'I can't control him. I'm appealing to you'— meaning Elliott—'the administration. I admit it. I can't control my class. If I can't do that, I can't teach. Take him out of my classroom. Get him off this campus. He's evil. He's corrupting these children.' And Elliott would smile his benign, grandfatherly smile, and say, 'They accused Socrates of corrupting the youth, George, and they exiled him.' And George would go absolutely berserk. 'You have the nerve to compare that maggot to Socrates?' And Elliott would smile some more and mumble, 'Freedom of Assembly. Freedom of

Speech.' And George would throw up his hands. They had these discussions all the time, George and our great Headmaster. Publicly, too. I'm sure Cap Spender heard of them and loved it."

Rina sat back in her chair and arched her back, lifting her chin so that she looked up at the ceiling. Her breasts pushed against her blouse. Then she looked at me. "Let's finish up this wine and get out of here," she said.

I found Charles with my eyes and moved my hand in a way I hoped he would not find patronizing. He came with the check on a little silver tray, which he placed by my elbow. "Thank you, sir," he rumbled. "I hope everything was all right."

"Great. Beautiful. Wonderful," I said.

I overtipped Charles outrageously, pushed my chair back, and stood up. I grabbed for the back of the chair. We had consumed a great deal of wine, I realized. It suddenly felt very warm in the restaurant.

I picked my way carefully around the table and held the back of Rina's chair for her. She stood, smiled, and fell against me for a second. "Oops," she giggled. I held her arm above the elbow and steered her ahead of me gingerly among the maze of tables and chairs through the restaurant and out the door.

The night air in the parking lot washed over me, cool, damp, and clean. I breathed deeply. Wisps of night fog drifted through the floodlights that were mounted under the eaves of the restaurant. Rina and I walked to where the cars were parked. I let my hand slide down her arm. She took my hand.

We found ourselves standing beside my BMW. "Whither, sire?" she said softly.

"Gee, I don't know. I mean . . ."

"You want me to go home now?"

"Oh, no, I just . . ."

"Good. I don't want to go home."

"Well, the thing is, I didn't plan . . ."

Her laugh tinkled like wind chimes. "Of *course* you didn't plan. I'm not accusing you of anything."

"Right. Well, where shall we go?"

Rina hugged my arm against her body. I could feel the softness of her breast against my arm. Then she rested the side of her head against my shoulder and murmured, "Wherever you want, sire."

I cleared my throat. "I understand Charity's Point is beautiful at night."

"So they say," said Rina.

"Can you show me how to get there?"

"Sure can."

"Well, lead on, Macduff."

We drove in silence. Rina lay her head back on the seat. Her eyes were closed. On the car radio a medley from *My Fair Lady* was playing. Rina sang the words quietly, her voice low, sexy, and clear. "I always wanted to play Eliza," she said dreamily when the medley ended. "Best I ever did was a spinster in an O'Neill play. Can't even remember the title."

"Broadway?"

"Nope," she said. "Way, way off Broadway. Every girl's dream. The stage. Boys want to be Mickey Mantle, girls want to be Eliza. See your name up in lights. I gave it three years. Supported myself modeling. Feet. Believe it? I sold a piece of my body in the Big Apple while I waited for the break that never came. You probably saw my feet in magazines. My feet were in great demand for a while there. I did sandals, pumps, sneakers. A national campaign for Dr. Scholl's even. My perfect feet. Also did a corn-plaster ad which was pretty big. This agency had a photographer who I swear ejaculated into his britches when I took off my shoes. Anyway, I gave it up, got my degree, and joined the other failures at dear old Ruggles. Those who can't, teach. You know?"

"I thought teachers detested that adage," I said.

"Oh, sure we do. But we're lying to ourselves. We're all bitter and angry at the world which rejected our real talents. Misfits. Look at Warren Baker. Or Bartley Elliott, for Christ's sake. Hey, look at me, directing a bunch of pimply kids through Shakespeare. Shit."

She fell silent. My mind drifted. The car radio gave us

soft strings. In the dark of the car, Rina suddenly said, "Oh, hell." Her voice was soft, melancholy. She sounded like one of those bad drunks whose self-flagellating monologues break up parties early. "Those who can, do. Most of us can't. 'We're lucky to teach. George always said that. 'We're lucky to have the chance to teach,' he always said. Thing is—*was*, I should say—George *could*. He was just a poor old goddam perfectionist, was his problem. Ah, screw it. He's dead. The rest of us, I guess we're only waiting around for it. Give the guy credit. He couldn't wait. Always the perfectionist. Old George. Old G. G."

After a while Rina started humming tunelessly. We drove through the misty night along the two-lane road that paralleled the ocean. "Right up ahead," she said suddenly, when I thought she was dozing. "You'll see a big parking lot. Turn in there."

I turned onto a big, flat, empty expanse of hard-packed dirt. The fog thickened in the headlights as I drove slowly toward a row of rectangular shapes which, as I neared them, materialized into big, green trash barrels. Beyond the barrels, the ground began to rise gradually into the fog and dark.

"You can park here," said Rina, sitting up straight and stretching her neck.

I extinguished the headlights and turned off the ignition, and then I could hear the muffled roar of the surf. It sounded very close, but the noise struggled through the heavy, moist air like the comings and goings of big trucks along a distant highway.

"North Cove Beach, straight ahead," announced Rina. "Just over the dunes." She opened the car door. "Coming?"

"This where . . . ?"

"Yes. Where George's body was found, they say." Rina shivered suddenly. "Look, you might as well take off your shoes. And do you have a blanket or something we can sit on?"

"Sure. In the trunk. I'll get it."

I slipped off my shoes and tucked my socks into them and left them on the floor in the front of my car. Then I found my raggedy old Army blanket. I shoved it up under my arm. Rina grabbed my shirt sleeve. "Come on. This way."

We followed a well-trodden path up over the sand hill. Somewhere above the fog the moon shone full, casting the scene into blurry shadows and shapes. I could see the white strip of breaking surf ahead, but the ocean beyond it merged with the dark sky. It was a watercolor wash in shades of gray.

"It's beautiful," I said.

"I think it's spooky," replied Rina. "A place for dead bodies to crawl up out of the sea."

We walked shoeless toward the surf. The sand warmed the bottoms of my feet with the heat it had stored up from the day's sunshine. Then its texture changed, and it was like setting cement, wet, cool, firm. I imagined the girl who had found George Gresham's body on this beach. In my mind I saw her jogging. The hard sand at the water's edge squeaked rhythmically under her feet, her toes kicking back little divots with each stride. She stuck close to that line where the tide lapped, splashing sometimes in the shallow sheet of moving seawater, savoring the cool splashes on the front of her bare thighs.

I pictured her, then, attracted to a formless mound on the beach where a flock of seagulls circled, croaking, angry at the disturbance. I saw her touch the dead man's hand, then draw her fingers back instinctively at the cold, clammy feel of lifeless skin. Perhaps she gagged; perhaps she screamed into the vast ocean. George Gresham's face was not pretty. I had seen the pictures.

Rina groped for my hand. "Come on. Charity's Point's about a mile down the beach."

We walked in silence, our hands clasped, toward a louder, angrier roar of surf. I was very much aware of Rina beside me, our arms brushing as we walked, the faint, clean scent of soap mingling with the sharp, briny smell of the sea and the fog.

"Make you think of George?" I asked.

She didn't answer. Instead, she dropped my hand and darted away, slipping ghostlike through the wall of fog. I stopped, momentarily disoriented, and felt a quick flash of panic.

I swiveled my head around and squinted into the murk. Suddenly a wet, clammy weight slammed against the back of my neck. My first thought was that I had been attacked by a seagull. Then Rina was rubbing a handful of the seaweed into my face, holding me strongly around the waist with her other arm.

"Hey!" I said. I reached for her, but she squirmed away and disappeared again.

From the fog her voice came, distorted, hollow, almost unearthly. "When shall we two meet again, in thunder, lightning, or in fog?"

"Come on, now," I said, clutching at my dignity in what I saw was a losing battle.

"When the hurly-burly's done, when the battle's lost and won," she called, her voice a cackle.

"Where the hell are you, pray?"

"Fair is foul, and foul is fair. Hover through the fog and filthy air."

"I'm hovering, already. Help me down, will you?"

Then she was at my side again, grasping my arm in both of hers, her head briefly pressed against my shoulder. "Scare you?" she said.

"Hell, no," I said. I could feel the roundness of her breast against my arm. "Where are we going, anyway?"

"This way." Her hand slid down my arm until she was holding mine. She swung it and began to skip, forcing me to increase my pace to keep up with her. After a moment I found it easier to skip, too.

So we skipped down the beach, hand in hand, the forty-two-year-old attorney with his pants legs rolled up and the younger woman in her swirling, peasant skirt, cutting through the fog and splashing in the water at the edge of the ocean.

Finally I stopped, holding her hand firmly so that she had to stop, too. When she did, she bounced against me.

"What's the matter, sire?"

"Tuckers me out," I panted. "Besides, I feel foolish."

"Nothing wrong with feeling foolish," Rina said.

"I'm not used to it."

"Well, we're there, now, anyway. We have to climb."

She led me obliquely away from the water line. I could distinguish the dark shape of what appeared to be a small mountain looming through the gray fog. We slogged over the dunes at first. Sharp grass cut at my bare feet and ankles. Then there were rocks, and we had to climb. Rina went first, her hand still holding mine behind her. Sometimes she tugged gently at me when I had to pull myself over a boulder. Once I banged my knee, and when I growled "Bastard!" Rina laughed.

She seemed to move effortlessly up the incline, slithering over and around the rocks, tall, slim, and lithe as a panther, and I became aware of the curves of her body—the breadth of her back contrasted with her tiny waist, her hips slim and angular, and the suggestion of her rump taut under her skirt as she stretched and pulled at me. I felt awkward in comparison to her. I had to cling to her hand for support. The folded Army blanket was still crammed under my arm. I thought of George Gresham climbing here alone not too many nights earlier, a man in a suit and necktie with a desperate purpose. I glanced ahead to check our progress. The fog, I noticed, was thinning, so that I could see our destination more clearly. The crashing of the surf came more sharply to my ears, each breaker a separate and distinct explosion of tons of water smashing against the hard planes of boulders.

Then Rina stopped. "We're here."

I looked out over the ocean. We seemed to be standing above the fog, which lay in a cottony blanket on the beach off to our left whence we had come. Before us stretched the Atlantic, shimmering with gathered points of light. I walked to the edge of the mammoth boulder and peered down.

"Jesus!" I whispered. The face of the cliff seemed to angle back under me, as if I were perched on a ledge, so that I could only see the thrashing of the confluence of current and tide far below me. Each crashing wave sent a sheet of white spray thirty feet into the air. A place for shipwrecks, I thought. A good place for suicide.

Rina was sitting, well back from the edge, arms clasped around her legs, head tilted so that her cheek rested on her knees. I went back and sat heavily beside her. I lit a cigarette. We sat without touching or speaking. I felt overwhelmed by the enormity of the place—the height, the awesome power of the ocean, the thunderous booming of the waves, the vastness of the sky. Rina beside me seemed small, vulnerable. I suppressed the urge to put my arm protectively around her shoulders.

"What're you really after?" she asked after a while. "What's in all this for you?"

"What? You mean the Gresham thing? Nothing for me. Not really. It's my job, that's all."

"You're a lawyer. I don't get it."

I flicked my cigarette away. "My client hired me. For advice. Legal advice. That's it."

"Umm."

"You don't approve."

I could feel her shoulders lift and fall beside me. "Not a matter of approval, my lord. I'm beyond judging. Way, way beyond that. Glass domiciles, you know. Just seems like a funny sort of thing for an attorney to do, messing around in the life of a dead man."

She leaned against me lightly. I glanced down and saw her face uplifted to mine. I did put my arm around her shoulders, then. She leaned her cheek against my shoulder and wiggled her body against mine. I rubbed my chin in her hair. Her face turned, and her mouth was a sweet fruit under mine, soft, promising, and languid. Abruptly, she turned away. I felt her shiver, and with my hand I urged her closer to me. Instead, she stood and walked slowly to the edge of the precipice. I felt a momentary panic. I thought, crazily, that she was going to jump. I stood and moved quickly to stand beside her.

"Sorry about that," I said.

"Sorry?" Her laugh was short, cynical.

"You know . . ."

"Want to kiss me again, good my liege?"

"Sure," I said. I did. The salt spray drifted up to us from

the chaos far below. Her hair was damp to the touch of my face. I couldn't tell if the salty taste on my tongue was from the mist rising from below, or if Rina was crying.

"Let's get out of here," she said, twisting away from me.

The descent from Charity's Point was easier. Rina didn't hold my hand on the way down. Instead, she bounced ahead of me, sure-footed and spirited as a young mountain goat. I hung back from her, glad for the space between us. Too much wine, I thought. That's all. A couple of nice, competent kisses, a very romantic spot for kissing, nice-looking woman, maudlin thoughts of death. Logical.

The tide was rising as we strolled back up the beach toward the parking lot. We didn't touch. I shifted the blanket to my other armpit. Waves broke out to our right, and the frigid, spring seawater hissed over the wet sand toward us, a shock to our feet, and then we felt the sucking erosion as it slid back to sea. We walked slowly, in no hurry. The fog was lifting from the beach, and the sky over our heads was a great bowl of stars. The moonbeams cut through the puffy little wisps of dissipating fog.

Sometimes as we walked our hips bumped. Once Rina grabbed my arm in both her hands as a wave crashed close to us. She dug her face into the front of my shirt to wipe off the water.

"Let's stop," she said suddenly. "Let's sit for a minute. Here, give me an end of the blanket."

I flapped out the blanket, and Rina grabbed the other end to spread it on the powdery sand. I lit another Winston. We sat in silence and stared at the moon. Then Rina stood up. Wordlessly, she stepped out of her skirt. I watched as she worked at the buttons down the front of her blouse. The moon's pale glow caught the white strips of nylon at her crotch and across her chest. She reached up behind her and shrugged her shoulders, catching the bra in her hand and dropping it to the blanket beside me. Then she hooked both thumbs into the band of her panties and drew them down her legs. She stood before me, legs apart, feet planted solidly in the sand. The moon's reflected rays played in her dark hair.

"Coming?"

I undressed awkwardly while Rina waited. Then she took my hand and we ran into the water. The shocking coldness of it stopped me, but Rina continued, high-stepping over the little breakers, and then, with a twinkling flash of her pale rump, she cut the water with a dive. She stayed under for a long time, and when her head popped out, silhouetted on the surface of the water, she was much farther from me than I had expected.

I followed her in my plodding crawl, too much arm and shoulder and too little kick. When I reached her, I was breathing heavily. She was treading water effortlessly, bobbing with the gentle swell of the ocean. I floated on my back, trying to restore my breathing to normal.

"You can swim like crazy," I puffed.

"Nearly made the Olympics."

"What happened?"

"Couldn't make up my mind. Loved the distances, but wanted to dive, too. Platform. Coach said if I'd specialize, you know, concentrate on one thing or the other, I'd be a cinch. But I wanted it all."

"So you didn't make it."

"Yeah. I should have. Really. I was good enough. But the judges, they knew what I was trying to do. They couldn't tolerate anyone being good enough that they could make it swimming *and* diving."

"But you were good enough."

"Yes. I was good enough."

"When was that?"

"I was fourteen. Eighth grader."

"Jesus!"

"And I haven't competed since."

She came into my arms, her naked body hard and cold against mine, her feet pedaling slowly. I tried to kiss her, and she bobbed away.

"Come on," she said. "Race you."

Her arms flashed, her kick thrusting her powerfully. I was no match for her, and when I finally staggered to the blanket Rina was sitting there hugging her knees and shivering.

I flopped down beside her. "I'm cold," she said, rolling

toward me. I moved onto my side and hugged her. My hand played on her back, tracing the planes and curves of muscle and the ridges and bumps of bone from her neck to the hollow places behind her knees. Her skin was taut and cold to my touch. Her hips began to move, tentatively at first, and then with a rhythm I recognized. She lifted her face to be kissed, then pushed me gently onto my back.

She slid over me, her breasts flattened against my chest, her mouth on my throat. Her legs straddled mine.

"Hey!" she said as I entered her. She lifted her face to smile at me. Then her mouth came down on mine, and then moved away. Her arms were tight around my neck. I held on, and moved with her.

I felt the muscles in her thighs spasm and her buttocks tense. "Oh, sire!" she whispered into the side of my throat, and then her whole body shuddered.

We lay that way long after it was over. She gave my chest little kisses, and I strummed my fingertips softly on her ribs as I watched the clouds drift past the moon.

"Look . . ."

"I know," I said.

"Just let's not . . ."

"Sure. The wine and all."

"Right. I mean, we're both . . ."

"Adults. Yes."

She rolled off me and propped herself up on an elbow so she could look down at me. The sudden rush of cold air where her body had been covering me made me shiver. I sat up beside her.

"Well," said Rina. "That was fun."

"Uh-huh," I agreed. "Jesus. It's cold," I said. "We should get dressed, don't you think?"

"Well, yes. Sure."

I found my clothes where I had dropped them beside the blanket, and hastily put them back on. I didn't look at Rina.

We each took two corners of the blanket, shook it out, and folded it, bringing our hands together carefully, trying not to touch.

We started back for the car. "God, it must be late," said Rina. "I've got classes in the morning."

"Umm," I agreed. "I've got work, too."

In the car Rina fiddled with the radio. There's not much there on Sunday nights. She finally settled for a fuzzy Country and Western program, its signal so distant that it kept fading and returning. She tried to sing along, but she didn't know the lyrics. She was able to join the refrain of one ditty, in which the words "love" and "you" figured prominently. She pronounced them "lerve" and "yew," mocking the hillbillies on the radio.

Her Pinto was the only car in Gert's parking lot. I pulled up beside it. Rina opened the door and slid out of my car, then bent down to look in at me.

"Well, thanks a lot for the evening. Great food, and everything. I really needed to get away."

"My pleasure," I said. We exchanged smiles.

"Guess I better get going, then," she said.

"Can you make it okay?"

She snorted. "Hey, I'm liberated, remember? No, I'm fine. Thank you."

"Well, then . . ."

"Yes. See you. Good night."

"Night."

She slammed the door to my car. I waited for her to climb into her Pinto. When I heard her engine start up and saw her headlights flash on, I started back to Boston.

At one o'clock on a Monday morning the highways seem like scenes from nuclear holocaust films. They're brightly lit and otherwise empty of human life. A few trucks passed by, northbound in the other lanes. I imagined them moving of their own volition, without men steering them. I drove in silence. Rina's hillbilly station had faded completely away. I listened to the static for a while, then snapped off the radio. It seemed as if Rina had faded away, too.

I parked in the garage under my apartment building and rode up the elevator to the sixth floor. Piped-in Muzak still filled the casket on cables. When the little bell dinged and the elevator eased to its cushioned stop, I twitched. I had actually dozed during the vertical trip.

I lurched down the corridor, unlocked my door, and flipped the light switch. My apartment looked as if it had been burglarized. It took me a moment to remember that it always looked that way. It was *supposed* to look that way. I still was surprised occasionally not to find Gloria's orderly influence on the place where I lived, where everything had its assigned place and God help the husband or son who put it in backwards, or upside down, or, most venal sin, neglected to put it back at all.

I loved the comfort of mess, disorder, untidiness, disarray. It helped define my place, identify it as Mine. Nothing had a special spot in my home, now. I gave everything the run of the house. If my books liked it under the kitchen table, I believed they had a right to rest there for a while. If spoons found their way onto the top of the television, and if shoes liked it in the bathroom, maybe just to get away from their mates for a while, it was all right with me.

Charlie had dropped by my place once to pick me up for a golf date. He had expressed envy at the mess I had achieved in my apartment. I told him that I hadn't been like that when I'd lived in my parents' house or when I had lived with Gloria. Charlie looked around, poking at a balled-up sweatshirt on the kitchen table, and said, "This is how you give the finger to Gloria."

So when I walked into my apartment in the early morning hours after my evening with Rina Prescott, I said, "Hello, Coyne's Place. This is why you'll never marry again."

I kicked my shoes toward the bedroom, let my jacket slide onto the sofa, found a can of Rolling Rock behind an almost-empty jar of pickled hot peppers, and made for my little balcony. One beer before bed.

I fumbled with the lock on the sliding glass doors that opened onto the balcony. I had taken my seat and lifted my legs tiredly up onto the railing before it hit me: The sliders had been locked! The sliding glass doors should have been unlocked. I never locked them. It was another way I had of flipping my middle digit at my ex-helpmeet, whose compulsion for security rivaled the one she had for tidiness. Gloria required me to tour the house every evening before I was allowed to retire. The cars had to be safely garaged *and* locked. I had to check each window and door. Bolts had to be thrown, chains secured, keys turned. She always said, "You can't expect me to make love to you unless I feel safe and secure. I just couldn't relax." There were moments toward the end of our marriage when I was tempted to unlock everything on one of my nightly rounds, go upstairs and screw her until she yelled "Uncle!" and then gleefully tell her the house was wide open.

I never did. By then I was beyond caring.

And now I found my sliding glass doors locked. I let the beer slide frigidly down my throat. The same moon that had shone on the ocean from Charity's Point only a few hours ago now hovered high over my city apartment building, illuminating the same ocean I had swum in, which now lay like a silvery blanket far below me. I felt depressed, uneasy, lonely. All that wine, probably. Postcoital ennui. I was tired.

How the hell could I have locked my doors?

I finished the beer, dragged myself to my feet, and wandered bedward. If I had locked my doors sometime before I departed for my rendezvous with Rina, I must have been more nervous than I realized. Damn! I was slipping.

CHAPTER *10.*

LEONARD WERTZ'S secretary, a solidly built, dark-haired girl with a pouting mouth and large astonished eyes, insisted that I fill out a questionnaire while I waited for the doctor to see me.

"I don't intend to see him regularly or anything," I protested. "I just need to talk with him."

She smiled, showing me the pink tip of her tongue. "A lot of people feel that way at first. You'll see. He's really *very* good."

"You misunderstand me, miss. I'm not here for treatment."

"That's perfectly normal, Mr. Coyne. Please fill out the form for us. There's no commitment."

I shrugged. It was easier to fill out the form.

The waiting room was furnished with two director's chairs separated by a magazine-strewn, glass-topped table on plastic legs, and the secretary's Danish modern desk. From where I sat her legs came into full display under her desk as her narrow skirt rode up her thighs—dimpled knees, pleasingly tapered calves, slim ankles. Part of the treatment, I supposed.

I took a copy of *Cosmopolitan* from the table and filled out the form on it, crouching awkwardly in one of the director's chairs. Those canvas contraptions are not designed for people over five foot six. Film directors tended to be short, I guessed. I got a backache after about thirty seconds of sitting in that one.

The items on the questionnaire were innocuous enough—occupation, marital status, health insurance. On the back page I found a statement for me to sign indicating that I understood that Dr. Wertz guaranteed no cure for whatever ailed me. I smiled. That might dissuade the average lay person from bringing suit, but I knew that a medical patient's signature on such a disclaimer had absolutely no standing in court.

An inner door opened, and through it stepped a man who appeared to be several years younger than I—a man constructed, it struck me, entirely of spheres and circles. The top of his head was bald and shiny. A reddish-brown fringe circled from behind up over his ears and continued down his cheeks in a neatly trimmed beard. He wore no mustache. His thick, rimless glasses magnified his eyes. The effect was that his head looked as if it had been placed upside down on his neck.

He wore prefaded designer jeans with hearts stitched on the rear pockets over his high, round, girlish ass and soft hips. A yellow jersey stretched taut across his pear-shaped torso. A little penguin was embroidered over his left breast. The square-toed, high-heeled cowboy boots that peeped out from under the boot-cut bottoms of his jeans had fancy stitching up the sides. He teetered uncertainly in them.

He moved, in fact, much like a penguin. Leonard Wertz was a *chic* shrink.

His fingers, as I shook his hand, felt like soft, uncooked sausages. In his voice I detected the hint of what I thought was probably a carefully cultivated British affectation.

"Mr. Coyne. Won't you come in."

He stood at the door, holding it for me. As I brushed by him to enter his office, the scent of English Leather assaulted me.

His office looked like a small living room. At the far end, a large picture window overlooked a small lawn bordered all around by a high stockade fence against which rambler roses were tied, leafing out and preparing to bloom. The inside of the office was conspicuous primarily by the absence of the usual accoutrements of an office—no desk, no telephone, no professional journals or books, no equipment, no diplomas on the wall. There were two easy chairs, a sofa, a rocking chair, and a coffee table. An undistinguished landscape done meticulously in oils was displayed over the sofa. On the opposite wall over the chairs hung a pair of matched prints—clown faces, one laughing and one crying.

"So, Mr. Coyne," began Wertz. He held the form I had filled out. "You're an attorney, I see. Divorced, eh?" He abruptly put the questionnaire onto the coffee table and fixed me with a magnified stare. "Why don't you just tell me about it."

"I'm not here for treatment," I said. "I thought you understood that. I'm here professionally. In regard to one of your patients. Former patients. George Gresham."

He nodded. "Mr. Gresham terminated with me some time ago, you know."

"He terminated, period," I said. "He's dead."

Leonard Wertz slowly removed his glasses. His eyes behind them were small, pink, porcine. He held his glasses in his upraised hand. "Oh, dear," he said.

"Suicide," I added quickly. "It appears to have been suicide."

"Oh, *dear*," he repeated emphatically.

"Yes. Mr. Gresham's mother—his next of kin—is understandably upset. She has asked me to try to sort out the details of his death. His frame of mind, that sort of thing. I thought you could help."

"Well, now, Mr. Coyne, you must understand that what passes between me and my patients is confidential. Strictly confidential. You, as an attorney, surely understand that. Without the assurance of confidentiality . . ."

"He's dead."

Leonard Wertz replaced his glasses slowly. "Yes," he said. He stared beyond me through the window into the back yard for a long moment. Then he focused his stare on me. "Well, I suppose if he's dead . . ."

I smiled and leaned back in the easy chair. "Good," I said. "I guess what I'd like to know from you is simply this: In your professional judgment, was George Gresham a candidate for suicide?"

"Suicide," Wertz repeated, pronouncing the word slowly, as if he were trying it out for the first time. Then he said, "George." He shook his head. "I wouldn't have believed it." He looked appealingly at me.

"Then you don't think . . . ?"

"No, Mr. Coyne, it's not that I don't think George was *capable* of suicide. Not at all. There are depths to the human mind that none of us can fathom. It's not that. I'm just trying to reconcile what I know of George with this fact you've given me."

I waited. Finally he continued. "I'm not an ordinary psychiatrist, you see. This sofa here is for my patients to sit on. I do very little retrospective analysis. No dreams, no stream of consciousness, no hypnosis. No psychotherapy, in the traditional Freudian sense. My specialty is A.C.R."

"A.C.R.?"

"Yes. Assertiveness Conditioning and Reinforcement. A.C.R. It's based on sound scientific principles—the culmination, really, of the works of Pavlov, Skinner, Krasner, and the others. Oh, there have been the popularizers, the *I'm OK, You're OK* crowd. Quack psychiatry. How to overcome depression and become rich and famous in five easy lessons. Mail-order sanity. But *we* are engaged in a legitimate branch of therapy." He looked at me, eyebrows lifted. I nodded to him. "We utilize the well-established principles of behavioral psychology," he continued. "We try to shape the individual's behavior—his personality, really, his entire repertoire of behaviors—in order to make him more assertive, more aggressive, a more successful person."

"Okay," I said. "I understand. So George Gresham wanted to become more assertive, then."

Dr. Wertz's eyes slipped past me to linger again on the garden outside the window. "He committed suicide, you say," he said softly.

"That's what people seem to think," I answered. I shrugged. "I hoped you could help me—help his mother, actually—to understand it."

"I told George—I used every trick of persuasion at my disposal, really—I told him that every gain he had made could be lost. You see, the first phase is the conditioning phase. We substitute a new galaxy of responses for the old. The second phase requires establishing that galaxy, firming it up, making those new responses part of the basic personality. That requires reinforcement—the second phase. George had completed the conditioning phase, and he had just begun some excellent reinforcing exercises when he left me. Quite suddenly. I was very surprised and very disappointed. He had made excellent progress. I told him he should finish. It's really quite dangerous to terminate in the middle of an A.C.R. program. The personality is in a change pattern, you see. Tends to be very unstable. If George had finished with me, I daresay he would be alive today."

Dr. Wertz spread his hands. "It's a tragedy."

"I agree," I said. "So are you saying that leaving in. the middle of treatment—in an unstable situation, as you put it—could result in a greater likelihood of the patient's committing suicide?"

"No," he said firmly. "Not by itself. But when an old pattern of coping—or compensating—has been conditioned away, and new ones aren't in place, the patient is left vulnerable to dramatic and sudden mood shifts. You can understand that, Mr. Coyne."

"Yes," I said. "Manic-depressive behavior."

He smiled. "You might say that," he said, as if *he* might never have said that. "The point is, it's the problems, the crises in one's life that are to blame, not the interrupted therapy. I don't honestly think George was any *more* suicidal when he left me than when he first came."

"I wasn't trying to blame you," I said. "Are you saying he was suicidal when you first began with him?"

"Everyone is suicidal, Mr. Coyne."

"Oh, come off it," I said. "You're not answering my question."

"Yes, I am. I'm just trying not to oversimplify things for you. Being suicidal isn't like having the measles or a broken leg. It's not a matter of being that way or not. It's a question of degree. You've heard of the death instinct, I'm sure. It's in us all. You, for example, smoke cigarettes. It's part of the human condition. George Gresham and Attorney Coyne alike."

"Okay, then. A matter of degree. Fine. to *what* degree would you say he was suicidal when he came to you? I really don't want to spar with you, Doctor."

"No, I don't want to spar, either. I'm trying to explain to you that George—like you and me—had an inherent predisposition to take his own life. It's there, in everyone. As I said, to some degree. You never know to what degree, until, well . . ."

"I see," I said. "But he came to you. To be more assertive, you said."

"Okay," said Wertz, sighing. "George had several conflicts in his life. Again, Mr. Coyne, you have to understand that we're not talking about an abnormal person here. George Gresham's conflicts were ones everyone has. His hadn't worked themselves out as comfortably for him as other people's do. But he was a good candidate for A.C.R. He could have been helped. He *was* being helped."

"Conflicts, you said."

"Yes." He patted the creases on his jeans. "He exhibited the classical Oedipal conflict, for one thing. There was a woman in his life—or on his mind, anyway—and he had, from all I inferred, a dominant mother—do you understand the Oedipal conflict, Mr. Coyne?"

"You want to screw your mother, but you know it's taboo."

He smiled. "Exactly. And when you, er, want to screw another woman, it can be a way of displacing that primal instinct, and your unconscious mind induces guilt. Which manifests itself, of course, in a sort of paralysis. Sometimes it's the inability to perform sexually. Impotence. Premature ejaculation. Sometimes the patient is unable even to approach the object of his feelings. That seemed to be George's case. He felt the need to become more assertive, to speak to this woman, to approach her."

"Did he tell you who this woman was?"

"No. Of course not. That would have been absolutely irrelevant. Even counterproductive. My treatment focuses on the patient. I would assume the woman had characteristics like his mother. Probably not a young woman. I would imagine she was distant, aloof, strong, aggressive. Certainly in George's mind she was, anyway."

"You said earlier he had several conflicts. Were there others? Besides this sex thing for his mother, I mean?"

"Nothing extraordinary. I would gather that his younger brother was an important factor in his life—a source of attraction and admiration, but also jealousy. Typical sibling rivalry. Again centering on the mother. And, of course, there was his father."

"Yes," I said. "Dudley. He committed suicide. Isn't that significant?"

"Surely. It's significant."

"Meaning, he'd be more likely . . ."

"Meaning, Mr. Coyne, that a boy admires and wants to emulate his father, because his father has succeeded in seducing his mother, you see. They're rivals, but the identity is powerful."

"So it's not simply . . ."

"None of this is simple. It's complicated."

I nodded. "What about Win? That was George's brother. How did he fit into all this? I mean, Win is dead."

"Only as I told you. Remember, my therapy does not require extensive dredging up of the past. George seemed quite fixated on his brother—his dead brother. This was somehow mixed up with the woman—and, of course, his mother. George directed considerable rage at his brother."

"Are you saying George didn't accept that his brother was dead?"

"No, I don't think that was it. It was an unconscious process, part of the old repertoire we had to condition away. That feeling that he was competing with his dead brother for his mother's love, as personified by this other woman."

I tried to understand all of this. I found a neat internal logic to it all, but I couldn't identify the place where it attached to the world where real people move. Psychology, in its presumption to comprehend the unconscious mind—indeed, even to postulate the dominance of the unconscious—immediately precludes rational criticism. "It's unconscious," the shrinks say. "Naturally you don't understand it. You *do* want to fuck your mother, of course, and you *do* want to murder your father, and it *does* fill you with guilt and self-loathing. So much guilt, in fact, that you have erected defense mechanisms to protect yourself from yourself by hiding it from your unconscious mind. It's there. *We* see it. We trained experts. But you can't expect to. Your defense mechanisms won't let you."

It seemed like a lot of mumbo-jumbo. Except, somehow, it seemed to work.

"I guess I understand," I said to Dr. Wertz. "Tell me. Why did he terminate with you?"

Dr. Wertz thought for a moment. "He missed an appointment," he began slowly. "Back in January. He had been seeing me every other Tuesday afternoon—after his classes had ended for the day. September through January—the program would have been finished in June. That's what I had promised him. So he had nine sessions, I believe. Nine out of the twenty. Anyhow, when he missed the January appointment and didn't call, I called him. To reschedule, you know. All he would tell me was that A.C.R. had become irrelevant for him. He had something else he had to devote himself to. I tried to persuade him to finish. I couldn't budge him." Wertz flapped his hands in a gesture of helplessness.

"You said he had something else. Meaning, he was no longer interested in the woman? Is that what you inferred?"

"Oh, it was no inference. He told me. Research. He would be needing all his free time to travel to Boston, he said.

An important research project which, he said, couldn't wait. I suggested we find another time to meet, but he just said he wasn't interested in the program any more."

"Interesting." I nodded, feeling very much as if I were the psychoanalyst and Leonard Wertz the patient on my couch.

"Of course," he continued—free-associating, it struck me—"it's all perfectly understandable. George was a historian, a cerebral man, a scholar. History was his first love. Before any woman, I'm certain. History was George Gresham's defense mechanism, you see. He knew it himself. Truth and justice, he always said, came before love and passion. So George's first passion, his first love, was history. This woman, this intrusion, you might say, into his concept of himself, his world view, had to be reckoned with, reconciled, so to speak. I think that's what he was telling me when he terminated. That he had reconciled her, found his place for her in his life, and he was then prepared to return to his real love."

"A neat theory," I said. "Makes sense, I guess. Tell me something. What was the date of his last appointment with you?"

He flipped through an appointment book that was on the coffee table. "Here we are. Tuesday, January 13, at four o'clock. George Gresham. The twenty-seventh was the one he missed. The last time I saw him was the thirteenth." He looked up at me. "Is that important?"

"I don't know." I shrugged.

Dr. Wertz was studying me. "Have I helped you?"

I spread my hands. "I don't know," I repeated. "To tell you the truth, I just don't know what to make of it all." I frowned. "Dr. Wertz, were you aware of George's having any enemies? Anyone who didn't like him, or was competing with him, or whom he didn't like?"

He ran his hand over his bald head. "Enemies," he repeated. "No, none beyond the usual ones, I think."

"What do you mean, 'the usual ones'?"

"Only his father. And, of course, his brother."

"But they are both dead."

"As I tried to explain to you, Mr. Coyne, in his mind—his unconscious mind, that is—they still lived."

I pondered this for a moment, then nodded and stood. I thanked Leonard Wertz, M.D., shook his sausage fingers, and walked back out through the waiting room. His stocky little secretary with the dimpled knees smiled brightly at me. I leaned close to her ear and whispered, "Your panties are a very saucy shade of lavender, my dear."

She didn't blush. In fact, she smiled wickedly, tilting her chin up and touching her throat with her fingertips, as much as to say, "I know. And what would you like to do about it, big fella?"

Her reaction startled me. Then it occurred to me that the graduates of Leonard Wertz's Assertiveness Conditioning and Reinforcement program probably walked through that door making similar comments to her all the time—testing out their new-found assertiveness.

Look at what I'd accomplished in only one session. I, clearly, was a quick study.

CHAPTER 11.

FLORENCE GRESHAM'S
home in Beverly Farms is nestled among those of descend-
ants of the Cabots, Lowells, Saltonstalls, and several other
moneyed, old Massachusetts clans. It's less than a fifteen-
minute drive from Leonard Wertz's office in Danvers. I decided to take a chance that she'd be home on Monday morning, see how she was making out, pick up the magazine article
we had discussed, and, in general, keep my fences in good
repair. House calls. Part of the service rendered by Brady L.
Coyne, Inc.

The Gresham estate in Beverly Farms is not visible from
the road. A high brick wall surrounds it. The sturdy iron gate
that admits visitors opens electronically.

I pulled the front bumper of my BMW up to the gate
and stepped out, leaving the motor running. Built into a brick
pillar to which the high gate was hinged was a metal box
painted flat black. Inside the box was a telephone. I opened
the box, put the phone to my ear, and pressed the button beneath the phone hook.

"Who is there, please?" came a man's voice.

"Brady Coyne, John. Mrs. Gresham available?"

"One moment, please, Mr. Coyne."

I waited for a couple of minutes before John's voice said,
"Mrs. Gresham will see you, sir. Please come in."

I hung up the phone and returned to my car. The gates swung silently open and I drove in. In my rearview mirror I saw them ease closed behind me. The tires crunched on the pea-stone driveway, which wound around an artificial pond up to an arched portico on the front of the Georgian mansion where Florence Gresham lived.

John led me to her where she sat at an umbrella'd table in the back garden amid a spectacular wash of blue and yellow late-spring flowers. I took the seat opposite her.

"Coffee, sir?" asked John, with a little bow to me after I sat down.

"No. Thank you," I said.

I lit a cigarette and spoke to Florence. "How are you?"

Instead of answering me, she thrust a tabloid-sized newspaper across the table toward me. "Look at this," she said.

It was a copy of the *National Tattler*, a popular scandal sheet which I confess to picking up from time to time along with my frozen dinners at the Stop & Shop. This edition featured on its front page a photograph in a grainy color of a hard-looking, blonde girl under the blaring headline: "Has Deborah Really Kicked the Habit?"

I lifted my eyebrows at Florence.

"Page three," she said.

I folded over the page. On the third page I saw a photograph of four young men dressed in military camouflage suits and wearing berets, kneeling side by side grinning into the camera. They reminded me of Cap Spender, the resident Nazi at Ruggles. Each of the men in the photo held a short, efficient-looking weapon which I recognized as an Israeli combat gun. The headline for the story read "Survivalists: Preparing for Armageddon."

The picture was captioned "Young Americans gird for their next battle."

"The radicals of the Eighties," I said to Florence. "The new generation of Abbie Hoffmans."

"Yes," she said. "I've been reading about them. They think civilization is about to come toppling down around our shoulders. They stockpile provisions and weapons and ammunition. They think the cities are going to collapse and all the people who live there will evacuate to the country. These people are prepared to kill to defend their property. They train their children to shoot strangers. They live on hatred—the Jews, the blacks, Easterners, urbanites, Catholics, whatever. Some of them say it'll be a Communist takeover. Others think it'll be a racial thing. They're organized in military fashion. Very big in the Midwest and West. Scary bunch."

"You've done your homework," I said, a little puzzled by it. "But I don't understand . . ."

Florence extended her finger to the paper spread open in front of me and pointed to the face of one of the armed young men in the photograph.

"That's Win," she said.

I looked at her, then at the picture, then back at her. "Win? Your Win?"

She nodded firmly.

"Oh, come on, Florence. Win is dead."

"That," she said, jabbing with her finger, "is Winchester Gresham."

I bent to examine the picture more closely. I had never seen Win Gresham alive, but I had seen pictures of the younger Gresham son. I remembered him as having Florence's strong features—a long, straight nose, heavy jaw, dark hair, and burning black eyes. The face in the fuzzy photograph I was looking at could have been anybody. The beret was pulled down over his forehead, and he wore a bushy black mustache. His smile showed strong, white teeth. I thought all four men in the picture looked pretty much alike.

I reached across the table and touched Florence's arm. "Your imagination's running away with you," I said. "It's not like you to indulge yourself in wishful thinking."

For an answer, Florence handed me a photograph in a heavy frame. I recognized it immediately. It usually sat on the grand piano in Florence's living room. Win Gresham. He wore his Army uniform. His hair was short under the officer's cap, and his expression was properly military.

"Yes, I know. That's Win."

"Compare them."

I tried to imagine the young soldier in Florence's portrait ten years older. I mentally crayoned a black mustache onto the face. I looked at Florence with raised eyebrows.

"It's the smile," she said.

"It could . . ."

"It's him," she said.

I studied the photo in the newspaper. I glanced back and forth at the two pictures. There was something about the smile, a kind of cynical lopsidedness, that struck me. And the structure of the faces—the noses, the jawlines, the cheekbones—all bore a vague similarity. I admitted to myself that if I looked for the resemblance, it was indeed there.

But that didn't mean they were the same person. I told Florence that.

She only smiled. "You haven't finished your job," she said.

"What do you mean?"

"Your first job. To find out what happened to Win."

"I did, Florence. Win died in Vietnam. Don't torture yourself." I reached across the table and covered her hands with mine. "You've got to accept it. Both of your sons are dead."

She stared at me for a moment, then averted her eyes. She pulled her hands away, reached under the table, and slid two postcards toward me. "Explain these, then."

I looked at them. They were picture postcards, the kind with spaces for a short message and an address on one side, and a gaudy, color photograph on the reverse. Florence's name and address had been printed by hand in capital letters on each. The places for the message had been left blank. One was postmarked November 10, 1973. It had been mailed from Ketchikan, Alaska. The second bore a postmark from Pittsburg, New Hampshire. Florence must have received it a couple of weeks earlier.

I flipped them over. The one from Alaska showed a snow-capped mountain. The New Hampshire postcard featured an autumn farm scene, resplendent with golden maples and a red barn.

I looked up at Florence. "I don't get it."

"They're from Win."

"What makes you think so?"

She smiled. "It's just the sort of thing he'd do. Even as a little boy he preferred little secrets and surprises and mysteries. He always signed my birthday cards, 'Guess who?' He liked to hide behind the furniture and jump out yelling 'Boo!' Besides," she added, "how else can you explain them?"

I shook my head. "I think there are probably several logical explanations. For example, people go on trips. They bring lists of people to send postcards to. They buy a batch, lug them back to their hotel, address them all at once, copying from their list, stick stamps on them, and drop them all in the mail without remembering to write, 'Having fun, wish you were here' on them."

Florence cocked her eyebrows at me.

"Or maybe," I said, "whoever sent them just assumed you'd know who they were from. Listen, there's no reason to believe they're even from the same person. The printing doesn't look particularly similar."

"I think they're from the same person. Win."

I sighed. "I suppose you'll believe what you want to believe. But I don't think it's healthy. Now that you've lost George, you're trying to resurrect Win. It's a sad, sad business, Florence. But you have lost both of your sons. You've really got to accept that."

She glared at me. "Win is alive."

"Look," I said. "If you believed this postcard from Alaska was from Win, why didn't you show it to me when you received it?"

She stared down at the table. "I wasn't sure it *was* from Win. Not then. I knew it could've been just wishful thinking. I mean, I knew I wanted it to be from him, you see."

"But now . . ?"

"Now I'm more certain. Now I've seen this picture in

the paper, and I've received this other postcard." She looked up at me. "Look, Brady. I know exactly how this must sound to you. A foolish old lady with all her heirs gone. A lonely old bag losing her grip, confusing her dreams with the facts. But that really isn't how it is. I think Win's alive. I've always felt it. Now I feel that I know it. These postcards, this picture, they just confirm what I've always felt. Will you find him for me? Or, if you can, prove once and for all that he's dead? Either one will put my mind to rest."

"What about George?"

"Okay," she said. "George first. Then Win."

I nodded. "I concede. But I think it's fruitless."

"Then prove it to me. If the man in that picture isn't Win, so be it. If I have some secret admirer who likes to send anonymous postcards, okay. I just want to know, once and for all."

I shrugged. I copied the dates and postmarks into my notebook. Then I handed the postcards to Florence.

She carefully folded the newspaper and placed it beside her on the table. She set the framed portrait of her son as a young soldier face down on top of it, and placed the postcards on the picture. Then she handed me a manila envelope. "Well," she said. "This is what you came for. I'll be damned if I know what good it'll do us, but you might as well have it."

I accepted the envelope from her, opened the flap, and pulled out George's photocopy of the *Atlantic Monthly* article. I glanced at it for a moment, then slid it back. I stood. "I'll take it along," I said.

She rose, and we walked together around the house to my car. "You still think George jumped, don't you?" Florence said.

"Seems that way. I talked with his psychiatrist this morning."

"Psychiatrist?"

"Doctor Wertz. His name was on George's Blue Shield forms."

"Was George disturbed?"

"Not really disturbed. A little depressed, maybe. The point is, George seemed to think he needed help."

"And you think that suggests he would kill himself."

"It fits."

We walked back to where I had parked my car. I climbed in and started up the engine. Florence stood by the door. I lifted my hand to her.

"I'll be in touch," I said. "And please try not to let yourself get too hopeful about Win. Let's just concentrate on George."

"And don't get too hopeful about him, either," she added sourly.

"They're both dead," I said.

She shook her head and turned away. I shifted the car into gear and drove slowly around the long, curving drive, then headed back toward Boston.

"Any calls?" I asked Julie when I walked into the office.

"That anything like 'Good morning, Julie, and did you have a pleasant weekend'?"

"Sorry," I said. I sat in a chair opposite her desk. "How was your weekend?"

"Shitty," she said. "Edward had to work. You?"

I thought about my evening with Rina Prescott. "I worked, too," I said.

"Frank Paradise. Waiting for your report, thank you very much; he'll be in touch. Mrs. DeVincent. Still on the dogs. Miss Prescott from the school. No message, will try another time. Mr. McDevitt reminding you of your luncheon date tomorrow. Office supply salesman. I handled him. Someone from the Bar Association about you joining some committee. I told him you'd get back to him." Julie slapped the pages in her notebook. "That's it."

"So who've I gotta call?"

"Mrs. DeVincent. I think you better call her. She sounded itchy. Bar Association guy—let's see—a Mr. Kelsey. I've got the number. The rest you don't need to call."

"Miss Prescott left no message?"

Julie glanced up at me. "I told you, no."

I heaved myself out of my chair. "Okay. We can do those calls later on. I've got some paperwork to go over. Why don't you put on the machine and get yourself some lunch."

"What's the matter? Can't answer the telephone yourself?"

"Sure I can. Don't want to. Anyhow, how do you think it would appear if I answered my own phone?"

"Appear?" Julie threw her hands into the air and flopped back into her seat. "*Appear*? Jesus, Coyne, is that what I am? An *appearance*?"

"Aw, you know what I mean."

"Sure I do. Damn straight I do. That any successful *male* attorney has to have a dumb-headed silly *fe*male to answer the phone for him, and buy *birthday* presents for his mistresses, and go get his *Red* Sox tickets, and all that shit. That phone answering is *beneath* any important *male*-type person. That . . ."

I held up both hands in surrender. "Whoa! I concede. Enough. I'm new at this equality stuff, you know. I'm learning everything I know from you, remember. I'm trying. Honest."

Julie grinned. "Yeah? Well, you're a damn slow learner. When it comes to this, I think you've got a severe learning disability. Okay. You want to do some uninterrupted reading while I'm at lunch, I'll put on the answering machine. Just don't tell me it has something to do with appearances, that's all."

I held out my hand to her. "Okay. Forgiven?"

She shook my hand. "Sure."

Julie began to move things around on her desk, and I went into my office. Something occurred to me. I opened the top drawer of my desk and rummaged among the pencils, half-opened packs of Winstons, bottles of aspirin and antacid pills, and assorted papers. I tried the other drawers. I went to the wall safe, spun the dial, and poked around. Then I went back to Julie.

"Do you remember what I did with that address book?"

She frowned. "What address book?"

"George Gresham's. The one I got when I was at the school with Florence. I put it someplace."

She shrugged. "I never saw any address book."

"Maybe I took it home. I'll check there."

"Right. It's probably there. I never saw it." Julie put on her jacket. "I'm off. The machine is on. You'll never miss me."

I leered at her. "The machine seems to lack a certain something."

"Slow learner, nothing," she said. "You're retarded." She blew me a kiss and swirled out the door.

I went back into my office, armed with a mug of coffee and the manila envelope Florence had given me. I sat on the sofa, slipped my shoes off, and put my feet up on the coffee table.

It bothered me that I couldn't find that address book. As I thought about it, I couldn't remember removing it from my jacket while I was in the office. I supposed I'd find it at home.

I lit a cigarette, sipped from my mug, and slid the *Atlantic* article from the envelope.

It was entitled "Who Are the New American Radicals?" Percy at the library had been pretty close. George Gresham, I assumed, had drawn heavy brackets around the first several paragraphs, and, for good measure, had added two big exclamation points in the right-hand margin. I read it.

Early in the morning of June 19, 1971, before even the milkmen had begun their rounds, the quiet of Norton Street in Queens was rocked by an explosion. Within minutes the five-story brick apartment building at number 72 lay in a smoldering heap of rubble.

When the Fire Department and the Bomb Squad and the NYPD and the FBI completed their investigations, the world was told that the blast had been produced by a group known to the radical underground as "The Sewing Circle"—an unlikely sorority of wealthy college girls devoted to the cause of creating anarchy and bringing the "corrupt establishment" to its knees.

In a joint statement issued to the press, the authorities reconstructed the event as follows:

"Five young women were constructing pipe bombs in the basement of 72 Norton Street, the apartment building owned by Martin Cashen, the father of one of the young women. Huge quantities of nitroglycerin, a very volatile and unstable explosive, were stored there. This material was accidentally detonated—probably as a result of careless smoking.

"It is believed that all five young women were killed by the powerful blast.

"The so-called 'Sewing Circle' has publicly claimed responsibility for three recent bombings of Federal buildings, in which a total of eleven people were killed—the courthouse in Chicopee, Massachusetts, a post office in Brooklyn, and an Army recruiting center in Concord, New Hampshire.

"In each of these three cases, the 'Sewing Circle' claimed to have acted 'on behalf of exploited victims of capitalist greed in Amerika (sic) and in Southeast Asia.'

"The five victims of the blast are: Melissa Cashen, Bennington, '72; Barbara O'Callahan, Bennington, '71; Carla Steinholtz, Brandeis, '71; Monica Pratt, Vassar, '73; and Evelyn Blondaro, Smith, '71."

George Gresham had drawn a circle around the name of Carla Steinholtz and written "SP" beside it in large, angry letters—just as he had on Harvey Willard's paper. Evidently both Harvey and the author of the article had trouble with spelling. It was the sort of detail, I concluded, that would annoy the careful scholar.

The article continued, no longer quoting the "joint statement":

What has fired the imagination of the American public—and what has struck terror into the heart of every American parent—is the background of the members of the "Sewing Circle." The five young women who met their death in that early morning explosion were America's future—bright, well-educated, popular, attractive.

Martin Cashen, father of one of the victims, said in a recent interview, "I thought I knew my little girl. And her friends— they seemed like nice kids. Clean-cut, polite. They had all the advantages. Where did we go wrong?"

Where, indeed, did we go wrong? What has happened to the fabric of American society, that five young women would set out to destroy it, and in the process, tragically, themselves?

The rest of the article reviewed the history of underground anarchists of the Sixties—the Weathermen, the Black Panthers, *et al.*—linking the phenomenon of their appearance with the "imperialist" war in Southeast Asia, the Civil Rights movement, and the Women's Liberation movement. The author found significance in the backgrounds of each of the five women. They had come from wealthy families, their fathers were upper-level managers of giant corporations, they had all been "model" students in high school. Two of them had been cheerleaders, and all five had been members of the National Honor Society. They had all been liberal arts majors at prestigious and highly selective Eastern private colleges.

I flipped the article onto my desk and sat back in my chair. So what? So it tells me that George Gresham was a painstakingly thorough teacher, willing to double-check the facts in a student's paper. Certainly if the paper dealt with an area in which George didn't feel especially competent, he might well want to educate himself further. That would explain the books on his desk. I could understand why he'd want to read the article. But why photocopy it?

I went over to my desk and found Harvey Willard's paper in the bottom drawer. I took it back to the sofa and read it. I glanced at the *Atlantic* article again. Then I reread Harvey's paper.

I went back to my desk and buzzed Julie. She didn't answer. I punched my palm. Still at lunch.

"Damn it, Julie," I muttered out loud. "I *need* you."

CHAPTER *12.*

        I WAITED in the outer office for Julie. When she returned she looked quizzically at me and said, "I'm not late. What's the matter?"

"Leave the machine on and come on in here, will you?"

"What'd I do?"

"Nothing, Julie. I need you."

"Ha! He needs me. You know how I hate shorthand."

"It's not shorthand. I want you to read something for me."

"Ah, come on. You know I'll fix up your spelling."

"I need your opinion on something."

Her mouth formed an O and her eyes widened in an exaggerated expression of amazement. "My opinion, he says." She looked at me for a moment. When I didn't smile, she nodded. "Okay. Let's go."

We went into my office. Julie sat at my desk and I took the chair in front of it. I gave her the *Atlantic* article. She read it slowly, her eyebrows knitted into a frown of concentration. When she finished, she looked up and said, "So?"

"Now read this." I handed her George's photocopy of Harvey Willard's essay.

She looked at it for only a moment, then jerked her head up to stare at me. "Finish it," I told her. I moved to stand behind her so that I could read over her shoulder. Harvey The Beast had written:

On the morning of June 19, 1971, before anyone was awake, an explosion rocked the quiet of Norton Street in Queens. Minutes later the apartment building at number 72 was a smouldering pile of rubble.

Julie flipped the page. Together we read on:

The Fire Department, the Bomb Squad, the New York Police, and the FBI investigated. Then announced that the explosion had been caused by a radical under ground group known as "The Sowing Circle"—a bunch of rich college girls who wanted to cause anarchy and bring "The Establishment" to it's knees.

When she finished it, she glanced up over her shoulder at me. I moved back to the chair in front of my desk.

"Well?" I said.

"He copied it."

"That's what I thought," I said.

"I mean, there are some misspellings, and some of the words have been changed, lots of comma faults, sentence fragments, like that. But he copied it, all right. No doubt about it."

"Notice how the magazine article and the kid's paper have been marked up?"

"Sure. Like Mr. Gresham was making notes on the similarities." Julie leaned forward in my chair, her elbows braced on the top of my desk. "What does it mean?"

I shook my head back and forth slowly. "I'm not sure. Let's try to be logical. Okay. Harvey writes this paper. George suspects it. He goes to the library, finds everything he can on the subject. Takes out all those books, looking for the part Harvey copied. Finally he finds the magazine. It rings the right bell. He makes a copy, brings it home, compares the two. And *voilà*."

I stopped. Julie regarded me expectantly. "Then?"

"Then—I don't know. Plagiarism. Some schools expel students for it."

"It gives Mr. Gresham an enemy," Julie said softly.

"It sure does."

"What are you going to do?"

"I'm going to think about it," I said. "I'm going to give it lots of thought."

Durgin Park is about the only thing that hasn't changed from the days when that part of the city known as Haymarket Square really was a marketplace. In the old days, the only people who went to Durgin's were the regulars from the financial district who were fanatical in their devotion, and the out-of-towners who were looking for an "authentic experience."

Now, in the "new Boston," it's all different. Where there used to be dank alleys and dirty meat-packing plants, today stand glass and chrome storefronts surrounded by brick-paved malls. You can wander around, buying hunks of pizza and hot fried dough from the stalls, drop into little bistros for a gin-and-tonic or a strawberry crêpe, or just sit on the wooden benches and watch the people.

The trucks still come with their produce, and other trucks come to take it away, and late at night you'll still see the old people from the North End with their shopping bags poking among the garbage to find a squashed tomato or a few stray leaves of withered lettuce after the trucks have gone and before the city's street cleaners come to sweep it all up.

They call it urban renewal, and I suppose it's a good thing. Still, I'm glad that they didn't tear down Faneuil Hall, and that Durgin Park remains. They've added an Oyster Bar downstairs, and the first-floor bar has been redone. But at Durgin Park it's still an experience in dining masochism. You can sneak up to the dining room the back way if you stop at the bar. The out-of-towners don't know that. They wait in line, chattering in nervous anticipation, sometimes outside the door and halfway down the street from the back entrance.

Charlie McDevitt and I had a couple of quick bourbons with the stockbrokers and bankers and slipped right up the stairs.

Our waitress's name was Stella. Most of the waitresses at Durgin's seem to have names like Stella or Sheila or Maggie.

145

They are carefully trained in rudeness. They majored in taunt and minored in insult. They sweat a lot, and their hair hangs in wet curls on their faces. They're from Southie, mostly, and they support their husbands who are laid off. They have lots of kids at home, and they worry about them. They move fast. Time is money. They shove food at you and tell you to pass it down the table. They're brassy, impatient, and crude.

Out-of-towners think they're charming. I just think they're vulgar. I go to Durgin's for the beef, which is still unsurpassed. The out-of-towners go there for the insults, and for the "family" dining, and for the sawdust on the floor, which, they are universally disappointed to learn, is now forbidden by the city's health statutes.

Durgin Park is a lousy place to conduct business. It's a lousy place for anything except eating prime rib.

Charlie and I sat across from each other at one of the long tables covered with a stained, yellowed tablecloth. Next to Charlie sat a fat couple from Arizona, each of whom was hunched over a big sirloin, well-done. The couple's two kids, a girl and a boy maybe eleven and nine, split a bowl of spaghetti. The boy complained that he hated spaghetti. The father told him to shut up, as he shoveled chunks of thick, overcooked beef into his mouth. The girl asked her mother for a french fry. The mother told her to eat her spaghetti first, then proceeded to gobble down all her french fries so that when the girl was finished there'd be none left.

"I had an interesting case last week," said Charlie as we waited for our beef to arrive. "Drug bust on the high seas, off Cape Ann. The Canadian connection. Complicated—had the Federal narcs, Coast Guard, local cops, and me, from Justice, all on this Coast Guard cutter. Supposed to intercept these guys in a tuna boat with a false hull stashed with hash." The waitress arrived with our dinner. "Hey, thanks."

The prime rib at Durgin's flops over the edges of the plate. When it's rare, the juices drip down onto the tablecloth. Stella held my slab onto the plate with her thumb as she handed it to me, which is how they're trained to do it at Durgin's, I think. Charlie received his cautiously, smiling at Stella.

He cut off a huge chunk and crammed it into his mouth. "Mmm!" he groaned. "As I remembered it. Anyhow, the boat was surrounded by gulls—hundreds of gulls, diving and swirling the way they do when the tuna fishermen are tossing hunks of dead fish over the side for chum. Man, this beef is fine."

I gave the kids next to me half a dozen french fries each, and smiled at their father. I have these gray eyes which Gloria used to call "baleful," and there's a scar through my right eyebrow, the result of an elbow I caught while trying to dig the puck out of the corner, so that I seem to smile in a way that discourages fat people from Arizona from being too critical of me.

So all the kids' father said was, "Thank the man."

"When we got close to the boat," said Charlie, "we could see these two guys at the stern tossing stuff into the water as fast as they could. We hailed them and pulled alongside, guns drawn and all. A couple of the Feds boarded the boat, and we made fast to them. Then we could see what they were doing. They had these bales of hash, and they were ripping chunks of it off and tossing it into the ocean. Disposing of their evidence."

"They knew you were coming."

Charlie nodded. "Guess so. Someone tipped them off. Suppose they figured if they tossed the bales off whole they'd float, so they tried to toss over handfuls. The birds went bananas."

"Hm," I mumbled around a mouthful of rare prime rib.

"So we asked one of the guys what the hell he thought he was doing, feeding the gulls like that. Know what he said?"

"What did he say?"

Charlie stared at me. "He said, 'I wanted to leave no tern unstoned.'"

"For Christ's sake, Charlie," I moaned.

"Honest," he said.

"Can we get back to business now?" I asked.

Afterwards Charlie and I found a bench along the edge of the brick-paved mall to sit on.

"Okay. You said you wanted to talk," said Charlie, appraising a tall, black girl with tight jeans tucked into high boots who was strolling by.

"Yup. Couple things. Think you could find out something for me on a guy who's supposed to have been killed in 'Nam?"

"Whadda you mean, 'supposed to'?"

I summarized for him the story of Lt. Winchester Gresham. "Florence thinks he's still alive, and she wants me to find him," I concluded.

"Jeez, I dunno, Brady. The Bureau keeps tabs on those survivalist groups, more or less. But they, you know, move around a lot, and they don't usually do anything overtly illegal, except maybe smuggle in guns. And that isn't the FBI's jurisdiction, really. Army won't be any help, for sure. He's dead, as far as the Army's concerned. I'll see what I can do for you, anyway. It'll probably cost you another meal, though."

"I appreciate it," I said. "This other thing that's bothering me—I need your brain."

"Such as it is," said Charlie. "Shoot."

I refreshed Charlie's memory of the story of George Gresham's suicide and my involvement in the case. I told him about Harvey Willard's history paper, and the *Atlantic* article, and my impression of Willard, and I described the people I had met at The Ruggles School.

I didn't tell him about my evening with Rina Prescott.

"Ah, yes," said Charlie. "The Sewing Circle. I remember it. Those poor, misguided, dead girls. Real mess. Sure I remember. I wasn't involved myself, but the Department was. They helped put the little pieces of those kids back together. Lotta guesswork. Had to identify the lower jaw of one of them. Feet, hands, scraps of clothing, pieces of jewelry. Teeth, scars, birthmarks, tattoos . . ."

"Tattoos?"

Charlie grinned. "Yeah. Those girls all had tattoos on their asses. Hip, actually. Praying mantis tattoos. You know about praying mantises?"

"We used to call them walking sticks."

"Right," said Charlie. "They're creatures of prey. Very

beneficial to farmers. Consume huge quantities of harmful critters. They look like they're praying, hence their name. All those girls had these praying mantis tattoos. On their left hip. Outside the cheek."

"Adorable," I said. "Actually, what I wanted to talk about was this plagiarism thing. I've been trying to imagine. Suppose George decided to turn Harvey in . . ."

"It's symbolic," said Charlie, ignoring me. "See, the female mantis, she's a very dominating broad. Like when she makes love, she eats her mate."

I raised my eyebrows. "That," I said, "could be worse."

"No, I mean it literally. At that very moment of orgasmic ecstasy, when the boy mantis has got it all the way in and the girl mantis feels him starting to come, she turns around and bites the poor guy's head off." Charlie grinned at me. "Pretty apt symbol for a bunch of female radicals, huh?"

"A pretty damn blatant symbol, if you ask me," I said. "Anyhow, suppose Gresham doesn't turn the Willard kid in right away, and instead . . ."

"They were blatant broads," continued Charlie. "The Cashen girl, I think it was, was pretty much intact from the waist down. Tattoo and all. Near as they could tell, these two girls—Cashen and the other one, O'Callahan, I think, who they had to identify by her teeth—they were assembling these bombs at a workbench in the basement, and when they went off, the top half of the Cashen girl was splattered all over the cellar. The bottom half of her was protected by the bench. That's what they found. The bottom half of her. The other one, O'Callahan, and the others who were in the room—I forget their names—they were blown all to hell, hardly enough left over to pin a name to. They took the full blast."

"Good God!"

"Yeah. Look, Brady, I'm not very good at creating scenarios with you. I mean, you know better than I do what this Gresham guy might have done. So the kid copied the paper and the teacher found out. Happens all the time. So what?"

"Here's what I think," I said. "See how it sounds. Okay. George tells Willard he knows about the paper. Willard panics. He's going to get tossed out of school, he thinks. Football scholarship to Duke, his whole career, down the tubes. So he . . ."

"What do you think? The kid killed him?"

I shrugged. "Could be, huh?"

Charlie picked a piece of gristle from his teeth with his fingernail. "Could be. So how does the suicide note fit in?"

I nodded. "I've been trying to figure that one out."

"Another thing. How does the kid get the guy up on the cliff there so he can toss him into the sea?"

"I don't know, Charlie."

"Pretty far-fetched, if you ask me."

"I've gotta talk to the kid, anyway, don't you think?" I said.

"What'll you say? That you know he cheated? Or are you gonna accuse him of murder?"

I shrugged. "I'll figure out something to say." Charlie shrugged and extended his arm in front of him to examine his watch. "Ah, shit, I gotta get back. Unlike some people, I've got a boss. Some people don't have any bosses. We public servants have to put in our hours."

"Okay," I said. We stood and started walking back to the MBTA station.

We lingered outside the stairway that led down into the subway. "What'd you say his name was?" Charlie said.

"Who?"

"The soldier. Gresham."

"Winchester. Lieutenant Winchester Gresham."

"Some name. Winchester. I'll see what I can get for you. And I'll think on the other thing. Don't count on anything eyeball-popping from me on that one, though."

"Appreciate the effort," I said.

"Friday afternoon still on?"

"Sure," I said. "Let's try to tee off at three. Beat the crowds."

Charlie waved his hand and disappeared down the stairs. I decided to walk back to the office. I had a lot to think about.

CHAPTER *13.*

IT WAS one of those spring afternoons that always makes me think of trout streams. I took my time getting back to the office. I wandered among the big, solid buildings of the financial district, where the narrow streets always seem to lie in shadows. When I got to Tremont Street, I cut across the Common diagonally toward Beacon Street.

By then the month of May had seduced me. Grave thoughts and suspicions drifted away from me like dandelion puffs. Spring had settled into the city. Late-blooming tulips and daffodils nodded their heads to each other with quiet sociability. Pigeons swarmed and fluttered around old men with bags of stale popcorn. I paused to listen to a boy wearing dark glasses sing and play his guitar. He looked and sounded remarkably like the young Bob Dylan. I didn't recognize his song.

When I got to the end of the Common, I considered strolling up Charles Street to window-shop in the self-consciously quaint shops and maybe buy an ice cream cone.

I reminded myself that I was an attorney with clients who depended on me. I had a lot of Important Business. I had trouble taking that premise very seriously. Nevertheless, I turned down Beacon Street, walked a couple blocks on the sunny side of the street, cut across at Dartmouth to Commonwealth, and kept on going to Newbury. I enjoyed looking at the chic ladies who toured the fashionable shoe stores there.

It was nearly four when I arrived back at the office. I felt good, refreshed and cleansed by the walk. I pushed open the door and regretted that I didn't wear a felt hat that I could toss onto a hatrack like James Bond while tossing a *double entendre* toward Julie.

"I've made an important decision," I announced to her.

"You've had an important phone call," she countered.

"My decision," I continued, "is to close the office this very minute, send you home to Edward, hang out the 'Gone Fishing' sign, and hie myself with all possible alacrity to the Squannicook River, where, with any good fortune, a hatch of Light Cahills should transpire shortly after my arrival, and where, given my consummate grace with the fly rod and intimate understanding of the feeding habits of the wily rainbow trout, I might capture half a dozen of those most worthy finny adversaries. Which," I continued loudly as Julie tried to speak, "I shall, sportsman that I am, return unharmed to their watery habitat to be challenged another day by another angler. And then, my brain clear and my limbs tired, I shall return to my abode to savor a large tumbler of Old Dungarees poured over ice cubes and fall gratefully into my bed for a soul-cleansing sleep."

I gave Julie a big grin. "How's that sound?"

"Good. You had a phone call."

"*Good?* It sounds wonderful. It sounds idyllic." I paused. Julie was not smiling. "What's the matter?"

"Harvey Willard called."

"Harvey?"

"You know. The boy who . . ."

"I *know* who he is, for Christ's sake. What the hell did he want?" I felt my afternoon on the Squannicook begin to slither through my fingers.

She shrugged. "He left a number. A pay phone, I gather. He said he'd be there every half hour to wait for your call."

"I wonder . . ." I looked at my watch. It was 4:07. "Damn it, Julie. I wish you'd said something when I first got in. I could have called him at four. Now I've got to wait nearly a half hour. I'll miss the hatch at the Squannicook. You should have told me."

"I tried to."

I sat heavily on the sofa across from Julie's desk. "Yeah, I suppose you did. Shit. It was such a nice day, too."

"Want me to try him now?"

"Sure. Please. Won't do any harm."

Julie poked at the buttons on the telephone, her forefinger stiff, her jabs sharp and swift as a woodpecker's. She snuggled the telephone against her shoulder and gazed at the ceiling. After several moments she returned it to its cradle. "No answer," she said to me.

"I could wait until tomorrow," I said.

"You could."

"I mean, whatever it is can certainly wait."

"Probably."

"I really owe it to myself to get in a little fishing. No reason why a man shouldn't go fishing."

Julie stared at me and nodded.

"It's not like this kid is a client or anything. Just some schoolboy. Probably worried about getting expelled. Thinks he needs a lawyer. He doesn't need a lawyer."

"Nope," said Julie, examining the backs of her hands. "Probably not."

"I mean, just because he plagiarized a history paper and George Gresham committed suicide . . ."

Julie looked at me, her eyebrows arched expectantly.

"Okay, goddam it. You're right. I'll wait until four-thirty."

"I didn't say anything," said Julie.

"Same difference," I muttered. I went into my office and slammed the door behind me. I sat behind my desk. Then I stood up and went back to the door. I opened it. Julie was hunched over some papers on her desk.

"Listen," I said, working hard to keep some anger in my voice. "Give me that number, will you? And go home, for God's sake. No reason for both of us to be miserable on a beautiful spring afternoon. Just give me that goddam telephone number and get the hell out of here."

Julie stood up promptly and handed me a piece of paper. "Don't mind if I do," she said. "Don't mind at all." She stood on tiptoes and kissed my chin. "Tight lines," she said.

"Ah, nuts!" I mumbled.

I smoked a cigarette and finished the dregs of the day's pot of coffee while I waited for the minute hand on the wall clock to fall to the six. It seemed to take forever. I forced myself to look at a magazine. My eyes grazed lightly over the *New Yorker* cartoons. Usually I thought they were funny, but my mind kept flipping to the little run below the bridge, where the river cut under the bank and the trout lay like cordwood at the tail of the riffle, waiting hungrily for a home-tied Light Cahill to float lightly overhead. I saw the silver flash, and my muscles remembered the throbbing tug of hooked rainbow trout on light tackle.

At twenty-nine minutes past four I tossed the magazine aside and called the number Julie had written on the scrap of paper.

"Yeah? Mr. Coyne?" It was Harvey.

"Yes, this is Brady Coyne. How can I help you?"

"Mr. Coyne, I gotta talk to you. It's very important."

"Okay, Harvey. Go ahead."

"No. Not now. Not on the phone."

"Come on, Harvey. It's all right. What is it?"

"I have to see you."

"You have to see me." I was losing what little patience I had left. "Look, Harvey. What is this all about, anyway?"

"I can't talk now."

"Well, damn it, you could have made an appointment with my secretary if you need counsel. I really don't care for this—this intrigue."

"I'm sorry. It's about Mr. Gresham. I really think you'll be glad you came out to hear what I have to say."

"You want me to go out there."

"Yes."

"It's got something to do with George Gresham."

"Yes. Something important."

"Important." I sighed. "All right, Harvey. Will tomorrow be all right?"

"Yes. Perfect. How about twelve-thirty? We can meet in the Student Union—you know where that is?"

"Yes. Near the theater. Okay. We'll make it twelve-thirty in the Student Union." I hesitated. "Do you want to see me professionally, Harvey?"

"Huh?"

"Professionally. As a lawyer."

"Oh. Yeah. I guess so. You could say that."

"All right, then."

"Thanks, Mr. Coyne." The line went dead.

I arrived at the Student Union at The Ruggles School at twelve twenty-five, again leaving my car at my very own slot by the Authorized Personnel sign. I bought a glass of iced tea at the counter, and found a table near the door so that I'd be sure to see The Beast when he came in.

The place was crowded and noisy. Boys and girls, all dressed in jeans or shorts and tee shirts advertising beer and restaurants—"I got scrod at Legal Seafoods last night"—moved from table to table munching hot dogs and squares of instant pizza. A girl with painted-on Gloria Vanderbilts dazzled me with a sunny smile and asked with her lifted eyebrows if she could borrow a chair from my table. Hoots rose from the corner where a bumper pool table had drawn a crowd. And above it all, loud, amplified rock music thumped its insistent, vibrating rhythm.

I felt isolated in this crowded chaos, middle-aged in my coat and tie and sensible shoes and graying temples, the more so since the kids all around me seemed unaware of my presence.

I nursed the iced tea. The ash tray accumulated several cigarette butts. I glanced at my watch. Ten of one. Evidently young Mr. Willard didn't appreciate the value of an attorney's time. I decided to give him ten more minutes, by which time the brain-searing music would drive me outdoors screaming anyway. I tilted the glass back and steered a pod of marble-sized ice cubes into my mouth. They seemed warm. I watched the kids playing around me. All of it, I decided, was sex—the music, the uninhibited movement of healthy bodies, the loud talk, the bumping and laughing. I felt as if I were aging visibly.

I gave him until nearly one-fifteen. The hell with Harvey Willard. I nearly tipped over my chair getting out of there. The bucolic peacefulness of the campus outside, the glorious quiet of it, startled me. I headed for my car. Before I got there, though, I acknowledged that, broken appointment or not, I wanted to see Harvey, even if he'd changed his mind about seeing me.

I found Bartley Elliott's office. In the corner, one elbow resting atop a four-drawer file cabinet, stood Alexander Binh. He was studying a sheaf of papers. I nodded my head to him. He glanced at me, twitched his head in minimal greeting, and returned to his papers.

A new girl sat behind the receptionist's desk. She eyed me suspiciously.

"Did you have an appointment, sir?"

"No. I've got to see Mr. Elliott. It's important."

I felt Binh's eyes on me. When I looked in his direction, his head was bent over the papers as if he were trying to decipher some fine print.

"What was the name?" The girl's voice was neither hostile nor friendly. Professionally neutral.

"Coyne. Brady Coyne. I'm an attorney."

She turned down the corners of her mouth and shrugged. "Big deal," her expression said. But she went to his door, knocked reverentially, heard a muffled response from within, then disappeared into the office. A moment later she reappeared.

"Okay. You can go in." She seemed to take it as a personal defeat.

Elliott's handshake was hearty. "Good to see you, Mr. Coyne." He gestured me to a chair. "Sit. Please. Now. How can I help you?"

"Harvey Willard. He called me. Asked to meet me. I waited over an hour for him, and he didn't show up. And I would like to see him. Any way we can track him down?"

"I'll have to check his schedule. Don't know if he has an afternoon class or not. What's it all about, anyway?"

"I'd really rather not discuss it just yet. Not until I've had a chance to talk with him. You understand."

"Oh. Surely." His frown said clearly that he didn't understand. "Make yourself comfortable. I'll go see if I can get him for you."

Then Bartley Elliott left, and I was alone in his office. Waiting again. I was not enjoying this day at all. An hour in the Student Union and now in Elliott's office. My rear end was getting tired, and my patience had a cramp in it, too.

I lit a Winston and glanced at the volumes that lined Elliott's bookshelves. Lots of important stuff on constructing relevant curriculum, disciplining adolescent miscreants creatively, and refining leadership techniques. Nothing that tempted me to pull it down and riffle through its pages. Not a single book on fishing for Oregon steelheads or hitting long irons from downhill lies.

I lit another Winston. I stared out the tall window behind Elliott's desk at the crisp, green campus dappled by the shade of the big old beeches and maples. In the distance I could see the fields where Warren Baker's baseball team practiced.

The door burst open.

"Come on! Something terrible! Come with me, Mr. Coyne." Elliott's eyes were wide. He gestured wildly with both of his hands.

"What is it?"

"The police. Harvey. Come on!"

I followed Elliott out of the office. As I hurried past him, I glanced at Alexander Binh. He hadn't moved from his place by the tall file cabinet. He was staring steadily at me with his narrow, expressionless eyes.

I jogged behind the running Headmaster to a green station wagon with "The Ruggles School" stenciled on the door. He leaped behind the wheel, and I jumped in beside him. When he turned the key in the ignition, the motor sputtered, coughed, belched, and died. "Oh, goddam shit," muttered the Headmaster. He banged the steering wheel with the heel of his hand. "Catch, you bastard," he ordered the automobile.

The engine obeyed on the second try. Gravel flew as Elliott spun out the winding driveway and under the arching old trees. Students, strolling the paths, stopped to stare after us. Then we were speeding through quiet, suburban streets. Elliott slipped through one yellow light, but he was forced to skid to a halt at the next light. He pounded his fist on the steering wheel, mumbling, "Shit, shit, shit." The way he was hunched over the wheel, goosing the accelerator to make the engine roar, made me decide it would be fruitless to ask him what had happened, and where we were going, and what it all had to do with Harvey Willard and me.

Elliott turned onto a divided highway and demonstrated that the green school wagon could do ninety with only a minor shimmy in the front end. Up ahead I noticed the flashing of red and blue lights. Elliott slowed down as we approached a cop in the middle of the road waving the traffic into the far left lane. Elliott stopped by the cop and leaned over me to speak to him.

"I'm Elliott. From the school."

The policeman glanced at the car. "Sure. Okay. This way." He gestured to the side of the road by a large sign announcing "Rest Area," where I counted three cruisers, all with lights flashing and doors hanging open, four ordinary sedans, and an ambulance.

Elliott pulled up behind the ambulance and we climbed out of the car. We were on a paved parking area. Beyond that lay a grove of big pines, underneath which were scattered picnic tables and green trash barrels. At the far end of the parking area, close to the highway, stood a tight knot of men. We trotted toward them. A narrow river passed through a culvert under the highway there. Elliott shoved his way through the crowd, saying, "Excuse me. Please excuse me. I'm from the school. Where is he? Damn it, *let* me through, will you?"

I stayed close behind him as he wedged himself between two uniformed policemen.

"Oh, Jesus!" The Headmaster's voice was a prayer.

The body of Harvey Willard lay on its back, legs in the slowly moving water, arms outstretched, head thrown back. His mouth gaped. His eyes stared up at the sky, which he couldn't see. On his cheek I saw an ugly, reddish-purple bruise, the color and size of a ripe plum.

Beside him knelt a white-haired man with a black bag by his side. He was holding a stethoscope to the boy's chest. Elliott and I stood with the quiet circle of policemen, watching.

". . . dead, all right," the old man was saying. He picked up Harvey's arm, which moved stiffly, and he grasped the fingers one at a time and wiggled them. Then he gripped Harvey's chin and pushed and pulled gently at it. He was talking to himself.

"At least twelve hours," I heard him mutter. He stood up painfully. His thinning white hair contrasted strangely with the brick red of his face. He moved slowly to where we stood and spoke to a barrel-chested man with the shadow of a heavy beard.

"Sometime last night, I should say," he declared wearily. "When your boys have finished taking their pictures you can move the body. Take it to the hospital. I'll have to order an autopsy."

The policeman nodded. "How do you figure it?" he asked the old doctor.

"Drugs, maybe?" He shrugged wearily. "Some small bruises on his throat. Big abrasion on his face. No broken bones that I can detect. Hard to examine him here. Could even be hit-and-run. He may be all mush inside. I've seen 'em like that. We'll know soon enough."

The doctor shook his head. His shoulders sagged. He pushed past us and climbed the slope. He looked as if he were mounting the stairs to go to bed after a long day. Elliott turned to the policeman who had been talking with the doctor.

"I'm Bartley Elliott," he said. "Headmaster at The Ruggles School. This boy was a student of ours. I appreciate being called."

The cop stared blankly at Elliott. "Oh, sure. Figured you were next of kin, so to speak. The kid had a wallet with the school as his address. You mind going to the hospital to make an official identification?"

"Ah, okay. That's fine. This—" he turned and gestured at me "—is Brady Coyne. Mr. Coyne is an attorney. Friend of Harvey's."

The big cop studied me. "That so? You got any idea what this kid was doing out here in the middle of the night, Mr. Coyne?"

"No," I said. "Harvey called me yesterday afternoon, wanted to talk with me today. So I came to the school to meet him." I glanced at the body, which two white-coated men were moving onto a stretcher. "He didn't show up."

"Suppose he didn't," said the policeman. "What'd he want to talk to you about?"

"I'm not really sure."

"Well, suppose we try to figure it out," suggested the policeman. "Why don't we come on over to my car and we can sit down, nice and comfortable."

I followed him up the slope. "You go ahead and follow the ambulance, Mr. Elliott," he said. "You can make the I.D. at the hospital."

Elliott nodded to me and shuffled away.

The policeman introduced himself to me as Captain Kevin Shanley. He was, for the time being, the officer in charge. He led me to his police cruiser, which was angled off the highway. The lights on its roof were still flashing blue and red, both front doors hung open, and the radio was crackling. We slid into the front seat. Shanley shut off the radio. He found the stub of a half-smoked cigar in the ash tray, lit it, and looked at me.

"Now," he sighed, "what's your story, Mr. Coyne?"

I told him. I told him about George Gresham's apparent suicide, Harvey Willard's plagiarized paper, and the phone call I had received from him the previous day. Once he interrupted to say that he would want me to make a formal statement later.

When I had finished he said, "So what do you make of it?"

I spread my hands. "I don't know. I *thought* I knew. I figured Harvey had something to do with George's death, that somehow the suicide maybe wasn't suicide at all, that Harvey had been caught cheating, and that he had—well, murdered George." I shook my head. "Doesn't look like we'll ever know now, does it?"

Shanley's thick black brows twitched. "Let's go down to the station so we can take your statement," he said.

CHAPTER *14.*

I RECOUNTED my story to Captain Shanley and a detective named Rossi. I was barely aware of the tape recorder on the table in front of me. They questioned me closely, and when Rossi said, "Where were you last night?" it occurred to me that I was being regarded as some sort of suspect. Despite my legal training and clear conscience, I felt the muscles in the back of my neck twitch and tense.

"I watched some TV and went to bed," I said.

"What time was that?"

"Ten. Ten-thirty, I guess."

"Anybody with you?"

"I live alone. I told you."

"Anyone call you on the phone last night?"

"No."

"What'd you watch?"

For an instant my mind saw only fog. I squeezed my eyes shut. "The news," I said. "The Channel 2 news. It's on at ten."

Shanley and Rossi were staring at me.

"You think I did something to Harvey Willard?"

Shanley grinned at me. "I doubt it, Mr. Coyne. Why? Did you?"

"Of course not."

"Okay. You can go. I appreciate your cooperation. If anything comes up, we'll want to know where to reach you."

I gave him my business card, scratched my home address and phone number on the back, and walked out of the police station into the May sunshine. I felt inexplicably elated, giddy. I paused at the bottom of the steps to light a Winston and savor the warmth of the sunshine.

A hand touched my arm. I whirled around. A young police officer stared into my eyes. He wasn't smiling.

"Mr. Coyne?"

I nodded.

"Captain Shanley asked me to drive you back to your car."

I grinned stupidly, embarrassed at the relief I felt. These guys could make you feel guilty for something you didn't do. They were very good at their trade.

"That's fine," I said. "Very thoughtful. Thank you."

He turned out to be a pleasant guy, a rookie on the force who was accustomed to assignments like patrolling school dances and directing traffic and operating speed traps. And driving people to their cars. "It's the shit work," he said as he drove, "but somebody's got to do it. Six years at Northeastern. I got a master's degree in Criminal Justice, for God's sake. And I get to help the cars out of the Itek parking lot at four-thirty in the afternoon. Know what I was doing while everyone else was looking at that kid's dead body? I was on the switchboard. Master's degree!"

I clucked sympathetically. My mind was elsewhere. I wanted to make sense of it all. Harvey's death could have been an accident, a malicious trick of fate, I knew. But the logical part of me had to reject that, and I needed to give my mind some space to operate. I resolved that when I got back to Ruggles I would climb into my BMW and drive straight home to my cell at the Harborside apartments. I would pour some Jack Daniels into one of my square, thick-glassed tumblers with three or four ice cubes and put my feet up on the rusting wrought-iron railing of my little balcony and watch the sailboats slide across the ocean.

I'd probably do that for a long time.

And then, if I had any sense, I'd go out and grab a Big Mac and a shake with large fries to go, lug it all back home in a bag, turn on the tube, and watch a Kojak or Columbo rerun and try to get it through that lead-lined cranium of mine that I was a lawyer, not a detective. I would resolve to let the cops do their job, and I'd do mine. And when I went to the office the next day I'd get back to my work. I'd call Jenny DeVincent's husband's attorney and we would settle once and for all the matter of the custody of the Labrador retrievers.

And I'd erase from my mind the image of Harvey Willard's dead, staring eyes and rigid, gaping jaw and the purpling bruise on his cheek. I'd try to forget the glossy eight-by-tens of George Gresham laid out on the chrome table.

I'd return to what made sense to me: the law.

I envied the chattering young cop beside me. Directing traffic seemed to me just the thing to keep a man's emotions on an even keel.

Sooner or later I'd have to call Florence Gresham. It would have to wait. I didn't know what I could tell her.

I took my copy of *Moby Dick* and a tumbler of Jack Daniels out onto my little balcony. I skimmed the book for the technical discussions of whales and whale hunting. I found the story of Ahab unbearably bleak. I watched the little sailboats and a couple of monstrous oil tankers move slowly across the harbor, and found it hard to imagine the days of the Nantucket whalers.

When I had sipped the last of the whiskey and crunched the last ice cube between my molars, I decided to do what I realized I had wanted to do ever since I had seen Harvey Willard's dead eyes staring into the sky. I called Rina.

It took them several minutes to get her to the phone, and when she answered she sounded as if she'd been running.

"This is Miz Prescott," she said.

"Hi. This is Brady."

There was a pause. "Oh. Well, hi."

"I hope you don't mind my calling you . . ."

"No. No, that's fine."

". . . but I was at the school this afternoon, and—well, I imagine you've heard about Harvey Willard—I was there. I saw him."

Rina didn't speak for a moment. Then she said, "We're all in shock here. I've just been with his girlfriend. I'm afraid I'm not doing a very good job of consoling her. Fact is, I could use a little consoling myself."

"Me, too, I guess," I said. "And I thought of you."

"Well, okay," she said. She cleared her throat. "Hey. I'm glad you called. I've been thinking of you a little bit, too."

"You have?"

"Yes. Matter of fact, I was thinking I might call you. To tell you it would be okay with me if we saw each other again." She hesitated. "Hell, I was going to tell you I *wanted* for us to see each other again. Is that too audacious of me?"

I laughed. "Audacious? No. Hell, no. That's what I called you for." I remembered the feel of her cold skin against the front of my legs.

"They're saying he got picked up hitchhiking and somebody killed him. My God! Isn't that awful?"

"Whatever happened, it's awful."

"Do you think it was something else?"

I sighed. "I don't know, Rina. I'm just a poor country lawyer. Listen, how's Friday?"

"Friday's good. Great."

"Dinner?"

"Wonderful. My treat this time, okay?"

"No way. There's a limit to how much of this equality and liberation stuff an unreconstructed old chauvinist like me can take. Anyway, I'll call it a business expense and write it off."

"Can you do that?"

"Sure I can."

"No, I mean, is that what it'll be? A business expense?"

"We can talk about George a little, and we'll try to fig-ure out how Harvey's death fits into it. I'll tell you the story of George's dead brother. You can tell me some more about the Ruggles folks. Then it'll be a business expense. Get it?"

She paused. "I see."

"Look," I said. "I didn't mean it that way. I want to see you. It'll be good to see you. Very good."

"That's better. Much better. Where shall we meet?"

"I'll pick you up. Okay?"

"Sure. I'll be free around seven."

"Seven it is, then."

Her voice softened. "Sire?"

"Yes, my lady?"

"I've missed you."

"Me too," I said.

After I hung up the phone I poured myself another generous shot of Jack Daniels, dropped in a couple of ice cubes, and resumed my seat overlooking the harbor. I was glad none of the sailors far below me could see the silly grin on my face.

The next morning when I arrived at the office, Julie said, "My turn," and brought me a mug of coffee. She even withheld her standard forecast of medical doom.

"You okay?" she asked.

"I'm okay."

"Right. Want to tell me about it?"

I told her, and when I finished she said, "Wow!"

"So now," I said, "it's in the hands of the police. Where it belongs. They know everything I know, and are a hell of a lot better equipped to handle it."

She smiled. "I'm not sure they agree with you."

"What do you mean?"

"You had a phone call before you came in."

"Who?"

"Dr. Clapp. The Medical Examiner."

I felt my resolve beginning to drain out of me. "No kidding! What did he want?"

Julie cocked her head and grinned at me. "You're leaving it all up to the police, right?"

"Ah, you know me. Anyway, he's probably just going to rehash what I told the cops yesterday. What did he say?"

"You know they never tell me anything. Wants you to call is all. Shall I try to reach him?"

"Hell, yes." The Labrador retrievers could wait.

There was something in Dr. Milton Clapp's voice, a hint of urgency when he said, "Thank you for returning my call so promptly, Mr. Coyne," that made me sit up straight.

"That's okay, Doctor. What is it?"

"Something I think might interest you. I received a report this morning on an autopsy performed yesterday afternoon. Imagine my surprise when I read that the deceased was a student at the same school where your Mr. Gresham taught. Reminded me of you and the Gresham case immediately, of course."

"Of course," I said. "Harvey Willard. I knew about that."

"I know you did. But you aren't aware of the autopsy report, I don't think."

"No."

"Mr. Willard was murdered."

I found myself nodding. "Are you sure?"

"We can say that it's my professional opinion. I would judge that he was murdered with clear intent by someone who knew exactly what he was doing."

"How . . . ?"

Dr. Clapp cleared his throat. I waited for his discourse. I wasn't sure I wanted to hear it. "His larynx was crushed by a sharp blow to the throat. Right below the hyoid bone—under your jaw, Mr. Coyne—there are little cactilaginous horns. Delicate little things. They were broken, as was the hyoid bone itself. What happens is this: A blow sharp enough to produce that kind of damage will overstimulate the carotid arteries, which are extremely sensitive to that sort of thing. They're like little pressure gauges. They send messages via the vagus nerve in the neck to the heart via the brain. What happened to Harvey Willard was that because of this sharp blow to the throat, his heart received an explosive set of nerve impulses. Cardiac arrest. Sudden, silent, absolutely deadly. We call this 'vagal inhibition.' I expect the boy was dead before he hit the ground."

"Good God!"

"Yes."

"I don't see . . ."

"The police are quite convinced that the boy was picked up while hitchhiking, and that whoever picked him up drove him to that rest area beside the highway and tried to rob him, or maybe made a sexual advance, and when he resisted, well, a man who knows his karate makes a quick jab with the tips of his fingers . . ."

"All right, but . . ."

"But I'm not completely convinced that that theory is accurate."

"You're not."

"No. I may be wrong—it's what we call an inductive leap—but I think there's a connection between the two deaths. Between this one and Gresham."

"Well, I wondered," I said.

"Yes. You may remember one of the several injuries Mr. Gresham suffered. The burst testicle."

I shuddered. "I remember. You said it was consistent with the fall."

"I said it was consistent. It's equally consistent with a karate blow. Or simply a hard kick to the testicles. Immediately and totally disarming."

"I should imagine so," I said. "So you think this same person . . . ?"

"A distinct possibility, yes. And in the case of Harvey Willard, he transported his body to the highway and rolled him down the slope. The body could well have gone undetected for a month. That's how often the highway department mows the grass."

"So if we find who killed Harvey, we've got George's murderer as well."

"Oh, it's not that simple, of course." The doctor sighed. "It's speculation. A theory to pursue—a useful theory, I think. Maybe the best theory, at this point."

"Except for coincidence."

"You're right, of course. The odds never favor coincidence, by definition. Yet they happen all the time. The police are following the principle that the commonest things most commonly happen. And that principle still suggests that Mr. Gresham committed suicide and the Willard boy's murder is unrelated to it, and that the possibility of a karate injury to each constitutes no more than a coincidence. And the scientist in me is obliged to agree, or at least to look at both sides of the sheep."

"The sheep?"

Dr. Clapp laughed. "One of those apocryphal stories laboratory scientists like to tell. A scientist is driving along a country road with a friend when they come upon a flock of sheep grazing on a hillside. 'Those sheep have been shorn recently,' observes the friend. 'On one side, anyway,' says the scientist."

"I get it," I said.

"That isn't to say that the good scientist doesn't *think* that the sheep are shorn on both sides. He just recognizes that he doesn't *know* it, that it's a theory, a hypothesis, based on evidence, that remains to be proved. I want to see the other side of the sheep in this case."

I thought about that for a moment. "I'm not sure why you're calling me," I said.

"Because I think you know who did it."

"Oh, wait a minute," I said. "I *don't* know who did it. I don't know who did anything. I *thought* I knew who killed George Gresham. If he was killed. I thought it was Harvey Willard. I was obviously wrong. The sheep aren't shorn on the other side. I don't know any more about this than you do."

"I didn't say you *knew* that you knew, or that you even knew *what* you knew. If you follow me. But you're the one with all the pieces to the puzzle, I think, now that I've given you this last one. The solution is there, on the table in front of you. *If* there's a solution. Move those pieces around. Make sure they're all face up and start trying to fit some of them together."

"I wouldn't know where to begin."

"You start with a couple of premises. They are, of course,

just premises. But it's what we have. One, George Gresham and Harvey Willard were both murdered. Two, they were murdered by the same person. That, so to speak, puts the border on the puzzle. Fill in the inside with the pieces you have. If the premises are reasonably accurate, the picture will emerge."

"I see," I said.

"You're an attorney. Use your training."

"Sure. I'll try."

"Call me any time, if I can help you move around the pieces that I've given you."

"I will," I said. I thought for a minute. "One thing."

"What is it?"

"This murderer—this alleged murderer. What do we know about him? What have your autopsies told you about him?"

"Two things, I think. One, he is obviously trained in karate or one of the martial arts. Knows that a blow to the testes is one of the most dependably disabling maneuvers one can make at close range. Knows that a thrust to the hyoid can kill, and will certainly render a victim unconscious."

"The second thing?"

"The second thing is that he has killed twice. That he has inflicted unthinkable pain on two men, and has, with cold malice and very possibly with clear-headed premeditation, killed them."

"Oh," I said.

"Yes," said Dr. Clapp. "Obviously."

"Okay."

We said good-bye and hung up. I buzzed Julie and told her that under no circumstances was I to be disturbed, and would she mind terribly bringing me the coffee pot because I didn't want to stop when I needed a refill.

I had to figure out how to climb up that hill and steal a look at the other side of those sheep.

CHAPTER *15.*

MUFFY TAYLOR, Harvey Willard's girlfriend, sat with me in Bartley Elliott's office, clasping and unclasping her hands in her lap. Her eyes were red, and her face was puffy. She was a tiny little thing, with a little, pointed nose, and a pointed chin, and small, pointed breasts. Cute, as my mother used to say, as a button.

"They're having a memorial service for Harvey," she was telling me. "At the chapel. Day after tomorrow at four. I don't know if I can take it."

Her inflamed eyes appealed to me.

"It's been rough," I said. I tried to imagine Harvey, all two hundred and twenty-odd pounds of him, making love to this child. He would, I thought, have riven her in twain.

"They're saying someone might have killed him," she said. "Who'd want to hurt Harvey? He was gentle, Mr. Coyne. A very kind, gentle person. Everyone liked him."

Okay then, I thought. If he was so gentle and kind, maybe he wouldn't rive her in twain. I said, "Muffy, that's the question. Who *would* have wanted to hurt him?"

"I talked to a policeman already. I couldn't think of anybody. Except poor Mr. Gresham. Harvey didn't like Mr. Gresham. I suppose—at least, Harvey *said*—that Mr. Gresham didn't like him either." She smiled forlornly at me. "But that doesn't help, does it? I mean, Mr. Gresham's dead, too."

"What about the Spender boy?" I asked. "Didn't Harvey have a fight with him?"

Muffy cocked her head at me. "That was a couple weeks ago. It was stupid. Cap was talking to me, that's all. Harvey got all bent out of shape and Cap said something and Harvey grabbed him by the shirt and Cap hit him."

"Hit him a pretty good one, by the look of Harvey's eye."

Muffy shook her head slowly. "Don't let Cap fool you, Mr. Coyne. He's very strong, and he knows how to fight."

"What did Harvey do?"

"Punched him in the stomach. Cap sat right down and started huffing away, trying to get his breath. That was it."

"So Cap Spender might want to hurt Harvey."

Muffy seemed to consider that. "I suppose so. But, knowing Cap, he'd go after Harvey with a gun."

"Or a gang?"

Muffy shrugged. "I don't think he'd do that," she said. Her eyes brimmed. "I don't know who'd do that."

"Did you see Harvey the night he died?"

"Yes. I usually saw him after dinner. Except for a few days a little while ago, when we were having an argument. We'd go for a walk, usually."

She bowed her head. I touched her arm. "Hey, now," I said. I fished out my handkerchief, which she took and blew her nose into. Then she looked up at me.

"I know this is hard," I said.

"It's okay. I'm sorry." She tried to smile. "Sometimes we'd walk down past the football field. There's a big grove there. It's quiet, private. Our special place, we always said. We pretended no one else knew about the grove. We went there to be alone. There's not many places around here where you can be alone, and sometimes we wanted to. Be alone. You know?"

I nodded. I thought I knew.

"Did you take your walk that night?"

"No. Harvey had something on his mind, I could tell. He was preoccupied. Said we couldn't go down to the grove. He had stuff to do, he said."

"What kind of stuff?"

Her eyes beseeched me. "I don't know, Mr. Coyne. Harvey was—" she seemed to be groping for the precise word "—he had been *weird* lately. Ever since he wrote that stupid paper."

"What stupid paper?"

Muffy dropped her eyes. "I shouldn't have said anything. I promised Harvey I wouldn't tell." She blew her nose into my handkerchief.

"Look," I said. "Harvey is dead. Maybe this paper has something to do with it."

"I can't say anything. I promised." She stared at her hands which moved in her lap, twisting and tugging at my handkerchief.

"Was this the paper he wrote for Mr. Gresham?"

She glanced quickly up at me. "How did you know?"

"It makes sense, that's all. He copied it, didn't he?"

Muffy nodded.

"And when Mr. Gresham found out . . ."

"Oh, he didn't find out. Everything might have been different if he'd been caught. I think Harvey *wanted* to be caught. That's what I meant. He felt awfully guilty about that paper. And scared, too, I guess. That he'd be caught. But at the same time wanting to be caught. Does that make any sense?"

I nodded. "Yes. I think it does. You say that Mr. Gresham didn't find out about it?"

"No. He never did. Harvey would have told me. No. He got a C on the paper. Harvey said to me, 'How could he give a C to the *Atlantic?*' Of course, he made some stupid errors on it to make it seem like it wasn't copied." She stopped. "I shouldn't be talking about this." She dabbed at her nose with my handkerchief.

I touched her arm. "Can you think of anything else, Muffy? Anything Harvey might have said that would help us know where he went that night, or who he might have been with?"

She shook her head.

"He didn't mention the paper?"

"No. Not that night."

"Or Cap Spender?"

"No."

"And as far as you know, nobody ever found out about his copying that paper?"

"Except me, no. I didn't really find out. He told me." She looked up at me. "And you. You won't tell, will you?"

"I guess it wouldn't do anybody any good."

Muffy managed a small smile. "Thank you."

"Well, okay," I said. "You've been a big help. Really. You could help me a little more if you'd tell me how I might be able to find Cap Spender today."

"What do you want him for? You don't think . . ."

"I don't think anything, Muffy. I'd just like to talk to him."

". . . because I guess I should tell you that I've been sort of seeing Cap lately. I mean, not that I stopped seeing Harvey or anything, you know. But . . ." She flapped her hands like butterflies.

"Did Harvey know this?"

"I told you. They had this sort of fight."

"I didn't realize you were seeing him."

"I guess you'd find that out soon enough, wouldn't you?"

"Probably. Look, Muffy. Is there anything else that you haven't quite told truthfully? It could be very important."

She shook her head back and forth several times like a stubborn infant refusing to eat her vegetables.

"Okay. Tell me how to find Spender."

"He'll be in the Student Union. There's a table near the back, beside the water fountain. He's almost always there in the afternoon."

Outside the office Muffy and I went in opposite directions. I stood for a moment to watch her go. She wore her grief proudly, I thought. She managed to walk as if she were bearing up bravely. I pictured her with her wrist to her forehead, head thrown to the side, while Tara burned in the background.

I turned and headed for the Student Union.

*　*　*

Spender was where Muffy said he'd be, with his back to the wall like a careful soldier. He wore his military clothes and his shiny head. He was hunched forward, his elbows on the table, talking intently to a dark-haired boy who was sitting with his back to me. As I maneuvered among the empty tables toward them, I saw Spender nod and sit back. The other boy reached across the table to punch Spender playfully on the shoulder, then stood up and turned to leave.

For the second time I had mistaken Alexander Binh for a student. He seemed to hesitate when he saw me walking toward him. Then he nodded his head at me.

"Mr. Coyne," he said.

"Hello Mr. Binh."

"May I help you?"

"I've come to talk to Mr. Spender, here."

Binh's eyebrows twitched. Then he flashed me his insolent grin. "Be my guest."

"Thanks," I said.

"You take care," he said to Spender.

"See you later," said the bald-headed boy.

I picked up an empty chair, twirled it around, and straddled it backwards.

Spender grinned at me. "So. Changed your mind."

"Right," I said. "Let's talk."

"Start with this," he said, thrusting one of his pamphlets at me.

I glanced at it. This one, too, featured a big red swastika on the cover. Part of a series, no doubt. I put it on the table between us, swastika side down.

"I'd like to talk, first," I said. "About the conspiracy."

He narrowed his eyes at me. "You're trying to put me on, right?"

"Wrong. I just want to make sure I understand. About the threat from the left. I want to understand your point of view. About the pinkos, the Jews, the liberal politicians, the antinuke crowd, the radical blacks. All the enemies of America. The ones who'll cause our defeat."

"They're weakening our country's moral fiber," said

Spender, a note of caution in his voice. "Yes. Those that aren't actively conspiring against us."

"And for our survival," I said, "these enemies have to be dealt with. It's a simple matter of ends justifying the means. Right?"

"You've got it. You do dig this stuff, don't you?"

"Yes. Harvey didn't, though, did he?"

"Willard?" Spender curled his lip in what I think he intended to be a sneer. "He was an enemy. Yeah." He stopped, glanced around, then leaned toward me. "Who the hell are you, anyway?"

"Friend of Harvey Willard. And George Gresham."

"Figures." He started to stand up. I reached across the table and gripped his wrist. Hard. "You better sit," I said. He remained motionless, half standing, just long enough to indicate that his decision to sit was the product of his own free will. Then, sneer still intact, he let himself fall back into his chair.

"So what do you want from me?" he said.

"Where were you the night before last?"

"You a cop or something?"

"More or less. Answer my question."

"I don't have to."

"Absolutely right. You don't have to. Not now. I just thought I'd make it easier for you. It's up to you."

He stared at me, then nodded. "Okay. What do you want to know?"

"Where you were the night Harvey Willard died."

Spender rubbed his hand across his bald head, as if he were testing it to see if he needed to shave. Then he grinned. "I was in the infirmary."

"The infirmary. Were you sick?"

He laughed. "I had a boil on my ass. Want to see?"

I pushed myself away from the table. "You want to play that way, sonny, it's all right with me."

"Wait," he said. I remained standing and looked down at him. "Please," he said. I sat.

"I really did have a boil on my ass. They lanced it and I had hot packs and a shot. That's where I was."

I nodded. "That's easy enough to check on. What about your friends?"

"Why are you asking me this stuff? What about Willard, anyway?"

"He's dead, you know."

"Everyone knows that. Got run over hitchhiking or something."

I shrugged. "Maybe. Where were your friends the night you were in the infirmary?"

The sneer threatened to return, but Cap Spender maneuvered his mouth into something like a smile. "I don't have *that* much control over them." His hand played with the pamphlet on the table. "Not yet, anyway."

He struck me, then, as just a pitiful, lonely kid, with a sad face and a bald head and a boil on his ass, and not to be taken seriously. I touched his shoulder as I stood. "Well, thanks for your time," I said. "I'll call the infirmary, you know."

He shrugged.

I reached down and took the pamphlet from the table. *When the Cities Burn* was its title. I thought of Win Gresham—or whoever it was in the photo Florence had shown me. Armageddon.

"Take it," said Cap Spender.

I tucked it into my jacket pocket.

He touched his forefinger to his eyebrow, a little salute. His mouth couldn't decide whether to smile or sneer. "See you later," he said.

Alexander Binh was leaving the Administration Building as I was entering it. "Nice day, Mr. Binh," I said to him as we passed. His mouth smiled and he nodded his head.

The door to Bartley Elliott's office was open when I got there. I put my head in and said, "May I come in?"

He was alone at his desk, his tie loosened and his jacket thrown over the back of one of the straight-backed chairs against the wall. He waved me in.

I sat across from him. "Rough times," I said.

He shook his head. "You don't know the half of it. Not the half. The trustees are getting nervous. The police are hanging around, asking questions. Parents are calling." He coughed and cleared his throat loudly several times. "Two deaths in less than a month, Mr. Coyne. Two *strange* deaths. Two fine people. Dead. And I don't understand any of it. You just can't expect to run an independent school, you can't attract students, you can't raise funds, you can't keep quality staff, when you have people dying. Violently. Mysteriously."

It was a lengthy speech for the Headmaster. He slumped back in his chair.

"I can imagine," I murmured.

"Oh, don't get me wrong," he sighed. "I feel badly on account of George and Harvey. As a human being, I feel very badly. But as the headmaster of this institution, I have other considerations as well."

"It would be to everyone's advantage to have these mysteries cleared up," I offered quietly.

"Oh, yes. Yes, indeed. It would."

I leaned forward. "That's what *I* would like to do. That is my goal."

"It is." He peered at me. "It is?"

"Yes. Oh, I know, the police say George's death was suicide. They say Harvey was murdered by somebody who picked him up hitchhiking. But I don't believe either of those things, and I'll bet you don't, either."

He spread his hands. "I just don't know. Certainly, George . . ."

"I know. I agree. That's what I mean. Suicide just doesn't make sense." I dropped my voice. "I'll tell you what I think, Mr. Elliott. I think that George didn't kill himself at all. I think somebody killed him. Threw him off the top of that big cliff by the ocean. And what's more, I think that the same person killed Harvey. And for the same reason."

"What reason?" Elliott's eyes were wide.

I sat back. "I'm not sure. I have some theories. I have no proof. But you can help me."

"Me? How?"

"Two ways, actually. First, I'd like you to check something for me. At the infirmary."

"The infirmary?"

"Yes. Just find out if the Spender boy was there the night Harvey was killed."

"Oh, do you think . . . ?"

I held up both of my hands. "I don't know. Don't jump to conclusions. It's just something I'd like to check out."

Elliott looked at me for a moment, then nodded. He picked up the phone, dialed three numbers, waited, then said, "Norma? Bartley Elliott here. . . . Yes, sad for us all. Reason I'm calling is this. Do you remember if young Spender— Calvin Spender—was admitted to the infirmary last Monday?" Elliott glanced at me and arched his eyebrows, indicating that he was exercising patience with Norma, who I gathered was the school nurse. "I don't know what his complaint might have been, but . . . well, wait a minute, then."

He covered the telephone with the palm of his hand and spoke to me. "Do you have any idea why he might have gone to the infirmary?"

I pointed to where I was sitting. "Boil on his ass."

"Oh," said Elliott, nodding vigorously. He glanced at the telephone he was holding, jiggled his brows for an instant, then spoke into it. "A, a boil, Norma. On his buttocks . . . Oh, yes, right. A skin eruption. To be sure. An abscess, I suppose. Could you check on that, please?"

He looked at me. "She doesn't remember. Checking her log."

His eyes darted back to the phone he was still holding to his face. "I see. No, not Friday, Norma. Monday. Yes. It's the day I'm interested in, not Mr. Spender's . . . condition." Elliott's eyes darted toward me. When he saw me watching him, his gaze quickly shifted to the ceiling. "You're quite sure, then. No, of course not, Norma. Your records are always impeccable. You've been a tremendous help. As you always are. And I'm sorry to bother you. Yes, I do know how busy things can be there. . . . Yes. I appreciate it. I appreciate *you*, Norma."

He hung up the phone, sighed, and stared at me. "He wasn't there Monday. Friday he was there, spent the night.

Abscess, as you said. But not Monday. Norma was definite about that. Norma is usually definite about such things."

I nodded. "Okay. Thanks. Now, the other thing . . ."

"Well, what does it mean? Is it important? That Spender wasn't at the infirmary?"

"I don't know. He lied to me. I don't know why he lied to me."

"But you obviously think . . ."

"I hope I'm not being obvious, Mr. Elliott. Because none of it's very obvious to me. I'm not keeping anything from you. Cap Spender and Harvey Willard had a fistfight a while ago, as I'm sure you know. That's all."

His shoulders slumped. "Okay. What else was it that you wanted from me?"

"I'd like to see your personnel files."

"Oh. I can't allow that."

"Yes, I know. They're confidential and all." I glanced at a four-drawer, green file cabinet in the corner of his office, and at a smaller two-drawer one pushed up beside it."

"Is that them?"

"Well, yes. The large one contains the records of the students, the smaller the staff. But, really . . ."

"Those are just students presently enrolled?"

"Oh, yes. It contains all of their school records right up from kindergarten. Test results. References and recommendations and forms from when they applied here. Medical records. Everything. We keep all of that material in one place." He paused. "Under lock and key," he added pointedly.

"I understand. And your staff files?"

"Can you tell me what you're looking for? Perhaps I can help you?" He compressed his lips and widened his eyes at me.

I could only shrug. "I don't know what I'm looking for. But . . ."

"But you'll know it when you see it?"

"Something like that, I guess. I need to see the files."

"Surely you understand, Mr. Coyne." Elliott frowned.

"It may be important. Crucial, Mr. Elliott."

"I understand. But I can't just . . ."

"You know the police can subpoena them."

"Even so . . ."

"That could be a mess."

He looked at me.

"Okay," I sighed. "You can't give me permission to look through your files. Fair enough. You shouldn't have to take responsibility for that. I understand. Perhaps, however, there's something you have to do somewhere else on campus for half an hour or so. I can wait in your office for you to return."

He stared at me for a moment, then turned his head to look out the window.

"Mr. Elliott . . . ?"

"Actually," he said slowly, "there *is* something. It's—let's see, it's ten after five now. I will need to be gone until, oh, say quarter of six. Yes. It'll take at least that long. I certainly couldn't be back before then. I trust you can make yourself comfortable in my office until then. I do have some magazines you can read."

"And your files—they're locked, of course. Very secure, safe."

"Oh, of course. Securely locked. The keys, they're in the top drawer of my desk—yes, very secure." He pushed himself back from his desk and stood up. He hunched his shoulders into his jacket and moved toward the door. "You make yourself comfortable, Mr. Coyne. I'll just close the door, here, and be back in half an hour or so."

The door clicked behind him.

I didn't move, at first. I smoked a Winston and stared at the green steel cabinets. Then I reluctantly stubbed out the butt and slid open the top drawer of Bartley Elliott's desk.

The two keys were there, where he said they'd be.

When Elliott returned, he found me sitting in the same place I had been when he left. I was smoking a Winston and flipping through his copy of *The Modern Administrator and the Independent School*. Fascinating stuff.

He closed the door behind him with a sigh. "Hope you made yourself at home, Mr. Coyne."

"Yes. Yes, I did. Thank you."

"Sorry to waste your time like that, running off in the middle of our interview. I know how busy you must be."

Elliott's eyebrows and mouth twitched violently, as if he were fighting the urge to sneeze.

"Not a waste at all," I said. "On the contrary."

"Good. That's good."

We shook hands and I walked out of his office. I kept the radio in my car turned off during the ride home. I had a lot of thinking to do.

I stopped for a Whopper, small fries, and strawberry shake at the Burger King down the street from my apartment. When I came out with the bag in my hand, I remembered I had some stuff to pick up at the dry cleaner's. It was located just down the street.

The girl who worked there, Molly, was a high school drop-out with a baby at home. She lived with her mother in one of the projects. She had received a little too much help with her algebra from one of her mother's boyfriends one night, hence the child, which she insisted on having and keeping. Her mother worked nights, Molly worked days, and between them they managed, although I didn't like the dull bruises around Molly's cheeks and jaw I sometimes saw, which her makeup failed to hide.

I had offered her legal services when the owner of the dry cleaning shop told me of her plight. I told her about her options, the legal aspects of abortion, the possibility of prosecuting her child's father, child support payments, welfare, alternative ways of earning her high school diploma.

There she was, sixteen, pregnant, handing out clean suits to people for eight hours a day, six days a week, shaking her head, smiling, and saying, "No. No thank you. I can manage."

So I made it a point to patronize the place regularly. I stopped in weekly. I took better care of my clothes because of Molly than I otherwise would have.

"How's the kid, Molly?" I asked as I entered the tiny shop.

"Oh, he's terrific, Mr. Coyne. Two big teeth. Right on

the bottom." Molly smiled beautifully. I hoped she'd continue to smile as the years passed. If she did, she'd have defied all the statistics.

She found the sports jackets I had left earlier. They were shrouded in clear plastic envelopes. She hung them on a hook beside her, unclipped the bill from where it had been pinned, and toted it up on the cash register.

"That's seven-fifty, Mr. Coyne. Oh, and you left something in one of the jackets." She reached under the counter and brought up a small notebook. "You should be more careful. These things can get lost real easy, you know."

I took it from her. I frowned. I started to tell her that it wasn't mine. Then I remembered. It was George Gresham's. I had slipped it into my jacket pocket the day Florence and I had cleaned out George's room. I flipped through it. Professional acquaintances, Florence had said. Former students. University professors. Publishers, editors. People at Ruggles. On the last page I saw the list of numbers. I stared at them. What was it we had decided? Safe deposit box numbers? But that didn't fit George, Florence had said.

"Mr. Coyne? Your change?"

"Oh. Thanks, Molly." I slipped the address book into my pocket.

"Don't leave it there, now, Mr. Coyne," said Molly.

I patted the little book where it rested against my chest. "I won't. Not this time," I said.

With my sports jackets hung on my forefinger and my sack from Burger King in my other hand, I shouldered my way out of the store. I decided to do some more thinking when I got home.

CHAPTER *16.*

I TOOK Rina to a restaurant I knew in Gloucester Harbor. The dining room is a veranda on stilts that sits out over the water. We were led to a corner table. Japanese lanterns provided a dull, orange light under a big canvas canopy. Waves lapped quietly at the pilings under us. The rich, not entirely unpleasant aroma of low tide drifted up to us. From somewhere out beyond the harbor a bell buoy clanged in slow rhythm, and an occasional sailboat chugged by under power, sails furled, running lights dancing on the quiet water. In the summer season this place would have been mobbed, but on a Friday evening in May the veranda was virtually deserted.

Rina sipped a glass of chablis and I nursed an Old Fashioned. We both stared out over the tranquil harbor and the purpling sky.

"It's pretty here," she said once, breaking the silence between us.

I nodded and smiled, and we lapsed again into silence.

A tuna-rigged party boat crept past us, its powerful engines burbling softly. We could hear the voices of the fishermen float over the water toward us, harsh male sounds. Beer and fish guts and sunburn and bristling chins.

We both had the baked stuffed filet of sole. We sipped

our wine and ate without talking, watching the lights out over the harbor. We agreed the stuffing was a bit too heavy on the breadcrumbs.

Afterward we wandered aimlessly through the streets of Gloucester Harbor, peering into the windows of the closed shops and walking out on the piers to examine the boats. Rina fumbled for my hand. We found a tiny courtyard at the end of a narrow alley. It was paved with brick. A high, stone wall bordered one side, with potted geraniums and petunias lined up along the bottom and Virginia Creeper draped from the top. We sat on a wooden bench by the wall. To our right the alley opened up to the harbor. Across the narrow patio from where we sat were three tiny art galleries with glass fronts, closed for business. But the paintings inside remained lit by dim spotlights on the floor and ceiling. Our bench, I realized, was intended to provide a place for serious study of the artwork.

One of the artists specialized in surf, one in clowns, and one in yellow and blue and green globs apparently thrown randomly at the canvas from some distance. Rina said she liked the globs best.

She sat close to me, her hands folded in her lap, her cheek on my shoulder. I leaned over and parted the short hair at the back of her neck to kiss her. She bowed her head and mumbled something I didn't understand.

I sat back and lifted her chin with my forefinger. "What'd you say?"

"I said, don't stop." She stood up. "Let's hie ourselves to the beach."

Rina was quiet in the car beside me. Once I felt her hand touch my leg. It fluttered there for a moment, then moved away. She leaned her head back against the seat and closed her eyes. She smiled, her lips parted. On the radio the Beatles were singing "Here Comes the Sun." Rina hummed along in the back of her throat.

The orange, three-quarter moon hung low over the horizon as we walked barefoot in its glow along North Cove

Beach. At the end hulked Charity's Point from where the crash of surf rolled over the quiet cove toward us.

I spread the blanket on the sand, then reached out both of my hands to her. She took them in hers and we stood under the night sky at North Cove Beach exploring each other's faces.

"My lord . . . ?"

I urged her close to me. She came into my arms with a little gasp. Both of her arms went around my chest, her hands flat against my back, holding me close to her. I sniffed deeply in her hair. She burrowed her face against my chest.

I grasped her shoulders and pushed her gently away. She stood facing me, her head cocked to one side, a little frown playing around her eyes. My fingers moved to the buttons of her blouse. Her arms hung at her sides. I stared into her eyes as I moved down, button by button. She shrugged her shoulders, eyes solemn, and I slid the blouse off her arms and dropped it. I reached behind her and found the little hook. I cupped both of her breasts in my hands and rolled my thumbs over her hardening nipples, and she said, "Oh, good sir . . ."

I reached for the waist of her skirt. She touched my hands and said, "Let me."

I felt a sudden rush of unbidden anger. I shook away her touch. "No!" I said in a harsh whisper. Her eyes questioned me, but she let her hands fall. I fumbled roughly for the zipper at her hip, tore it open, and tugged her skirt down over her roundness. She stepped out of it with touching grace, her eyes still wondering. I hooked the band of her silky, pale panties at either side and yanked hard. I heard the elastic give. I knelt and pulled them down.

When I stood up Rina seemed to have shrunk from me. One arm was raised across her chest in childlike modesty. The other she held half bent toward me, palm raised.

I began to unbutton my shirt, my eyes fixed on hers. She reached to help me. I pulled back from her, and she sank to her knees on the blanket. I threw my clothes into a pile on the sand, then dropped beside her. Her legs were tucked under her as she sat on her heels. Her head was bowed, and she had folded her hands in her naked lap. She looked like a seventh grader at dancing school waiting demurely to be asked to waltz. Except she had no clothes on, and her pale body glowed in the moonlight. And the ripe maturity of her could never be mistaken for a seventh grader's.

When I reached for her she came hard against me, a cry in the back of her throat. I forced her onto her back and rolled onto her, my legs pinning hers. I heard a grunt of protest or surprise, and I silenced it with a hard kiss. My teeth cracked against hers and cut into her lower lip. I could taste her salty blood. I held her arms down with my hands and forced her legs apart with my knees. I moved against her, and when I entered her she cried "Oh!" and when I exploded inside of her I could feel her body shrivel and withdraw from me.

Her hands moved aimlessly on my back, her fingers wandering, feeling for answers. I lay heavily atop her for a moment, trying to regain control of my breathing. I found that my anger, my unreasoning urge to hurt her, had seeped out of me, and all that was left was an empty, tender, lonely despair. I rolled off her and stared at the sky. She drew away from me, and I sensed that she might be crying. I moved up onto one elbow and looked down at her. She was lying on her side, her back to me. Tentatively, I reached to trace the curve of her hip. Her left hip. I bent to her, my lips pretending kisses as I looked.

The mantis prayed there. It was etched clearly in the moonlight. As I knew it would be.

She rolled toward me. Her wet face caught the rays of the moon. Her eyes glittered. She reached one hand timidly toward me.

"I'm sorry," I said.

"Fie," she whispered. "It's okay."

I lit a cigarette. She lay flat on her back, her eyes closed, her breasts rising and sinking in rhythm with her breathing. I watched her for a moment, filled with an ineffable sadness. My mind flashed images, like a high-speed slide show. Pipe bombs exploding. A body tumbling through the misty night air. Florence Gresham's sagging face. Harvey Willard's blind, staring eyes and gaping mouth. George on a chrome table. The bottom half of Melissa Cashen. A praying mantis snapping the head off its mate.

I bent and touched Rina's forehead with my lips, then turned to stare at the sea.

Her hand touched my back, fingers soft, hesitant.

"What's the matter? What's happened?"

"Shh," I said. "Nothing."

The receding tide left a splashy white line where the tiny waves broke against the sand. The film of sea water at the water line shone like glass. I felt Rina sit up and move her shoulder against mine.

"Want to swim?"

"No," I said. "I want to walk."

She stood wordlessly and gathered up her clothing. We dressed quickly, not looking at each other, and, carrying our shoes, we began to walk along the hard-packed sand toward Charity's Point. When we got to the rocky part we stopped and slipped on our shoes. The moon, low in the east, lighted our way. The climb was easy. Once atop the great rock, the angry attack of the surf far below sounded clearly in our ears.

We sat. I smoked another cigarette. We didn't touch. I snapped my butt over the edge. George Gresham's route. I began to speak without looking at her.

"Carla," I said. "Carla Steinholtz."

"So that's it."

I turned to look at her. A smile played at the corners of her mouth. "Yes. That's it. You find it amusing?"

She shrugged. "So. My little secret's out."

"It's been out for some time, hasn't it? George? Harvey? They found out, too, didn't they?"

She nodded and looked straight into my eyes. "Yes."

I forced myself to break away from her stare. I walked to the rim of the great rock at the tip of Charity's Point and stared down into the boiling surf below. I saw George Gresham cartwheeling down, and the rocks and water rising up to smash him, and George tossing and twisting, gulping in sea water, grasping for the moss that grew on the rocks, puking into his own lungs, gagging, and the lights flashing their last in his brain before his heart trilled and died. And then Harvey, in an agony of surprise at the sudden explosion of pain, openmouthed, gasping, eyes wide, as his pulse galloped out of control and his nerves short-circuited in his brain.

Rina's fingers. They had traced the outlines of the tight muscles of my shoulders, held my face still so it could be kissed, flitted and fluttered like butterflies around my eyes. They had struck adder-quick into the soft larynx of Harvey Willard.

And her feet, those sand-walking, surf-kicking path-climbing instruments of ball-crushing, pain-screaming horror.

She was standing close to me. I felt her hand tentatively touch my shoulder. I shook it away.

"My lord . . ."

"Come on, Rina," I said wearily. "Don't Shakespeare me."

"How did you know?"

My laugh sounded harsh to my ears. "How did I know?" I turned to look at her. "Sabrina. That's the name you chose. Rina from Sabrina. Obviously. Sabrina, who saves maidens from drowning in the river Severn. Still the Sewing Circle. You never gave it up, did you?"

She was shaking her head. "You don't . . ."

"See, it was your initials. S. P. Not for 'spelling' at all. S. P. Sabrina Prescott. George told me. On Harvey's paper. He found you out. He put it all together. Then what? Did you become his lover, so you could get close to him, learn what he knew, until you got the chance to get rid of him? And Harvey—what, the same thing? Were you Harvey's lover too, for God's sake, so you'd know when he knew? And me, too. That's what you did to me, wasn't it? It took me a while to figure it out. When I was in George's room. Suddenly, there you were. Checking up. To see what I knew. And after I went back to the school to see Harvey, that must have worried you. Enough to kill him."

I walked away from her, away from the edge of the precipice. She followed me. "So what exactly do you think, then?" she said. Her voice was soft, calm.

"Think? I think you killed them. Both of them. George and Harvey."

"I killed George and Harvey? You actually think that I . . . ?"

"Yeah. That's what I think."

Her laugh startled me. It was a clear, genuine, guiltless, little girl's laugh.

"Jesus," I said. "You're crazy. Now I understand."

"No," she said. "No, you don't. I'm not crazy." She was shaking her head, still smiling. "You've got it wrong, sire."

"I think I've got it right, Rina."

She cocked her head at me and shrugged elaborately. "Okay, then. So now what?" she said.

"Now I've got to take you in."

Her mouth twisted, transforming her smile into a scornful sneer. "Take me in. Yeah. The lawyer and his justice. Right." She studied me for a moment. "I could have loved you. You know that?"

"You can't bribe me," I said. I started to reach for her. "Come on, Rina." She stepped back beyond my grasp. "For Christ's sake, come on, now."

I suddenly sensed the other presence up there atop Charity's Point, and my body tensed an instant before my knee cracked and the pain burst behind my eyes. A scream stuck in my throat. As I began to topple forward I saw Rina looking calmly at me. Her hands were on her hips, her legs spread apart, as if she were a mother staring her loving disapproval at her misbehaving child.

A hand grabbed my shoulder and pivoted me around. And then my head exploded, a new and different pain that spread upward from a sharp spike on my jaw to my eye sockets and my ears and the middle of my brain where the deepest pain lives. I felt myself lifted softly on a sweet red cloud, spinning, turning, drifting. I was a feather, rising on warm currents of air through a foggy twilight. And then, abruptly,

I plummeted. The ground zoomed up to me and smashed itself against me, and I tumbled into a spinning emptiness.

I felt hands on my body. The thunder of surf below me seemed to fill my brain. Someone held me under my arms. As my body was lifted, I heard a scream. It was my own. I was being dragged. I knew in a moment I would tumble over the edge of the cliff to my death, and my pain and fear paralyzed me. I felt the sharp edges of the ledge under my back scraping me.

"Leave him." It was Rina's voice.

"We can't." A man, a voice I had never heard.

"Just leave him. He can't hurt us. Let's get the hell out of here. Come on."

Then he let me go. I opened my eyes. Rina was standing over me, straddling me. She smiled. I tried to speak, but a dart of pain shot through my face. I let my eyes close.

"You'll be all right here," I heard her say, before I spiraled down a drain of dark unconsciousness.

Sometime later the blackness shifted to gray. I opened my eyes to see the moon straight over my head staring down sympathetically. I tried to lift my head. White-hot spikes stabbed through my eyes. I let my head fall back, welcoming the dark, numbing blanket that fell over me.

I lapsed in and out of consciousness. I vaguely marked the passage of time by the movement of the moon. Once I managed to rise on one elbow, and my stomach flopped over and I retched miserably, each spasm bringing with it a hammer of pain to the back of my head. When I tried to open my mouth to spit out the acid bile, I realized my tongue had swollen horribly and my jaw was rigid. I began to gag on my vomit, but I was able to let it ooze out of the holes where I used to have teeth.

Again, later, I climbed up through my pain to see an apparition hovering over me. "It's God," I thought, and the thought did not sadden me.

"What happened to you, man?" said God.

I heard a low moan, the sound of a man bellyshot dying slowly on the barbed wire.

God knelt beside me and stared into my face. "Man, you drunk? Some bad spill, there, man. You just let me take a look here." I was aware of his moving my body, although it seemed to be detached from the focus of pain in my head. Then he stood, holding something in his hand. I lay helpless, watching him through narrow eyes. The sky over his head shone pearl gray.

"I'll get some help for you, old friend," he said. "This here'll pay me for my troubles. Don't you move, now." He cackled and was gone with my wallet.

Later I felt the sun pounding down on me. I tried to swallow and couldn't. I welcomed sleep. Then there were gentle hands on me, and voices far away, lifting, and then a softer bed under me, and I swayed and rocked as they carried me, and a new pain rose up through my body from my knee. I began to gag. Someone helped me hold my head over the side of the stretcher. My stomach pumped convulsively, but nothing came. I sank back.

"I think he's coming around," said a voice. "You better come on over here."

I focused on the shape hovering over me. A kindly face with dark eyes and a bushy red beard frowned down at me.

"I'm Dr. Frye," he said. "You're going to be all right. We're going to have to wire your jaw, and you'll be staying with us for a while. Do you think you can talk?"

I tried to say yes. What came out was a groan.

"Okay, never mind. Take it easy. You don't have to. I'll tell you what's wrong with you and what we're going to do, and then Captain Shanley here would like to try to get some information. I think you can answer him by saying, 'Uh-huh' for 'Yes' and 'Uh-uh' for 'No.' Think you can do that, Mr. Coyne?"

"Uh-huh," I grunted.

"Good. Okay, then. Let's start where it probably hurts the most. Your jaw has been broken. Badly. Shattered, I should say. But not to worry. We'll be able to set it for you. Like I said, we'll have to wire it up. You'll be on liquids for a month. Give you a chance to lose some weight, though you don't look like you need to. You've lost five teeth. Convenient, actually, since you'll be drinking through a straw. Saves us the trouble of taking one out. Couple others have been loosened, but I think those can be saved. Your tongue needs a few stitches. Lucky you didn't bite it off. You've had a severe concussion. I was afraid there'd be a skull fracture, and there's still the possibility of clots, so we'll be watching you closely."

I squeezed my eyes shut as a flame of agony shot through my head, from temple to temple and back again. Dr. Frye was smiling when I looked back up at him.

"Bad, huh? We'll get you onto pain-killers soon enough. The police are anxious to talk with you first." He paused, and then said something over his shoulder. I heard another voice, and the doctor said, "In a minute, I told you. The man's in pain, can't you see?"

Then he spoke again to me. "The other thing is your knee, Mr. Coyne, and frankly, I haven't looked too closely at it yet. It's your head that's our first concern. The orthopedist will be in later to take a good look at that joint of yours, though, so don't you worry about it." He patted my arm. "You're going to be just fine."

The bulky frame of Kevin Shanley took the doctor's place. "Remember me?" he said, grinning.

"Uh-huh," I said. I tried to return his smile. It brought tears to my eyes.

"I'd like to ask you some questions, Mr. Coyne. I'll be as quick as I can. Do your best for me. Okay, now, first, we found no money, no wallet, or anything in your clothes. Did a mugger do this to you?"

"Uh-uh."

"No, eh? Hmm. What were you doing up there on Charity's Point last night, anyway? No, sorry, let me rephrase that. Did you go up there alone?"

"Uh-uh."

"With somebody, then. That the person who did this to you?"

"Uh-uh." I wanted to tell him it was more complicated than that.

"And not the one who took your money?"

"Uh-uh."

Shanley frowned. "So you went up there with one person, a second person beat you up, and a third one robbed you. These three people were together in some way, then."

I shut my eyes and sighed.

"For Christ's sake, Mr. Coyne. These are not difficult questions." Shanley paused, took a breath, and spoke again in a quieter voice. "Okay. Let's talk about the first guy you were with, the guy who . . ."

I interrupted him, grunting "Uh-uh" as loudly as I could.

"What? Oh. You mean it wasn't a guy?"

"Uh-uh."

"A woman? You went up there with a woman, then."

"Uh-huh."

"A woman didn't do this to you, Mr. Coyne. The second guy, then . . ."

I tried to shrug, to explain. It hurt. I moaned. I closed my eyes.

The doctor's voice said, "That'll have to be enough, Captain. I really am concerned."

I welcomed the warm womb of sleep.

CHAPTER *17.*

I DREAMED through the next several days on a pink cloud of Demerol, interspersed with moments of fuzzy, painful consciousness. There were flowers. Faces hovered over me. Julie came with her Edward, and when she left she kissed me sweetly on my swollen lips. There were doctors and nurses shining lights into my eyes, invading me with thermometers, bathing my body, rolling me gently onto clean sheets, jabbing my butt with needles.

Clear liquids dripped through tubes into my veins. I sucked chocolate shakes through straws. They tried vanilla first, but I grunted "Uh-*uh*," until they brought chocolate. I had no coffee, no Winstons, no Old Grand-Dad. I thought, in a moment of lucidity, that the drugs weren't bad. I had no desire for the others.

Then one morning I woke up and cautiously opened my eyes and—*mirable dictu!*—my head was clear, the pain only a dull, aching memory. A nurse materialized, a hefty, gray-haired matronly sort, all bluster and gentleness.

"Well, now, Brady, are we feeling better today?"

I tried to answer her. "Mff," I said.

"You still can't speak. My kind of patient. No complaining. We're going to get along just fine. You'll be happy to know that you're out of Intensive Care. You've had some lovely brain scans, and your jaw is set beautifully. You'll be as handsome as ever. Of course," she smiled, "you're nothing to take home to Mother quite yet. Why don't we just sit you up a little and see if you won't try some nice buttermilk."

"*Uh-uh!*"

"Don't care for buttermilk, eh?" Her eyes crinkled. "Between us, Brady, I can't stand it, either. Vile stuff. Let's try some hot soup."

I found I was able to nod my head and smile with my eyes.

Later in the day they brought me books and newspapers. In the afternoon Kevin Shanley returned. He gave me a package of yellow legal pads and a fistful of ballpoint pens.

"I thought you'd like to try telling us what happened, as well as you can," he said. "I have a strong suspicion that this assault had something to do with the Willard case."

I nodded.

"Also," he continued, "I got a call from the headmaster at the school, Elliott, reporting that one of his teachers has been missing for five days. Seems like more than coincidence. Miss Prescott. She the one who was with you that night?"

"Uh-huh."

"Okay, then. If you're up to it, write it all down for me. I'll come back tomorrow. Meanwhile we've got an APB out on Sabrina Prescott. We'll get her, don't worry. It would help a lot, you know, if you could identify the other two who were with you that night."

I closed my eyes and opened them again. Shanley shrugged and turned to leave. I grunted as loudly as I could. He stopped and turned back.

"What is it?"

I reached for the package of pads and tore the cellophane wrapper from it. Then I took a pen and printed on one of the sheets the words: CARLA STEINHOLTZ. I tore it off and handed it to Shanley.

"Who's this?" He handed the paper back to me.

I wrote: SABRINA PRESCOTT.

Shanley looked at the name, frowned, and then began to nod his head. "They're the same person, right?"

It was very tiring. I nodded. I wrote: "Call Charlie McDevitt. Justice Department. Boston." Then I dropped the pen and the pad and sank back onto my pillow.

The next day a squad of green-frocked nurses wheeled me into an operating room so that the orthopedic surgeon, Dr. Connolly, could peer at the damage in my left knee through his arthroscope. Later he told me, "You were lucky, Mr. Coyne. Your legs are strong. You received a hell of a blow on the outside of the joint. Could have ripped you up beyond repair. As it is, a couple of ligaments are torn, and the others are stretched, but the cartilage seems intact. You'll always have a bum knee, I'm afraid, but if you are faithful to your therapy you should eventually be able to resume all your activities."

"Jogging?" I wrote.

"No jogging for a while, I'm afraid," he said.

"Good!" I wrote. "Hate jogging."

After two weeks they sent me home, my mouth still wired shut, the skin hanging from my bones. I could swing myself along on crutches for short distances, but I found myself exhausted most of the time. Nurses watched over me twenty-four hours a day, bringing me broth and frappes and each noon a vile mixture which they insisted was very good for me. Extract of malt, wheat germ, dessicated liver, cod liver oil, and various vitamins. "It'll build up your strength," the nurses said, and they stood watching me so that I wouldn't dump it out onto the floor.

To my dismay they tidied up the place until I scarcely recognized it. I lay in my bed or on the sofa steeling my mind to resist the impulse to grow accustomed to the new appearance of my living quarters. I vowed never to like it neat.

Billy and Joey surprised me with a visit one afternoon. Julie had called Gloria. I was disappointed that Gloria hadn't come, and then I was surprised at my disappointment. Billy brought a bottle of Jack Daniels. Joey gave me a first-edition volume of Edmund Ware Smith fishing stories. Typical of both of them. The boys seemed ill at ease. Their conversation was awkward, the more so because I could only write them notes, and they seemed relieved when I wrote, "Real tired. Thanks for gifts. Great to see you. Hi to Mom."

Julie phoned me each day, assuring me that all was well at Brady L. Coyne, Attorney-at-law. The nurses insisted on answering the phone. They'd say, "Mr. Coyne's residence. Who is calling, please?" And when the person on the other end replied, they'd say, "Mr. Coyne is tired. You may talk to him, but he will be unable to speak to you. Please be brief."

It didn't matter how tired I felt, or who it was calling me, or what their business was. And it felt strange to listen to a familiar voice on the other end of the line without being able to respond.

Three or four times late at night the telephone rang, and when the nurse answered, she'd frown and slowly replace the receiver on the hook. "Hung up on me," she'd shrug. "Wrong number, I suppose."

After two weeks at home, I was driven back to the hospital to have the wires removed from my jaw. I found I could barely open my mouth at first, but I worked at it, flexing and straining to move it.

The nurses stayed with me another week. By then my strength had returned. I was able to maneuver my way around my rooms with the aid of a cane. I ate soft foods. I spent a great deal of time out on my balcony, watching the sailboats and thinking.

"I'm going to work tomorrow," I announced one day, bracing myself for the argument.

"Good!" said Helen, my day nurse.

"What do you mean, 'good'?" I said.

"I mean," she said, "that we've got plenty of sick people to take care of."

On the third night after the nurses had been gone, the telephone jarred me from my sleep.

"Yeah?" I muttered.

"Prithee, m'lord."

"Rina." I felt no surprise that she had called.

"You must wear your rue with a difference. Pray you, love, remember."

"Where are you? They're looking for you."

"I'm safe." She paused. "Are you?"

"I'm alive."

"I tried to call you. Many times. There was no answer for the longest time. I thought you were dead. He never will come home again, I thought. Fennel for you, and columbines. Then a woman answered."

"A nurse. I had nurses."

"Ah! Nurses. I thought . . ."

"No, I had to have nurses. They *were* nurses."

"I called to tell you that you were wrong."

"About what?"

"George and Harvey. You've got it all wrong."

"So tell me."

"Okay. Listen. I went up there with George. It was his idea. He held my hand as we climbed up there. And then he took off his jacket and folded it for me to sit on. Always the gentleman. And then he started. He knew who I was, he said. He had an obligation—a moral obligation, he called it. He was all bluster and self-righteousness. He wanted to turn me in. For the crimes of Carla Steinholtz. I tried to tell him that it wasn't me. He didn't understand. He tried to grab me, to hurt me. So I had to kick him. Just to get away. Not a mortal blow."

"And then you pushed him."

"No. No, I didn't push him. He grabbed himself, and I said, 'I'm sorry. But I have to go.' And he looked up at me with this beatific smile on his poor old face and he walked backwards, all bent over, to the edge of the cliff, and then he just straightened up and let himself go. He just disappeared. No scream. He fell. I didn't push him."

"He did kill himself, then. You're telling me that it was suicide."

"Yes. I didn't want him to die. I'm no killer."

I hesitated. "Rina, is that the truth? It really doesn't matter, now. You can tell me the truth."

"That is the truth. In faith."

"And the note?"

"The note," she repeated. "At the time, I didn't know about any note. But it was like George to write a note. Not to explain his suicide. The note was for me. George was not a direct man. He had trouble coming to the point. He avoided confrontations—or at least personal confrontations. He welcomed intellectual ones. So I think this was what he was doing. He asked me to take a stroll on the beach that night. That was okay. We were friends and it was a nice spring night. But his intention, I guess, was to tell me what he knew about Carla Steinholtz, to bring me to justice, as he would have put it. But he didn't trust himself to say it. Whether it was his diffidence, or . . ." She hesitated.

"Love," I said.

"Maybe. Maybe his love. I never suspected love, but maybe that was it. Maybe that's why he suggested we go to Charity's Point. Anyway, George thought he might fail to raise the subject with me. We'd take our stroll and exchange pleasantries, and he'd take me home, and he never would say what was on his mind. So he wrote a note. Maybe to slip into my hand as we said good night, or maybe to slide under my door later. So he had it with him. A hedge against his own cowardice."

"And Win?"

I heard her draw in a quick breath. "What *about* Win?"

"George's brother."

"How do you know about him?"

"It's a long story, Rina. Shall I call you Carla?"

"I'm Rina, now."

"Okay. There were several things. I've been putting them together. When your jaw is wired shut and you can't move around very well, you have lots of time to put things together. When you and I went to Charity's Point—that was Win up there, wasn't it?"

"Yes."

"And he was your lover?"

"Was. Yes."

"And George knew, didn't he? And he approved, I think. Until he found out who you were. And then . . ."

I heard her short laugh. "Yes. George knew. He introduced us. Of course, he didn't tell me Win's real name, or that they were brothers. I didn't learn that until later. After we became lovers."

"Why did Win go to Ruggles? To visit George?"

"Partly. He and George had been in contact with each other for a long time. They really did care about each other. George sent Win money sometimes. I know he didn't approve of what Win was doing. He was violently opposed to it philosophically. But he protected Win. Win was in hiding. A fugitive. Like me." She laughed again.

"I don't understand," I mused, "why George wouldn't have at least told Florence that Win was alive."

"Their mother? Win wouldn't let him. Said his mother was better off thinking he was dead than knowing what he had done and how he was living. They argued about it. But George would never have told her without Win's permission."

"So you and Win . . ."

I heard her sigh. "Win is a very attractive man. Smart, worldly, exciting. We—we became close before I knew anything about him except that he was George's friend. He was just George's mysterious friend, that's all. And then he found out about me. I don't know how. He promised he'd never tell George. And he told me about himself. So we realized we had a lot in common. We had to trust each other, two people hiding from their pasts, so to speak."

"But George found out anyway."

"Yes. Harvey's paper tipped him off. Then he did his research. He was so meticulous about his research. He put it all together. And then when George died—when he stepped off the edge of Charity's Point—it ended between Win and me. Win blamed me, of course. We stopped being lovers.

But we still needed each other, depended on each other, had to trust each other with our secrets. So he stayed around."

"And then Harvey found out."

"Ah, poor Harvey. Not such a dumb beast. He figured it out from that paper of his. The same way George did."

"Because I encouraged him to work on it some more," I said.

"Blame yourself, then," said Rina.

"Not likely," I said. "So then Win took care of that little problem for you."

"Yes. Win took care of it. For me."

"And when I became a problem . . ."

"Yes." She paused. "But you didn't answer my question. How did you know about Win?"

It was my turn to laugh. "George had an address book. In the back of it was a list of numbers. Nonsense numbers, they looked like. I didn't know what to make of them. Actually, I didn't know if I should *try* to make anything of them. Then Florence—George's mother—showed me a couple of postcards. She said they were from Win. She insisted he was still alive. I didn't believe it, but while I was recovering from my injuries these past weeks I had a flash. I checked. Do you know the zip code of Ketchikan, Alaska, or Pittsburg, New Hampshire? That's what George's list of numbers was—post office boxes and zip codes. Where he could reach Win. They matched the places Win sent postcards from. George even kept a zip code directory in his room. He and Win were communicating all that time."

"That book. He couldn't find it."

"Who? What do you mean?"

"Win. He went to your apartment. He couldn't find it. You hid it well."

I laughed. "No, I didn't hide it. I left it in my jacket when I took it to the cleaners." I stopped. "He locked my doors."

"Huh?"

"Never mind." I thought for a moment. "That was the night—the first night—on the beach . . ."

I heard her sigh. "I'm sorry."

"Calculated. To keep me away from my apartment. So he could search it."

"Yes."

"How did he know I had it?"

"Me. I saw you take it. The day you were in George's room."

"Right," I said. "Of course." I paused, thinking. "For a while I thought it was just you who killed George and Harvey. Until we were up there. You saved my life. He would have thrown me over."

"Yes, he would have."

I tried to sort out the half-formed thoughts that swirled around in my head.

"Tell me where Alexander Binh fits into it."

"Binh? Nowhere. Matter of fact, I always thought he was the one I had to worry about, that he'd be the one to find out about me, the way he would look at you as though he could see right into your mind. He always made me feel exposed. I really think he knew that I—that I had a secret."

"That's funny," I said. "He made me feel the same way. Except I didn't have any secret."

"Everybody has a secret," she said softly.

"Yeah," I said. I paused. "Okay, then, what about Cap Spender? I know he fits into this somewhere. One of Win's recruits?"

"I said Win came to Ruggles to visit George. That was only part of the reason. Win is a true believer. He's always trying to find converts—disciples to help him spread the word. One day he got a look at Cap in that weird costume he wears and I guess he figured he'd found another soul brother."

"Even though Cap antagonized George every chance he got?"

"Yes. As I said, George didn't even try to change Win's ideas. And he couldn't change what he did. Win took Cap under his wing, and Cap started trying to convert the other kids. He was good at it, too."

"And the night Harvey died?"

"When we learned that Harvey had found out about me, Win said he had to die. That was how he said it. 'The boy must die.' It wasn't my idea."

"But you didn't try to talk him out of it."

I heard her sigh. "He told me there was no other way. I couldn't think of another way. Anyway, Cap and Harvey had had that fight. So it was easy. Cap lured Harvey off the campus, on the pretext of having it out. They were supposed to meet at this place off the highway."

"Except," I inserted, "Win was there instead of Spender."

"Yes."

"And in the same fashion, you lured me to Charity's Point because you suspected I knew too much."

"It was your idea to go there," she said quickly.

"But it was your idea that we go to the beach."

She paused. "Yes."

"And Win was waiting for us there."

"Yes."

"Rina," I said, "why didn't you let Win kill me?"

She hesitated. "I don't know. Maybe I should have." I waited, sensing she had more to say. "Why did you take me to the top of Charity's Point?"

"I don't know."

"You were giving me a chance, weren't you? You thought I'd—you thought I had killed George and you thought I had killed Harvey, and you went up there with me anyway. Why?"

"Same reason you didn't let Win kill me, I guess."

"Good," she said. "That's good."

"Now what are you going to do?"

"Do? I'm going to live. Go on living. What else is there?"

"All those crimes. Those bombs. The Sewing Circle. My God, Rina. You can't just go on living as if there were none of that."

"That was Carla," she said in a small voice. "Not Rina. Those were my salad days, when I was green in judgment, cold in blood. I'm Rina now. Not Carla. That was ten years ago. A different person."

"Are you?"

I heard her sigh. "Yes. Yes, I am a different person. People change. When that bomb went off, when my friends were killed, it killed all that anger in me. I was supposed to be with them. But I went out for bananas and beer for us. I was in the store a few blocks away when I heard the explosion, and I just walked out and that was the end of the Sewing Circle. I saw all at once the absurdity, the futility of it. We used to pretend we had a philosophy, and that the establishment—that's what we called everybody who was working in some constructive, functional way, you know—the establishment was the enemy. School, parents, not just the government. And that violence was the only way. Dumb little college girls reading their Marx. But when that bomb went off, when I heard that horrible explosion, and I knew that Melissa and Evelyn and Barbara and Monica were in there, not some nameless establishment types—that's when it suddenly became clear to me. So I became Rina."

"Just like that."

"Yes. Just like that. Everyone figured I'd been killed along with my friends. Well, in a way I was. I stayed in New York. Best place in the world to disappear in. I modeled my feet for a while. Then I came to Ruggles. I just wanted to teach and be Rina Prescott. That's all I wanted."

I didn't speak. I had nothing more to say.

"Adieu, then," she said after a long moment. "You'll not hear from me again. Dry sorrow drinks our blood."

I touched the button on the telephone with my forefinger and disconnected myself from her.

A week or so after Rina's phone call, I was at my desk trying to catch up on my correspondence when my phone buzzed.

"Yes, Julie?"

"Two gentlemen to see you, Brady."

"They have an appointment?"

"They're FBI."

"Aha! Well, send them in, then."

Mr. Sousa and Mr. Olanoff shook hands formally with

me and sat side by side on my sofa. Each carried a thin, dark-leathered briefcase which he balanced on his knees. Mr. Olanoff seemed to be the spokesman. He was a tall, balding man with elusive, smoky eyes and an angular beak of a nose. Mr. Sousa sat tensely, burning me with his dark eyes, his mouth hidden beneath an enormous black mustache.

"We understand you have some knowledge of Carla Steinholtz and Winchester Gresham, Mr. Coyne," said Olanoff.

I nodded. "I've told the police everything I know."

"Everything?" I felt Sousa's eyes.

I hesitated. "Yes. Everything."

"We want those two, Mr. Coyne." Olanoff's lips, I noticed, barely moved when he spoke. "We think you know where they are."

I looked from one to the other. They were both staring steadily at me. "I have no idea where they are," I said, looking from one to the other as I spoke. "They nearly killed me, as you must know. She called me the other night. I told the police that, too. I don't know any more than I've told. Don't you think I want you to find them?"

"No, Mr. Coyne. We don't think you do. Your relationship with Steinholtz is hardly a professional one."

"Was," I said. "Before I knew about her, we were friends." Olanoff's eyebrows twitched when I said that. "I'm a lawyer," I continued. "I know what has to be done. It's as I said. I don't know anything else."

Sousa leaned forward, his black eyes glowing. His teeth appeared beneath that mustache. He reminded me of a Northern Pike I reeled right up to the boat once on Lake Champlain before it grinned at me and bit through the twenty-pound leader. "Why *didn't* they kill you?" said Sousa.

I laughed. "They came goddam close, don't you think? I spent nearly a week in Intensive Care, another two sucking milkshakes through a straw. I still don't walk very well."

"They killed the other two," persisted Sousa. "They could have killed you. Right?"

"Sure. I guess so. They didn't need to," I said. "They got away."

"Exactly," said Olanoff. "That's the point. They got away. Because they knew you'd cover for them. Gresham's mother is your client. Steinholtz was your playmate."

I stared from one to the other. "Look," I said. "I don't think I like what you're implying here. You think I *helped* them? You think this was some kind of setup?"

Olanoff shrugged. Sousa showed his teeth. I stood up and limped over to my desk. "End of interview," I said. "Good day, gentlemen."

Olanoff leaned back into the sofa. "Look at it from our point of view, Mr. Coyne," he said, his voice soothing. "You had plenty of reason to suspect that your girlfriend was actually Carla Steinholtz. Who you also knew was a fugitive. McDevitt tipped you off to that. But did you call us, or Shanley, like anybody—especially an attorney, for God's sake—would do? No. What you did, Mr. Coyne, is you let her take you up to the top of that big rock so that Gresham could beat the shit out of you." Olanoff spread his hands, as if in apology. "What are we supposed to think?"

"Think whatever you want. I told you what I know."

"*Some* of what you know," said Sousa.

"I've told you everything. Now I think you better leave."

Olanoff smiled bleakly under that great nose. "We think you're lying."

I moved back so that I was standing in front of them. They both looked up at me from their seats on my sofa. "Gentlemen," I said, my voice tense, "get the fuck out of my office. Just get out."

Olanoff and Sousa nodded and stood up slowly. "Okay. Have it your way. But you better understand one thing." Olanoff's grin was harsh and completely mirthless. "You'll be watched. We're very patient. You'll slip."

They left without shaking my hand.

I returned to my chair behind my desk and lit a Winston. I noticed that my hands were steady. I picked up the pile of papers that lay before me. I had work to do.

By the end of July most of the stiffness had left my knee. I affected a cane now and then. Julie said it made me seem decadent—her word—like an effete English lord or a tragic war hero.

My poor, emaciated corpse of a body made me *feel* decadent, although I was able to chew real food. I felt about ready to tackle a steak, but hadn't hit upon the proper occasion for such a celebration.

I called Gloria.

"I'll cook it for you," she said. "Here. In our home."

"Your home," I corrected her.

"Shall I invite the boys?"

"No. Don't."

We made a date for early August. Gloria had a very busy social calendar. I was to bring the wine.

I rediscovered the blissful elegance of coffee and Old Grand-Dad sipped from a mug or tumbler rather than sucked through a glass straw. I had never appreciated fully the sensual exhilaration of ice cubes clicking against teeth, or the powerful sense of control in being able to take one into your mouth and roll it from cheek to cheek with your tongue, then purse your lips and slide it back into the glass.

You learn a lot from having your mouth wired shut for a month. It would have been a challenge to argue a case, grunting "Uh-uh" and "Uh-huh" and scribbling terse notes to His—or Her—Honor.

Winstons tasted best of all, now that I could chew on the filter again.

In due course, Dr. Clapp, the Medical Examiner called me to confirm what I expected: The inquest into George Gresham's death was going to be reopened. My testimony would be crucial. When I explained to him what Rina had told me—that George seemed to have stepped off the tip of Charity's Point purposefully—Dr. Clapp said that testimony of that sort would not be admissible, even at an informal legal proceeding like an inquest. "You know what hearsay is," he said to me in that patient tone of his that made me feel like a college freshman. I admitted that what Rina told me over the phone was definitely hearsay. "The significant fact here is that Miss Prescott—Miss Steinholtz, I should say—was present at Charity's Point with Mr. Gresham, and that she apparently did strike him with what appears to be malicious intent, and that he did fall to his death. And the note, from what you've reported, was not a suicide note at all. It doesn't add up to suicide. Murder, maybe. Accident, at least. In either case, a double-indemnity situation."

"Have you been in touch with Jefferson Mutual?" I asked.

"Mr. Gresham's life insurance company? No." Dr. Clapp chuckled. "I thought I'd leave that pleasure up to you."

So I called Parker Barrett and summarized for him all that had happened. He interjected a "Hmm" and an "I see" periodically as I talked.

"Anyway, the death was not a suicide," I concluded. "No matter how you look at it."

Barrett was a good sport. "We'll wait for the verdict, of course," he said. "We'll honor the decision of the inquest, naturally. But from what you've told me, I think Mrs. Gresham can begin to think about what she'll do with another million dollars."

Less ten percent, I thought. My cut. "I'll share the news with her," I said.

It's more than a six-hour drive from Boston to Florence's "cottage" in Bar Harbor, Maine, most of it along the unbearably monotonous Maine turnpike, which cuts straight and flat northward across the sandy summer landscape. Scrub pine, pin oak, occasional glimpses of rural poverty, and that endless flatness.

Heat mirages shimmered on the highway and evaporated as I neared them. The miles burned away, too, and for once I found myself in no hurry to get there. I stopped at a Howard Johnson's outside of Portland for coffee, and lingered there longer than I needed to, trying to sort out my thoughts. I had been putting Florence off since I had what she and I had tacitly agreed to call my "little accident" atop Charity's Point. By the time I had limped out of the hospital, she had moved to her summer digs, and when I talked to her on the phone long distance, as I had several times, I simply reassured her that I'd fill her in when I could get up there.

I contemplated withholding my knowledge of Win from her, at least for a while. But I knew I couldn't do that. I had no right. My attorney's ethics wouldn't permit it. And, anyway, Florence couldn't be fooled.

I found her tending the big pots of geraniums that she had lined up along the low brick wall that surrounded the big terrace attached to the back of her house. Her hair was bound up in a big orange kerchief, and she wore baggy jeans and a white sleeveless blouse bearing several smudges on the front. When I greeted her she blew a wisp of hair up off her forehead and said, "Well, you don't look any the worse for wear."

"You're looking pretty good yourself," I said.

"For a decrepit old hag," she said. She turned to John, who was standing deferentially to the side. "Build one of your mint juleps for Mr. Coyne, please," she said. She cocked her head to measure the angle of the sun. "Seems to have passed over the yardarm. You might as well bring me one, too."

John nodded and disappeared. I sat in a white wicker chair and studied the ocean. Florence returned her attention to her flowers. "You have to pinch out the old blossoms," she said without turning to me. "Remove the dead heads so the new ones will come in. Otherwise the plant will make seeds, not flowers. Take out the old blooms and it'll keep making new ones. All it wants to do is to reproduce itself."

"You ought to wear gloves when you work," I said.

"You ought to mind your business, Brady Coyne," she retorted. "Besides, I like the geranium smell on my fingers. It's not a delicate, perfumy fragrance. Not subtle at all. But it's strong and alive, and I like it."

When John brought out the drinks Florence took a seat beside me. She lifted her glass and held it to me.

"Your health, Brady."

"And yours, Florence."

We sipped. Florence placed her glass on the table between us and turned to look at me.

"I'm prepared to hear what it is you have been trying to avoid telling me," she said.

"Now, Florence. I haven't . . ."

"I can take it. Just tell me."

So I told her. I told her that George may have jumped, but that the official verdict would probably not be suicide. I told her that the one-million-dollar insurance settlement would be forthcoming.

And I downed my drink, took a deep breath, and I told her about Win. I told her everything I knew about Win.

When I had finished I watched her face. She gazed out over the ocean for several minutes. Then she turned to look at me. Tears glistened in her eyes.

"I knew all that," she said. "I just knew it."

"Yes, I guess you did."

"Those postcards."

"Yes. And do you remember the address book you found in George's room? That mysterious list of numbers? Those numbers were post office boxes and zip codes. Places where Win could be reached. He and George were in touch with each other the whole time. One of those zip codes matched the one of your postcard from Ketchikan, Alaska. Another was for Pittsburg, New Hampshire. When I studied those numbers I was able to see a zip code in them. And I remembered that George had a zip code directory in his room. The rest was easy."

"And you didn't think you could do detective work," she said, smiling.

Florence was silent for a long time. When she spoke, her voice was soft, and her eyes still lingered on the ocean's horizon.

"What will you do with your windfall, Brady?"

"The insurance money? Oh, the boys will be off to college soon. That'll take a big chunk of it. And they say the trout fishing in New Zealand is out of this world. I think I'll try to sneak away in September."

She turned to face me, and I saw some of the old snap in her blue eyes. "Before you go, you have some work to do."

"I do?"

"Yes. There's the matter of my will. I seem to have a dilemma. My only heir is now dead. But a previously dead heir turns out to be alive. On the other hand, he is a fugitive from justice, as they say. Now. Should he ever be captured, he'll need the very best legal defense available." She squinted at me. "That must be provided for. However, he doesn't seem to be the most logical candidate to manage the Gresham estate. Or, I guess, to inherit it. That leaves us with a problem."

She touched a little button under the table and John appeared. "Another drink, madam?"

"Yes."

"How will you want to handle it?" I asked her after John left.

"I don't know. I want to give it some thought. I want you to give it some thought, too. Give me some options. Not today, and not tomorrow. Later in the summer, after I've had a chance to digest all of this. You plan to come up and spend four or five days. Bring lots of pencils and those big pads of yellow paper. While you're at it, you might as well bring a friend with you."

"A friend?"

"We certainly won't want to work all the time," said Florence coyly. "Thank you," she said, as John appeared.

I took my fresh drink from John and sipped deeply. "I'll bring the pencils and paper, and I'll do the research," I said. "I don't know about the friend."

And I stood up and carried my mint julep out onto the lawn so that Florence wouldn't argue with me.

Frank Paradise had a new scheme, something which he said would "revolutionize the word-processing industry." I was booked on a flight to Washington for the second week in August.

Jenny DeVincent's husband settled for generous visitation rights to the litter of labs, with a special provision for the duck-hunting season. His lawyer and I finalized that agreement over fresh bluefish fillets at Legal Seafoods in Chestnut Hill. Mine was delicious. But it still wasn't steak.

Julie requested a two-week leave in September for her

honeymoon trip to London. I gave her four weeks—the same four weeks I would be in New Zealand. "We'll just close down the damn office," I said when she began to protest. "If we're lucky, we'll lose a few of the more boring clients while we're gone."

At The Ruggles School, Bartley Elliott took the month of July to vacation in Canada. Alexander Binh stayed on to supervise the summer maintenance crew. Warren Baker was coaching an American Legion team. I took Billy to one of the games. Warren greeted me warmly and clapped Billy on the shoulder. "We're winning more than we're losing," he said. "Nice bunch of kids here."

Jenny Wolcott resigned from the school. She was taking a fellowship to study for her doctorate in Athens. I was sorry I hadn't had the chance to wish her well.

The police decided not to prosecute Cap Spender. His parents came for him at the end of the term. They loaded all of his stuff into their big station wagon and drove him home to Pennsylvania. They already had him enrolled in a Main Line prep school, a little closer to home.

I treated Charlie McDevitt to dinner, to repay him for all he'd done for me. We hit the spaghetti special at the Howard Johnson's on the Fresh Pond rotary in Cambridge. All you could eat for a buck ninety-nine. Charlie swore he'd get me for that.

I picked a cloudless night to drive to North Cove Beach. I wanted to watch the moon rise from a place high above the world. I had to climb Charity's Point one last time. To vent my folly, as Rina might have said.

$2\frac{1}{2}$